Mark Hopkins, Russell Herman Conwell

The Life, Speeches and Public Services of Gen. James A. Garfield of Ohio

Mark Hopkins, Russell Herman Conwell

The Life, Speeches and Public Services of Gen. James A. Garfield of Ohio

ISBN/EAN: 9783337055165

Printed in Europe, USA, Canada, Australia, Japan

Cover: Foto ©Raphael Reischuk / pixelio.de

More available books at **www.hansebooks.com**

THE

LIFE

SPEECHES AND PUBLIC SERVICES

OF

GEN. JAMES A. GARFIELD

OF OHIO,

BY

RUSSELL H. CONWELL,

AUTHOR OF "LIFE OF PRESIDENT HAYES," "LIFE OF BAYARD TAYLOR," ETC., ETC.

WITH INTRODUCTION BY

REV. MARK HOPKINS, D. D.,

EX-PRESIDENT OF WILLIAMS COLLEGE.

BOSTON:

PUBLISHED BY B. B. RUSSELL & CO., 57 CORNHILL.
PHILADELPHIA : QUAKER CITY PUBLISHING HOUSE.
NEW YORK : CHARLES DREW.   PORTLAND : JOHN RUSSELL.
CHICAGO : J. FAIRBANKS & CO.   INDIANAPOLIS, IND :
FRED L. HORTON & CO.

1880.

DEDICATION.

TO MRS. ELIZA GARFIELD, AND TO HER SISTER, MRS. ALPHA
BOYNTON, PIONEERS AND CO-WORKERS IN THE DE-
VELOPMENT OF A GREAT STATE, THIS BOOK IS
GRATEFULLY DEDICATED.   FROM SUCH
SPRANG THE NOBLEST AND MOST
POWERFUL RACES OF MANKIND.

PREFACE.

It is a delicate and difficult task to write the record of any man's life under any circumstances, and the work is the more arduous and perplexing when he of whom we write is still in active fields of labor and engaged in Political contests. To measure a man's success and pass an unbiased judgment upon his career, while the events of a single day may mar the picture, and while great political parties have much to gain by misrepresentation or falsehood concerning the subject of the biography, is an undertaking full of perplexity and anxiety. Such a task was this when the writer entered upon it. There was a sudden and unusual interest taken in the History of General Garfield owing to his nomination for the Presidency of the United States by a strong political party, and a great demand created for a trustworthy account of his life. That fact coupled with the probable benefit which the biography would be to the thousands of young men in America who need the encouragement which the success of General Garfield gives, led to the preparation of this work. The writer asks the indulgence of the reader in view of the difficulties and the haste in which this volume was written, but assures all who read it, however, that the facts herein stated have been collated with much care, and the conclusions herein drawn have been inserted without political or social bias. It is the earnest hope of the writer that the biography of General Garfield in some form may find its way into every library and that the interest in it may long outlive any political excitement concerning it; for the lessons it teaches, the courage it imparts. the love of honor and truth it awakens, and the sweet pictures of domestic affection, filial devotion, patriotic heroism and religious faith which it reveals in our American life, cannot be valued too highly in the education of future generations. Of such a life it is a duty and a pleasure to write, and of such, he believes it will be a duty and a pleasure to read.

INTRODUCTION.

Williams' College, July 14, 1880.

R. H. Conwell, Esq. :

Dear Sir: — You ask some account of the college
life of General Garfield. I remember no incidents
worthy of note, but some characteristics may be
given. Any thing that may aid the people in forming a judgment of his fitness for the office to which
he is nominated, they have a right to.

My first remark then is, that General Garfield was
not *sent* to college. He *came.* This often makes a
distinction between college students. To some, college is chiefly a place of aimless transition through
the perilous period between boyhood and manhood.
Without fixed principles, and with no definite aim,
with an aversion to study, rather than a love of it,
they seek to get along with the least possible effort.
Between the whole attitude and bearing of such,
and of one who *comes,* the contrast is like that between mechanical and vital force. In what General
Garfield did, there was nothing mechanical. He not

only came, but made sacrifices to come. His work was from a vital force, and so was without fret or worry. He came with a high aim, and pursued it steadily.

A second remark is, that the studies of General Garfield had breadth. As every student should, he made it his first business to master the studies of the class-room. This he did; but the college furnishes facilities, and is intended — especially in the latter part of its course — to furnish opportunity, for gaining general knowledge, and for self-directed culture. To many, the most valuable result of their college course is from these. What they have affinity for, they find, and often make most valuable acquisitions in general literature, in history, in natural science and in politics. Of these facilities, and of this opportunity, General Garfield availed himself largely. Of his tendency towards politics in those days, we have an illustration in a poem, entitled "Sam," which he delivered while in college, and in which he satirized the Know-nothing party. He manifested, while in college, the same tendency towards breadth which he has since; for it is well known that he has been a general scholar and a statesman, rather than a mere politician.

And as General Garfield was broad in his scholarship, so was he in his sympathies. No one thought of him as a recluse, or as bookish. Not given to athletic sports, he was fond of them. His mind was open to the impressions of natural scenery, and as his constitution was vigorous, he knew well the fine

points on the mountains around us. He was also
social in his disposition, both giving and inspiring,
confidence. So true is this of his intercourse with
the officers of the college, as well as with others, that
he was never even suspected of any thing low or
trickish ; and hence, in part, the confidence I have
always felt in his integrity. He had a quick eye for
any thing that turned up with a ludicrous side to it,
and celebrated a trick the Freshmen played on the
Sophomores, by a clever parody, of Tennyson's
" Charge of the Light Brigade," published in the
Williams' Quarterly. Respecting always the individ-
uality of others, and commanding, without exacting,
their respect, he was a general favorite with his associates.

A further point in General Garfield's course of
study, worthy of remark, was its evenness. There
was nothing startling at any one time, and no special
preference for any one study. There was a large,
general capacity, applicable to any subject, and sound
sense. As he was more mature than most, he naturally had a readier and firmer grasp of the higher
studies. Hence, his appointment to the metaphysical oration, then one of the high honors of the class.
What he did was done with facility, but by honest
and avowed work. There was no pretence of genius,
or alternation of spasmodic effort and of rest, but a
satisfactory accomplishment, in all directions, of
what was undertaken. Hence, there was a steady,
healthful, onward and upward progress, such as has
characterized his course since his graduation. If

that course should still be upward, it would add another to the grand illustrations we have already of the spirit of our free institutions.

The above views were substantially held by me, as far back as 1864.

Truly yours,

MARK HOPKINS.

CONTENTS.

CHAPTER I.

CHAPTER II.

THE OLD HOMESTEAD.

CHAPTER III.

BIRTH OF JAMES AND DEATH OF HIS FATHER.

CHAPTER IV.

HABITS AND INCIDENTS OF HIS BOYHOOD.

CHAPTER V.

YOUTHFUL OCCUPATIONS.

CHAPTER VI.

EFFORTS TO OBTAIN · AN EDUCATION.

CHAPTER VII.

SCHOLAR AND TEACHER AT HIRAM.

CHAPTER VIII.

LIFE AT WILLIAMS COLLEGE.

CHAPTER IX.

A PREACHER AND PROFESSOR.

CHAPTER X.

POLITICIAN AND LAWYER.

CHAPTER XI.

THE EVENTFUL YEAR OF 1861.

CHAPTER XII.

CAMPAIGNS IN KENTUCKY AND TENNESSEE.

CHAPTER XIII.

REVIEW OF HIS MILITARY CAREER.

CHAPTER XIV.

SERVICE AS A LEGISLATOR.

CHAPTER XV.

EARLY SPEECHES.

CHAPTER XVI.

· EULOGIES OF NOTED MEN.

CHAPTER XVII.

PERIOD OF UNPOPULARITY.

CHAPTER XVIII.

LABORS IN CONGRESS.

CHAPTER XIX.

HIS PRESENT POSITION.

LIFE OF GEN. CHESTER A. ARTHUR.

LIST OF ILLUSTRATIONS.

THE LIFE,

Speeches, and Public Services

OF

GEN. JAMES A. GARFIELD

CHAPTER I.

GENEALOGY OF THE GARFIELD FAMILY. — EARLIEST MENTION OF THEM IN ENGLAND. — ASSOCIATED WITH ROBERT DUDLEY, EARL OF LEICESTER, FAVORITE OF QUEEN ELIZABETH. — THE FAMILY IN WALES. — THE HOME OF EDWARD GARFIELD IN CHESTER, ENGLAND. — THE FIRST OF THE FAMILY IN AMERICA. — THE COAT OF ARMS. — HISTORY OF CAPTAIN BENJAMIN GARFIELD. — ABRAHAM GARFIELD AT THE CONCORD FIGHT, IN 1775. — EMIGRATION OF SOLOMON TO NEW YORK STATE. — DEATH OF THOMAS AT WORCESTER, N. Y. — BIRTH OF ABRAM GARFIELD. — HIS REMOVAL TO OHIO. — HIS MARRIAGE WITH ELIZA BALLOU. — BROTHERS MARRY SISTERS. — THEIR REMARKABLE CHARACTERISTICS. — EARLY MARRIED LIFE ALONG THE NEW CANAL. — BIRTH OF THE FIRST CHILDREN. — SELECTION OF A HOME IN THE WOODS.

SHOULD the time ever come when it shall be proven by scientific investigators that man, as a being, is but "the aggregation of minute developments and of varied experiences," the genealogical history of his ancestors will be shown to be of the first importance in forming an estimate of his ability and character. If it be true, as now claimed by scientific leaders of modern thought, that the child is born with all the experiences and mental accumulations of his progenitors, paternal and maternal, latent in his brain and system ; then, to gain a knowledge of his physical mould and of his mental peculiarities, the student of biography would need to secure impossible information about the lives of the generations past in order to measure the physical power and mental capabilities of the man whose life he studies. Whether the writers and scholars who devote so much of their time to genealogical studies take this scientific view of the matter or not, it is certain that, for some reason, the study of genealogy is taking a prominent place in the pursuits of scholarly men.

Having, however, no faith in the theory that the men of to-day are but the aggregations of experiences and developments in the past, and giving but little credit to the aristocratic claim that ancestry makes the nobleman, we give the line of the Garfield family for the benefit of such as may deem it important. The tendency of this record is to show that all the individuals of the different races are born into the world with very similar characteristics and with much greater equality in mental endowments than aristocracy is willing to admit. It shows, too, that it is not what our fathers were so much as what we make of ourselves, that determines our right to nobility or praise. Ancestry and health wield a perceptible and sometimes a strong influence ; but the capital we are born with may be increased a hundred fold by our own exertions. It is this increase which constitutes the noblest claim to human greatness.

The earliest known mention of the Garfield family is in 1587, when it appears that one James Garfield (or Gearfeldt), was given a tract of land on the borders of Wales, near Chester, England, through the influence of Robert Dudley, Earl of Leicester. A natural inference would be that he had performed some military service on the Continent, under that celebrated favorite of Royalty, or was of some special service to Robert at Kenilworth or London. The estate thus conferred is said to be situated near Oswestry, and not far from the most beautiful and celebrated vale of Llangollen, on the border of Wales. What was the nationality of James Garfield, whether Welch or English, German or Dutch, does not appear. The most probable conjecture is that he was Welch, and was a warrior of some note, perhaps a descendant of the old Knights of Gaerfili Castle. The estate conferred upon him was either released by him, taken from him, or for some reason his children did not inherit it, and no mention of them appears, so far as is now known, in any record of the Garfield family until 1630, when Edward Gearfield, of Chester, England, came to America, in a company of colonists, who embarked with his family under the auspices of Governor John Winthrop.

The name appears again at Watertown, Massachusetts, in 1635, and is probably the same man. He was born in 1575. Of this Edward Garfield (or Gearfield) quite full accounts come down to us, and curi-

ous searchers into the family history claim to have
discovered his Coat of Arms. If the following description of the family escutcheon be correct, as
claimed by those who have given the matter study,
it goes far to confirm the previous conclusion that
the Garfields were a martial family of wealth and influence in the days of Queen Elizabeth, and perhaps
in the Crusades. It had three horizontal bars of red
on a field, or background, of gold in the center of
the shield, and a red Maltese cross on an ermine can-
ton or corner piece. The crest consisted of a helmet
with the visor raised, and an uplifted arm holding a
drawn sword. For a motto were the words: " In
cruce vinco," (by the cross I conquer).

This Edward Garfield, from whom the present
large Garfield family in America has descended, appears to have taken no great pride in his lineage or
lordly titles, for he took a personal and laborious
share in the manual labor connected with the clearing
of his land in Watertown, and left but a meager trace
of his armorial badge. His house was built on a
beautiful spot in Watertown, overlooking the Charles
River, and the site is still pointed out to visitors,
near the railroad station of the Fitchburg railroad.
In this house he lived but a few years before he was
able to purchase a much larger estate in the western
part of Watertown, near the present location of the
Waltham town line. On this land he erected a capa-
cious mansion, and surrounded himself with all the
comforts and elegance of the "gentleman" of that
period; and the estate now known as the " Gov. Gore

place," still holds its position as one of the most beautiful and valuable estates in Massachusetts. Edward Garfield, Sr., had two sons, viz., Edward, Jr., and Samuel. The latter lived a bachelor's life, but Edward, Jr., was a selectman three years, and married a lady of Newton, Massachusetts, who died April 16, 1661. She had, however, before her death, given birth to three sons and two daughters, viz., Samuel, the date of whose birth we cannot ascertain, but who died November 20, 1684; Joseph, who was born August 14, 1691; Rebecca, who was born March 10, 1640; Benjamin, who was born in 1643, and died November 28, 1717; and Abigail, who was born June 29, 1646.

BENJAMIN GARFIELD, Edward, Jr.'s fourth child, remained at home in the old mansion, and married Mehitable Hawkins, in 1673. After the birth of two children, viz., Benjamin and Benoni, she died December 9, 1675, and her gravestone is still standing in the cemetery at Watertown. Benjamin married Elizabeth Bridge, of Watertown, for his second wife, January 17, 1677. By this second marriage there were born to him Elizabeth, whose birth was June 30, 1679; Thomas, born December 12, 1680, and who died in Weston, Mass., February, 1752; Anne, who was born June 2, 1683; Abigail, who was born July 13, 1685; Mehitable, whose birth was December 7, 1687; Samuel, whose birth was September 3, 1690; and Mary, who was born October 2, 1695.

Captain Benjamin Garfield, the father, was a distinguished citizen of Watertown, and was given a captain's commission by the Governor, in the Colonial Militia. He held numerous town offices, and was elected nine times to the Colonial Legislature. He was a stout, broad-shouldered man, with an open, cheerful countenance, and most affable and kind in his manners. His light complexion, and especially the light hair, appear to have descended to the present generation.

It appears, from the old records, that Captain Garfield's house and barn were burned on the night of March 29, 168–, by his negro servant, Joshua, and on the night of April 9th, Joshua was discovered with his throat cut, a knife clasped in his hand. He had, perhaps, committed suicide out of remorse. In 1684 the captain's fence was burned by Christopher Thompson, who was ordered to be sold into a neighboring colony. Both of these were probably slaves.

His eldest son by his second wife, LIEUT. THOMAS GARFIELD, was married to Mercy Bigelow, daughter of Joshua and Elizabeth (Flagg) Bigelow, January 2, 1706, and he also made his home at the old homestead. At his death, the estate passed out of the family. He appears to have inherited many of his father's natural qualities, and to have won for himself the esteem and friendship of the people of his town. He was commissioned a Lieutenant in the Militia, and saw active service in a campaign against the Indians. His wife died February 28, 1744. He died February 4, 1752. They had twelve children, viz., Elizabeth, born August 10, 1708; Eunice, born August 23, 1710; THOMAS, JR., March, 1713, and who died January 3, 1774; Thankful, born February 15, 1715; Isaac, born February 19, 1716; John, born December 3, 1718; Samuel, born April 11, 1720; Mercy, born June 17, 1722; Ann, born June 1. 1724; Lucy, October 5, 1725; Elisha, November 11, 1728; and Enoch, June 23, 1730.

THOMAS GARFIELD, JR., married Rebecca Johnson, daughter of Samuel and Rebecca Johnson, of Lunenburg, Mass., and moved to Weston, and afterwards to Lincoln, Mass., where he owned a large farm, and where he died, January 3, 1774. Their children were born as follows, viz., Solomon, July 18, 1743; Rebecca, September 23, 1745; Abraham, April 3, 1748; Hannah, August 15, 1750; Lucy, March 3, 1754.

SOLOMON GARFIELD, the eldest son of Thomas, Jr., married Sarah Stimson, of Sudbury, May 20, 1766, and soon after his marriage they moved to Worcester, Otsego County, N. Y., where he purchased a farm. He was accidentally killed by falling from a beam in his barn, in 1806. His children were Thomas, Solomon, Rebecca, Hannah, and Lucy.

Solomon's brother Abraham was an earnest devotee of American independence, and lived at Lincoln, Massachusetts, when the Revolutionary war began. He was one of the first volunteers who enlisted in defense of the Colonies, and was in the fight at Concord, and was side by side with the ancestors of many illustrious Americans, including Judge E. Rockwood Hoar of Massachusetts. The signature of Judge Hoar's great-grandfather, John Hoar, and Abraham

Garfield are still preserved, and the curious document they signed was an important matter in its time.

At the beginning of the revolution, separation from England was not generally meditated, and it was deemed important to endeavor to fix the responsibility for the beginning of the conflict, showing which side struck the first blow, in the event of a settlement of the troubles. Therefore the affidavits of many persons concerned were secured and preserved. Their deposition, showing how the attack on Concord Bridge began, was as follows : —

LEXINGTON, April 23, 1775.

WE, John Hoar, John Whithead, Abraham Garfield, Benjamin Munroe, Isaac Parker, William Hosmer, John Adams, Gregory Stone, all of Lincoln, in the County of Middlesex, Massachusetts Bay, all of lawful age, do testify and say that, on Wednesday last, we were assembled at Concord, in the morning of said day, in consequence of information received that a brigade of regular troops were on their march to the said town of Concord, who had killed six men at the town of Lexington ; about an hour afterwards we saw them approaching, to the number, as we apprehended, of about 1200, on which we retreated to a hill about 80 rods back, and the said troops then took possession of the hill where we were first posted ; presently after this, we saw the troops moving toward the north bridge, about one mile from the said Concord meeting-house ; we then immediately went before them and passed the bridge, just before a party of them, to the number of about 200, arrived ; they then left about one-half of their 200 at the bridge, and proceeded, with the rest, toward Col. Barrett's, about two miles from the said bridge ; and the troops that were stationed there, observing our approach, marched back over the bridge and then took up some of the planks; we then hastened our march toward the bridge, and when we had got near the bridge, they fired on our men, first, three guns, one after the other, and then a considerable number more ; and then, and not before (having orders from our commanding officer not to fire till we were fired upon), we fired upon the regulars and they retreated, On their retreat through the town of Lexington to Charlestown they ravaged and destroyed private property and burnt three houses, one barn, and one shop.

Signed by each of the above deponents.

Solomon was also a strong advocate of American Independence, and met with a company on training-day, but for some reason was not called into the militia.

Solomon's eldest son, THOMAS GARFIELD, was born in 1775, and lived a farmer's life at Worcester, Otsego County, N. Y., and married Asenath Hill, of Sharon, N. Y. Their children were Polly, Betsey, Abram, and Thomas. Abram was named for his patriotic uncle, who fought at Concord.

This Abram Garfield was the father of James A. Garfield, the subject of this biography. Abram was born December 28, 1799, at Worcester, Otsego County, N. Y., and, as his father, Thomas Garfield, was an industrious man, and not a wealthy farmer, he kept Abram at close and hard labor during his early years. Abram had but little opportunity for obtaining an education, although naturally a gifted and thoughtful

3

man.   The construction of the Erie Canal gave employment to a large number of people along the line during the time of Abram's later youth and early manhood; and the first money he was able to save, is said to have been in connection with a job as a laborer on the Erie Canal.

When the Government decided to construct the Ohio Canal, and thus open to communication with the East the beautiful lands of Ohio, many people living in the State of New York moved into Ohio, and quite a number of the contractors and laborers who had found employment on the Erie Canal, sought the same opportunity on the Ohio Canal.   Through the influence of friends who had moved from Worcester to Ohio, Abram Garfield and his half-brother, Amos Boynton, secured an interest in a contract on the Ohio Canal, and they went to Ohio when Abram was twenty-one years old.

At the town of Perry, Muskingum County, Abram met again with one of his old playmates, Miss Eliza Ballou, who had accompanied her family to Perry a year or two before.   They had been confidential friends in Worcester and the friendship of youth ripened into the love of maturer years.   Miss Ballou is represented to have been an unusually attractive young lady, petite, sprightly, and possessing the spirit of tireless activity.   Eliza and her sister Alpha were such industrious, intelligent girls, as to cause the "Ballou Sisters" to be held up by parents in the neighborhood as examples of neatness and activity.

It appears that Abram and his half-brother Amos,

did not have a very easy courtship, so far as communicating or meeting with their sweethearts affected their happiness, for their work was arduous, and their abode much of the time away on the banks of the unfilled canal. However, with but little capital and less household furniture with which to begin life, Abram married Eliza, and Amos married Alpha.

Abram and Eliza immediately after their marriage in 1819, removed to the town of Independence, Cuyahoga County, Ohio, where Abram was engaged in excavating for the canal. From the first day of their marriage, Eliza entered upon the work of gaining a livelihood with a will, and by weaving, knitting, keeping as boarders the workmen on the canal, she contributed her full share to the gains of the partnership. She inherited many of the noble qualities of her ancestry; and the heroism of her brother, James Ballou, in the war of 1812, or of that distinguished uncle, Hosea Ballou, in his controversy with his Baptist brethren over his Universalist belief, was never greater nor more worthy of respect than the ceaseless, and good-natured self-sacrifice of their little niece on the banks of the Ohio Canal. Many of the Ballou family have held high positions. In New Hampshire where the family first settled, in Vermont to which one branch early emigrated, and in Boston, where, as the President of Tufts College, as the Editor of the *Universalist Magazine*, as the preacher of sermons, now classic, as the author of the *History of the Crusades*, the editor of *Ballou's Pictorial*, and *The Flag of our Union*, and as the editor and founder of the *Boston Daily Globe*, they have been known and honored; but neither the Ballou family, nor the Ingalls family, from whom they descended on their mother's side, throughout all their scholarly ranks can show a more lovable and admirable character than that displayed by those remarkable sisters Eliza and Alpha, in the wilds of Ohio.

But it is somewhat aside from the purpose of this volume to give in lengthy detail the life of the parents and we turn with regret from a chapter that may never be written. After the canal was completed at and near Independence, Abram moved to Newburgh, a town which has since become a ward of the city of Cleveland, Ohio. Meantime, there were born to him three children, viz., Mehitable, now Mrs. Trowbridge, of Solon, Ohio, Thomas, now a farmer at Jamestown, Ottawa County, Michigan, and Mary, now Mrs. Larabee, of Solon, Ohio, her husband being a second cousin of General U. S. Grant.

Those early years of their married life from 1819 to 1829 were full of unremittent toil and hardship, and after ten years of such self-denial, Abram and Amos found themselves with a very meager sum on hand for future capital. They had labored diligently, they had saved scrupulously, they had availed themselves of every known opportunity, yet the result of the decade's work was most unsatisfactory. They had no home. Abram and Eliza had built air castles, planned, discussed and dreamed of a home in which they and their children could dwell in the sweet retirement of domestic love and joy. Yet their children were growing up without the sweet influences and hallowed associations which brighten the life and sharpen the intellects of those who enjoy the ownership of a country home, while the presence of boarders and the objectionable people, who, for a time, sought employment on the canal and congregated at its terminus, made it almost imperative for these upright, devoted parents to seek other associations for their children.

Just at that time, 1829, there was quite an excitement over the advance in the prices of land in Ohio, which very naturally turned the attention of the people toward the purchase of wild land and toward the desirability and profitableness of a farmer's life. With a view to locating somewhere, and clearing a tract of land for a farm, Abram with his half-brother Amos made many excursions into the interior for the purpose of selecting a site; and in the summer of 1829 they concluded a bargain for fifty acres of land for each, at a cost of $2.00 per acre, and situated in the township of Orange, about sixteen miles south-east of Cleveland. It was a heavily wooded tract of land of the "forest primeval," and it must have required a very active and hopeful imagination to have foreseen in the gloom of that silent woodland, a future farmer's home, with waving fields of grain, cows feeding in the pastures, and children sporting on a wide door-yard lawn. Yet they were happy in such dreams; and our history will begin by an account, in the next chapter, of their removal to their forest home where James was born.

CHAPTER II.

THE OLD HOMESTEAD.

THE OPENING OF OHIO TO SETTLERS. — THE EARLY HABITATIONS. — THE PRIMITIVE FORESTS.—WILD BEASTS.—APPEARANCE OF CLEVELAND. — FERTILITY OF THE SOIL. — ABRAM GARFIELD AND HIS WIFE. — EXCURSION OF THE BROTHERS INTO THE WOODS. — SELECTION OF A HOME. — THE FIRST CLEARING. — SMALL QUARTERS. — ARRIVAL OF THE BOYNTON FAMILY. — THE FIRST CABIN. — THE REMOVAL OF THE GARFIELD FAMILY.—THE FOREST ROAD.—TWO FAMILIES IN ONE. — JOY OF THE SISTERS. — NO PLACE LIKE ONE'S OWN HOME.—THE GARFIELD LOG CABIN.—SETTLEMENTS OPENED ABOUT THEM.—CLEARING THEIR FARM. — THE SCHOOL-HOUSE.

OHIO, as early as 1803, had taken her place among the States of the nation, and the " Western Reserve" lands, belonging to the State of Connecticut, had been nearly all sold to settlers and speculators when Cleveland was incorporated as a village, in 1814. But the State had not, as late as 1828, assumed that thrifty and mature appearance which to-day reminds the traveler so forcibly of that New England from whence so many of the people came. The tracts of land which had been cleared had not parted with their primitive stumps, and the towns were composed largely of log houses, or low, one-story wooden dwellings, put up in the cheapest and most hasty manner, as if for a mere temporary stopping place, to be occupied but for a few weeks. There were vast forests still untouched in which the bears, deer, raccoons and foxes still found hiding places; and there were prairies still unbroken, where the wildest and fiercest of wolves secreted themselves by day and howled hideously by night. Cleveland, now such a stately, populous city, with a shipping that equals many old seaports of the Atlantic, was, in 1828–9, a village with several small stores, and three or four diminutive churches. The highways were few and most rudely graded, and it was not an uncommon thing to hear of settlers whose little cabins were twenty miles from any passable highway; in which case, they worked their way across the country to the public road as best they could, choosing their own route. The Indians had not been so completely exterminated by General Wayne as to be altogether unknown, and Indian squaws and Indian hunters were frequently met in the forests and seen begging at the cabin doors in the clearings. It seems hardly credible that within the memory of men and women living, such a condition of things existed in that Ohio, which to-day is so stable, so dignified, so enterprising in all the arts of this progressive age, having the appearance of centuries of civilization.

But one cannot trust to his eyes in a country like this. Ohio possessed a soil so surcharged with vegetable life, that the grains of civilization felt instantly its vivifying touch, and leaped like intelligent beings into luxuriant maturity, and danced as they ripened in the breezes of the lakes.

To clear the forests, to break up the prairie, to

construct the canals, railroads, highways, dwellings, barns, fences, and sow the grain, was at first a task that required strong arms, persevering minds, and fearless spirits. Ohio had many of them in 1828. But the equal of any man, and the superior of many was Abram Garfield. He was large, robust, of light complexion, auburn hair and with a high forehead. Physically, he was one of the strongest men in Ohio. He seldom met his equal in feats of physical strength; and if there was found any huge boulder, or large log which the men on the canal or in the woods could not handle, they called for " Abe Garfield," and the obstruction was removed. He was a fearless, frank, energetic man, less rude than the majority of his associates, and giving the heartiest expressions of his love for his family, and his good will toward his neighbors.

Such was the man, who, with his younger half-brother, Amos Boynton, went into the wilderness of Cuyahoga County, Ohio, to clear a spot for their homes. Their land was two miles and a half from the nearest open road, and they were obliged to cut the way for their ox team through the underbrush, and to build a rude hut to occupy at night. It is said the two young pioneers shook hands as they took the axes to fell the first tree on the line between their lands, and said they would live and die together there. They had never owned a foot of land before. This was their own. Wolves might howl, and bears might threaten, they were happy in the consciousness of superior strength and right.

The forest steadily and surely melted away before the vigorous woodsmen, and the proper logs having been saved from fire and axe for the purpose, the work of constructing a log house for Amos was begun. They had no thought of pride then, and but little of convenience; but, influenced by the overmastering desire to get a home of their own as soon as possible, they constructed a building which was said afterwards to be too small for a convenient loom house.

A few days after their first arrival, Amos concluded to bring his family and lodge them in a log shed or weaving-cabin belonging to their nearest neighbor, about a mile and a half from their clearing. So the family were brought and stowed away in that little cabin, scarcely twelve feet square, and there on the ground they set their rude furniture and waited day by day for the completion of their new home. One child, Mr. Henry B. Boynton, was born in that little structure.

When the cabin for Amos was covered, and a floor laid in one end of it for the beds, Amos moved his family in, and, according to the previous understanding, Abram went to Newburgh for his family. It was New Year's day, 1830. There was a heavy fall of snow, and in the clearings it had drifted badly. He was obliged to unyoke the oxen often, and drive them wallowing over a ravine, and returning drag the rude ox sled himself through the snow. The road had improved somewhat before his return, but what was gained in more solid snow banks, was lost in being heavily loaded with his household goods and family. That trip from Newburgh to their clearing in Orange away back in January, 1830, Mrs. Garfield never has forgotten, notwithstanding the subsequent bitter and dangerous experiences. The oldest boy, Thomas, was then nine or ten years of age, and, inheriting his father's hardy qualities, gave considerable assistance. But it was a long, weird, cold and exciting journey through an almost unbroken forest, on a road such as the woodmen now would consider to be unfit and unsafe for the transportation of wood.

Yet the whole family, with a feeling akin to that the traveler on the ocean feels when longing for land, looked forward with joyful anticipation to the establishment of a home and the erection of those household gods with which all childhood homes abound.

It was a joyful meeting at the log hut there in the woods. Two brothers, two sisters and their families, with the one distant neighbor, were to be a community, a State, a law unto themselves, and they determined that love should abolish the need of law. Rough in manners, some of them might have been, and probably were; uncouthly dressed, perhaps, if judged by the standards of the Boulevards or Broadway, rough hands there must have been; but the great hearts and strong brains which make nobles of the laborers, and found great nations, were there also.

"Is this your house. Uncle Amos?" asked the children,

"Yes, and yours, too, for a while," said Amos.

Mrs. Garfield is said to have been delighted with the consciousness that she could stand on their own soil.

"Is this our own land, Abram?" said she. "I cannot realize it."

Years afterward, and even to this day, the sisters visit frequently the spot where first they set foot on their own land, and each lives over again the sensations of those good old days. So frequently did Alpha visit the place where she first stopped and asked: "Amos, is this our land?" and so sacred did she hold it, that the children gave it the name of " Mother's retreat," and always scrupulously left her to herself whenever they saw her put on her bonnet and start in the direction of the place. Births, marriages, deaths, have come since then. The strong men are laid low, the children are scattered, and the trees have been cleared away and grown again, but the two women live to visit their sacred "retreats," and to recite the tales of their early adventures in the ears of a wondering generation.

When the two families were safely packed away in the little cabin with one room and one fire-place, the brothers began the construction of Abram's house.

They selected a spot about forty rods from the other cabin, and on an elevated mound, behind which was a little ravine and a diminutive streamlet. A short distance down the ravine was a living spring, which was found afterward to be a most convenient and valuable household appendage.

There, with the ox team for the transportation of timber from the adjacent forest, and with their own natural Yankee skill to hew it, and their own strong arms to raise it, they constructed the old log cabin, without a "raising," and, as Amos always took pride in adding, "without whiskey."

This log house was nearly square, with the front door in the middle, and the windows, about two feet square, in each end. It was ready for occupancy in the early spring, and in time to sow the front yard with wheat. During the summer other cabins were erected within a circuit of a mile and a half, so that they did not long feel the weight of an almost complete isolation. It required the closest management for the new farmer to secure a livelihood through the months preceding the sale of the first crop, and no little watching to keep his family from the wolves and from the possible visits of fiercer beasts. But all seem to have willingly endured all the privations of poverty and isolation with cheerfulness, often making jokes of their greatest hardships. The brothers often exchanged work, and so together cleared the fields of stumps, constructed fences, and set out fruit trees. Such saplings, seeds, or stock as they needed, one or the other procured at Cleveland. So that at the close of the autumn of 1830 both farms were in a prosperous condition, giving promise of rich harvests in the year to come.

Other relatives, and many of his former acquaintances, purchased tracts of land in the county and in adjoining counties, and the three years which fol-

HOME OF GENERAL GARFIELD'S CHILDHOOD.

lowed Abram's removal to his new home saw many clearings and improvements made in that whole region. His fifty-acre tract of land underwent a complete transformation. Early and late he toiled with the oxen; and such a share did those beasts of burden have in the establishment and improvement of his home that Abram regarded them ·with affectionate fondness, and treated them with the most friendly and patient consideration.

It was a grand thing to see the forest and wildwood give place to the garden of vegetables, the fields of grain, and the orchards of apples. Abram and Eliza appreciated the wonderful change. Those were their sweetest, best days, when they watched for the sprouts of corn and wheat with the eagerness and innocence of children, when the whole family joined in the gathering of the harvest, or when about the roaring winter fire they sat and talked of the past or planned for the future.

Soon a log school-house was constructed, across the ravine at the back of Abram's house, and at one corner of his clearing. This furnished a means of education for their children, and Abram and Eliza were happy.

CHAPTER III.

BIRTH OF JAMES AND DEATH OF HIS FATHER.

BIRTH OF JAMES. — THE FOURTH CHILD IN THE FAMILY. — REJOICINGS. — HUMBLE SURROUNDINGS. — NAMED AFTER HIS UNCLE AND HIS FATHER. — DEATH OF HIS FATHER. — THE EFFECT OF THAT CALAMITY. — THE SYMPATHY OF THE NEIGHBORS. — IN DEBT. — WIDOW ADVISED TO GIVE AWAY HER CHILDREN. — ATTEMPTING TO SAVE THE HOME. — FINISHING THE RAIL FENCE. — INDUSTRY OF THOMAS. — HIS SELF-SACRIFICE. — OCCUPATIONS OF THE WIDOW. — HER LOVE FOR READING. — TEACHING LITTLE JAMES.

NOVEMBER 19, 1831, nearly two years after Abram had taken his family to their new home at Orange, the household was made happier by the birth of another son. Yet, so far as the child was concerned, it cannot be said to be a very auspicious beginning of life. It had been a difficult task to feed the children already in the family. The gloomy log cabin, made more shadowy by the attempts to shut out the cold winds of November, could not be said to be an augury of future brightness. The crying of a child within the humble abode, and the barking of wolves in the woodland near at hand, suggest nothing unusual, prophetic, or propitious. Such circumstances have surrounded the birth of many men, and will attend the nativity of many more. These circumstances neither make nor unmake men. But they do present the encouraging thought that if, from such humble beginnings, a useful life may be made, then there are none so poor and humble but they may improve their condition and become benefactors.

Yet the infant was welcomed heartily by his large-hearted father, and his appearance was made the occasion for congratulations among all the neighbors. For in the woods then, there were loving and honest neighborly sympathy and interest in each other's welfare, which the non-conducting brick walls of a city prevent or destroy. Then, if a person died within twenty miles, all the farmers, in sincere sympathy, left their work, and appeared at the sad rites. If there was a birth or marriage all rejoiced. If there was a "raising," where help was needed, all were there. Children of the cities often grow up be narrow, useless, weakly men and women, for the lack of this wholesome large-hearted spirit which nature and freedom impart.

When the time came to name the baby, he was given the name of James Abram, the first being that of his uncle in his mother's family, and the last being that of his father. There could have been none of those poetic high hopes of the child's future greatness on the part of his parents, which we often find mentioned in biographical works, or they would have selected some other name than James, which in that region was simply a suggestion to call him "Jim." Neither his father nor his mother had any loftier hopes than that he would become an honest man and a good citizen.

But when the child was about a year and a half

old an event happened which suddenly left the family in the greatest gloom.

Abram Garfield had been fighting fire. From several heaps of burning brush, a conflagration had spread to his fences, woodland, and fields, and threatened destruction to everything around. In the contest, which lasted for many hours, the strong man became so heated and fatigued, that he eagerly sought the shade and breeze of his cabin doorway. He had been warned of the danger that lurked in cold drafts of air, but, trusting in his robust health and past escapes, sat in the draft and fanned himself with his hat. It was a fatal mistake. For in three days the husband and father lay in the log cabin a corpse. Who can imagine the shock to the wife and mother? So unexpected and so terrible. The neighbors could not for a while credit the rumor that Abram Garfield was dead. He had been the most certain of a long life, of any man they knew. Could it be that Abram Garfield had actually died of disease?

To the widow it was for a while a paralyzing shock, which she could not comprehend. But when little James, just toddling about and beginning to speak whole words, pulled at the sheets of his father's bier, as the body lay on the boards across two chairs, and piteously called for his papa, she must have felt the keenest agony. The other children, Thomas, Mehitable, and Mary, were older, and could understand what death meant. But little Jimmy would not be quiet while his papa slept such an unusual sleep. He could read in the sorrowful faces and sobs of all about him that something sad had happened; so from one to another the baby wandered, with his large eyes filled with tears, touchingly and hesitatingly saying to each, "Papa."

"What a pity," said one, "that such a helpless little child should be left fatherless!"

"His mother cannot support him," said another; "at all events, some of the children will have to be given away or bound out."

"She must sell the farm at once," said a third, "for there is no one now to complete the fences nor cultivate the farm. Poor soul! This will kill her!"

Yet the sorrowing woman did have one comfort. Her husband was loved by all and she had deep and hearty human sympathy. Have you ever been poor and imprisoned in a great city, with the body of a child, or wife, or husband, or a mother, or a father lying in death in your front room? Have you ever in your grief glanced at the passing crowds, and longed for one look of sympathy? Have you ever wished that your next neighbor would stop the piano, or his loud, careless laughter, or quiet his noisy children at play about your door? Did not the persistent calls of traders, market men and beggars harrow up your stricken soul and cover your cheeks with the hot tears of unutterable woe? Like the "Ancient Mariner's" surfeit of water with none to drink, you sat wretched and lone, friendless and unnoticed in your sorrow, while around you an ocean of humanity surged and rolled, wasting its superabundance of sympathy on poodle pets and hardened criminals; and caring not if the dirty gamins in the gutters pelted your meager funeral procession with sticks and stones.

If you have experienced this not uncommon woe, your heart will bless those Ohio pioneers, whose children whispered about their doors and hushed their voices in the plays of school recess, saying, ' Poor Jimmy's father is dead," you will have a sincere yearning for their friendship, as you hear how the hardy plowmen came from many miles away, and with tears coursing their rough cheeks, offered consolation and help. All mourned in sincerity, all remembered the widow and the fatherless in that hour of trial.

The funeral which soon followed was unostentatious and simple, but called out a large attendance of friends and neighbors. Little Jimmy was the recipient of many a sad caress on that occasion, and tears freely flowed at the sight of his helplessness and artlessness, from fountains which even the presence of the stricken widow had not unloosed.

In that same year Sir Henry Taylor wrote "The world knows nothing of its greatest men," and his true saying would have been a wiser one had it passed into literature that " The world knows nothing of its greatest women." The situation in which Eliza Garfield was left, was peculiarly disheartening because she was a woman. To a man, with physical strength, with opportunities for gain, with power to compel respect for himself and his children, the cir-

cumstances which follow the death of a consort are
not so appalling. But the utter despair which must
have filled that widow's heart, when with her fatherless little ones she entered alone their log home after
the burial, cannot be known to those who have not
had a like sorrow. The phantoms which his pres.
ence had kept aloof from their cabin, the shadows
which his face had ever dispelled, came boldly in at
the door, and lurked in the corners at the approach
of every evening. The farm was not fully fenced.
The stock was not paid for, and the orchard of trees
which Abram had planted had not reached its fruit-
age. There was but a meager stock of provisions or
clothing on hand, and the crop which had been sowed,
she seemed helpless to gather. The reader may say
that there is nothing very uncommon in their situation, and may say that other women have been in
even worse circumstances; but such facts do not
make this experience any the less interesting, nor
these evidences of womanly heroism any the less
striking. If she sold all their personal property to
pay the debts, she must still leave some unpaid. To
the men of business, there seemed no way but to sell
the farm and everything of personal property con-
.nected with it, put the children out into families
where they could be adopted, or be made to pay their
way doing errands and light work, while she could
probably support herself by weaving, or by household labor in the families of those who knew her.

It does not appear that the brave woman ever
entertained the thought of following their advice.

Her love was too strong, her capabilities for self-sacrifice too great to admit of a separation without a struggle to maintain her family. In her resolution she had the sympathy of every one, even of such as looked upon it as a foolhardy undertaking.

In order to pay the outstanding debts, she concluded to sell a part of the little farm and finally disposed of twenty acres, for a sum which left her thirty acres and two cows, free of debt. The dimensions were reduced but it was still their home.

Thomas was a robust and active boy, and appears to have taken hold of labor with a heroic devotedness worthy of his mother. It is said that he and his mother actually attempted to complete the unfinished rail fence along one side of their farm, but she was too light and small to be of much use at a man's work of driving stakes or splitting rails. Yet the attempt shows the determined and independent spirit with which she took upon herself the office of father in addition to that of mother. With the help of kind neighbors and her brother-in-law, Amos, who was still her nearest neighbor, the first crop was gathered, and odd jobs of employment found for Thomas. Living on the plainest food, wearing the coarsest clothing, and denying themselves every luxury, the little family struggled on from day to day managing so as to keep out of debt and retain their hold on their home. Mrs. Garfield sought employment for herself among the people of that vicinity, and appears to have earned considerable in spinning, weaving and knitting, at which she was an expert.

While she was engaged at work, little Jimmy was left in the care of the girls, or, in case the girls also found some work, he was left with the family of his Uncle Amos. She occasionally had an opportunity of letting a few acres of her land to be cultivated on shares, and secured some of her firewood in that way, while the remainder was brought in by herself and children by hand from the borders of the wood-land.

Of Thomas, whose industry as a boy, and whose self-denying faithfulness to his mother in her needs was remarkable, the people still retain most praiseworthy traditions. Whenever he could work extra hours and earn a few pennies more, he never neglected the opportunity, and always with most touching indications of joy carried home to his mother with alacrity every cent of his earnings. He seemed never to have thought that he was entitled to any share of it for amusement or luxury. It is still related of him, how he walked to Cleveland and back on an errand, saving the small cost of a horse, with a determination to "get money enough extra to buy Jimmy a pair of shoes," so that the little fellow could go to "the Sunday meetings in the School-House." However, the clothing for the family was usually secured by Mrs. Garfield in exchange for her work. When shoes became a necessity she would weave or sew for the shoemaker, and he would come to her cabin and make the shoes on the spot and fit them as he put them together.

Yet it seems that amid all this excessive labor and

mental strain, Mrs. Garfield found time to read papers
and books such as the neighborhood contained.   Her
Sabbaths, doubly sacred for the gathering of her
family about her, were also improved by her in reading, and often she read aloud to the children.   In
this way, no doubt, young James gained that-first
love for books which afterwards led him into the
higher walks of life.

CHAPTER IV.

HABITS AND INCIDENTS OF HIS BOYHOOD.

NOT PRECOCIOUS. — HIS PLAYS. — HIS GARDEN. — THE PETTED YOUNG-
EST CHILD. — HIS EARLY TASKS. — ABSENCE OF A FATHER'S DISCI-
PLINE. — HIS ABSOLUTE TRUTHFULNESS. — COULD NOT LIE TO HIS
MOTHER. — ASHAMED TO BE CALLED A COWARD. — HIS UNCLE
AMOS. — WHOLESOME FEAR. — LOVE OF POETRY. — NAMES THE
TREES AND ROCKS AFTER HEROES AND HEROINES. — THE APPLE
ORCHARD. — AMBITION TO BE A SAILOR. — CARELESS USE OF TOOLS.
— READING AT HOME. — COUNTRY LYCEUM. — MOTHER'S WATCH-
CARE.

THE boyhood of James is interesting and encouraging to the youth of our land, inasmuch as it lacks
those extraordinary and unusual features which
would adorn a romance or a fable. It was so much
like the life of many other boys, and so little varied
from the common experience, that it shows the possibility that goodness, greatness and fame are within
the reach of many other poor country lads. The
hardihood and intelligence of his mother may have
contained a blessing which is exceptional in such
circumstances; but the life he led in his earlier
years was, in its daily routine, very similar to that of
other fatherless farmers' boys. He brought in at
night the wood for the morning fire; his bare feet
made solid the often trodden path down to the

spring; and he was not unusually precocious in his desire for knowledge or in his willingness to work.

He constructed mud dams and set up rude toy mills at the little stream in the ravine below the spring. He sought out the shady nooks in the near woodland for summer shade, and made caves in the woodpile in winter, to secure a sheltered playhouse. He planted his little garden in the spring, and often lost his interest in it after the wonderful resurrection of the beans and cucumbers had ceased to astonish him. He was the pet of his mother and the pride of his brother and sisters, but poverty prevented anything like a dangerous indulgence. Yet its tendency was to make him less inclined to work either in school or in the field. But he often entered into the sports of the boys in the neighborhood with enthusiasm, and sometimes with unhealthy zeal. If he was given a job of work to do, and a certain time was allotted him in which to perform the task, his whole soul engaged in the work, and the job was pushed to completion with startling vigor.

His early life lacked, however, that energy and promptness which is ever the result when a boy loses the discipline of a father's presence and example. It is a surprise that he was so active. Many boys have been led away into laziness and its consequent vices and crimes, for the lack of a father's stern and dignified commands.

But there was one feature of little James's character which will account for his final triumph under all these discouraging circumstances of his life. His mother's training, his inherited disposition, and the habits of the rather remarkably religious neighborhood of Orange at that time, kept his boyhood life in the way of the most scrupulous truthfulness. He did not and would not lie. While that anchor held, his character and future were safe. No boy or man can be selfish, self-indulgent, or lazy, without being dishonest. He cannot steal, nor cheat, nor play truant, nor indulge in vicious habits, unless he will lie. Absolute truthfulness and a useless or vicious life are incompatible and impossible.

A traditional incident, illustrating his love of truth, is related of him, which may or may not be exact in its details, yet which is an apt illustration of his whole character in that early day. His uncle, Thomas Garfield, lived three or four miles from his mother's house, and the road led through a lonely country, a part of which was thickly wooded. It often happened that he was sent on errands, to and fro, over this road. One evening, while he was at his uncle's, there came up a sudden shower which turned into a storm, and darkness came on suddenly. He had probably heard the usual ghost and Indian stories which terrified the youth of his time and was somewhat timid. He disliked to traverse the road alone in the night, yet he felt that he must go home. His cousins and aunt tried to persuade him to stay all night, but he would not. He started boldly out into the night. It was wet, cold, and pitchy dark. The wind groaned among the maples, and the great beech trees cracked and creaked ominously. It was too much for his boyish courage, and, after going a half mile, he turned back.

But on reaching his uncle's house he felt ashamed of his weakness and determined to start again.

"I would not try it again, James," said a workman.

"But mother will worry about me," said the little fellow.

"O stay all night, and tell her the mud was too deep to get home," said the workman.

"I shall not tell her that, and I won't tell her I was afraid," said James. And off he started a second time. This time he went bravely through the dark woods to his home, and it may be that his mother never knew how much he endured that night rather than tell her a falsehood or confess that he was afraid.

That tradition is in accord with many others and shows that truthfulness requires a brave spirit and a self-sacrificing life. The *truth* was his good angel. It kept him from everything which he would be ashamed to confess. It overcame his indisposition to labor. It guided him safely over the dangerous bar of a petted boyhood. Inasmuch as he was more true in his speech and actions than other boys, just that much was his boyhood nobler and more promising than theirs, and no more In all other things he was like the multitude. The determination and habit of speaking the simple truth was a badge of honor, more honorable and more respected than the kingly ermine on the heraldic shields of his ancestors.

Wild and rough oftentimes, rude in his sports and awkward in the presence of visitors, often in rags and dust he had carelessly made, with no other title or claim to respect and no other capital to begin life upon, he found in his truth-telling an infallible guide to nobility and human greatness. This was the only very remarkable thing about his young life, and we shall see how curiously and surely it guided him upward.

Romances have been constructed about the boyhood of James, in which he has figured as the heroic representative of Ohio boys. But the dress of fiction adds nothing to the moral of his noble life. He was no more of a hero, loved his books no better, enjoyed hard labor no more than the hardy boys of his neighborhood. There was nothing in his boyhood, save that single characteristic of honesty in speech, which could be said to be indicative of superior gifts.

Fortunately for James, his uncle, Amos Boynton, had a heart broad enough to take in more than his own family; and the uncle's example, precepts and threats were most efficacious in keeping the children of the Garfield family decorous and respectful. James was not always good-natured nor always in the mood for immediate obedience to his mother's commands. But when he was inclined to mischief or willfulness, his mother had but to say, "I will tell Uncle Amos," and he was as meek as the lambs.

Uncle Amos was a valuable man in the community, and appears to have had, in his eccentric way, a most excellent influence over the young people of

Orange township.   He was a devoted member of the Disciples' Church, loved the Bible, and despised lazy or dishonest people.   He took an active part in organizing and sustaining local lyceum debates among the young men at the school-houses.   The singing-schools, spelling matches, out-door games, and religious gatherings had his personal assistance, and his encouragement and advice had a great influence with James, who stood in most reverential awe of his uncle.

His early school-days were not remarkably brilliant, nor did he particularly distinguish himself at that time, in any direction, beyond the majority of his school-fellows.   He possessed a good memory, and made reasonable progress in such rudiments as were taught in the log school-houses of that time. He loved to hear his mother read poetry, and committed many verses to memory.   His nature was poetical, and he loved to wander alone in the fields and woods, and in imagination act the part of some of the poetical characters of which he had heard. When he was old enough to read story books for himself, he found, somewhere, the "Pirates, Own Book," "Tales of the Sea," "Indian Stories," and other kindred volumes, in which he seems to have been greatly interested.   Pet calves and sheep were named by him after some favorite hero or heroine mentioned in romance, and even the rocks and highlands came in for a share in the titles of nobility he conferred.

The apple orchard of one hundred trees, which

his father planted and which had already spread wide its fruitful branches, and in the shade of which he passed the happiest days of his boyhood, was to his active imagination an army of warriors, or a host of Indians. Every tree soon had its name by which it was known, not only to him, but to all his playmates in the neighborhood. Each tree was named after some noted Indian warrior, or after some old saint; or, as was occasionally the case, for the lack of other names, he applied those of neighbors, preachers and school teachers. He appears to have felt no lonesomeness when left to himself, but was able to imagine the presence of others with him, or himself to be in some distant and attractive place, and "was never less alone than when by himself."

Very early in his life some story of the sea awakened his keen interest in the sailors' lives, and he formed many plans concerning a visit to the great ocean, to be carried out when he should become a man. He dreamed of the surging billows and longed for a sight of the white-fringed breakers. He would some day be a sailor. He would climb to the top of the masts. He would one day command a man-of-war. He would fight battles and win victories on every ocean and sea. He was often overheard repeating the commands of the heroic captains, about whom he had read, and with a stern and loud voice he often bade his imaginary men to "clear the deck for action."

He early imbibed a love for the Bible, which he found was always his mother's dearest companion.

Its warriors, prophets, saints and apostles were characters as real and familiar to his active imagination as were the people he had actually met. In his work and at his play he saw and felt more than some other boys, because of this power to call about him imaginary characters.

It may have been this habit of thinking on distant things that caused him, as a workman, to meet with so many accidents.

He found much comfort in the society of a little black dog, which seemed to understand the language and wishes of James, like a human being. The dog was considered a wonder by the other boys. For several years the little creature was seen with James at all his work, whether chopping wood, riding the horses for the plow, or going to the pastures for the neighbors' cows.

To all the beasts of the farm he was a kind and patient instructor, teaching them many curious and useful things. In all this he was, however, under his mother's careful oversight, and most faithfully did she watch over the "four saplings," of which James was the youngest, and which her husband, on his death-bed, had said he must leave to her care. For him she felt and exhibited that special solicitude which mothers usually feel for their youngest child. She was determined that he should avail himself of the school privileges during the few winter months in which it was held, and she labored very hard to supply him with the necessary clothes and books. The teachers of the school parted with Mrs. Garfield in the spring with great reluctance, for the school-house being on one corner of her farm, they were often obliged to seek favors from her, and thus became familiar friends. At no place in all the district was the teacher more welcome than at Mrs. Garfield's cabin, and although the loft in her home was perhaps more lonely, and the bed less easy than many others, they were glad when the time came in their "boarding around," to go to her abode. Many years afterwards they told of her love for learning, and of her desire that her children should have a thorough education.

James was favored with opportunities for reading which the other members of that industrious family did not get. It was usually accidental, however. He was a careless, awkward boy in the use of tools in his work, and was often laid up by self-inflicted wounds. He cut his feet with his axe or scythe. He wrenched his back by the fall of a fence rail upon him. He fell from the barn upon a pile of wood. So that while he was not perhaps more careless or awkward than boys of his age usually are, yet he was more often confined to the house as a result of accidents, and the hours of his retirement he most earnestly employed in studying all the books they had in the house, and all he could borrow of the neighbors. It was to his credit that he used his books with great care, and any neighbor was willing to intrust their volumes to him. His neighbors say that he learned much more in his early days by reading history and studying stories of scientific discov-cry out of school than he ever gained from teachers. He was greatly interested in the debates and literary exercises which were often held on winter evenings at the school-house ; and it is said that, as a critic, he was dreaded by some of the old men before he was ten years of age.

In 1842, when he was about eleven years old, the boys in Orange, by the advice of "Uncle Amos," organized a lyceum of their own, and it was the first place of the kind in which James ever ventured to speak.

His speech was not preserved, even in tradition. But the speech of the last disputant has never ceased to be a funny circumstance in the minds of the old people who heard of it at the time. The subject for discussion contained a clause in which it was resolved that navigation was of superior importance to some other branch of human industry. The young orator "supposed a case" where a meal of victuals awaited a hungry, drunken man, but he could not get to them. " Now," said the speaker, "that man is too drunk to navigate himself. He will have no supper. Now, of what use are all the beans, potatoes, sausages, pork and doughnuts to a man who can't *navigate?*" That speech was conclusive, and by a unanimous vote it was seriously declared that it was of the highest importance that men be able "to navigate."

These debates quickened James's desire for reading, and in less than two years he had read and remembered so much concerning the current topics of lyceum debates that he successfully held his own as a "principal" debater with the old men. Those evenings at the lyceum were the happiest, perhaps, in his youthful life. It was an escape for an hour or two from his hard and incessant toil. It was a place where he knew his mother was proud of him, and where even "Uncle Amos" was inclined to be more sparing of his critical suggestions than usual. It was the opening of a new life to the poor boy, and was suggestive of possible achievements which, until then, he had considered wholly beyond his reach. How many of our American statesmen can trace the beginning of their career to the lyceum in the country school-house! On the popularity of that humble and crude institution, the safety of the nation has often rested.

During his training in those evening schools of debate, he searched the neighborhood and drew upon distant relatives for books and papers. He put his soul into the work ; and with an eager longing looked forward to each debate with ever increasing interest.

There was a high ledge of broken rocks in the woods, about a quarter of a mile from his home, where one large shaft of rock rose considerably above its larger neighbors. To the top of that rock James used often to climb, and from its summit deliver to the rocks and trees around his prepared addresses or impromptu harangues. The trees and stones were an audience to him, and in his imagination they listened, sighed, and applauded, as, with excited tones, he approached his peroration. He called that rock his pulpit ; and never in the sacred desk or in the halls of the national councils found he a place in which there seemed to him such necessity for dignity, for grammatical accuracy, or for stirring illustration, as on that forest rostrum among the aged maples. Where will the American country youths find another such an audience as they saw in the waving corn, the rows of potatoes, the forest trees, or the astonished herds, in those youthful days when the spirit of oratory first touched their lips with its inspiring fire?

CHAPTER V.

YOUTHFUL OCCUPATIONS

EARLY MATURITY. — BOILING SALTS. — A MAN'S WORK AT HARVESTING. — AMBITION TO BE A CARPENTER. — SELF-SACRIFICES OF THOMAS. — THE NEW FRAME HOUSE AT ORANGE. — LEARNING THE TRADE. — OUT OF WORK. — CHOPPING WOOD. — WISHES TO BE A SAILOR. — VISITS A SHIP AT CLEVELAND. — ABANDONS THE IDEA OF BEING A SAILOR. — FINDS EMPLOYMENT ON THE OHIO CANAL. — A DRIVER BOY. — FEVER AND AGUE. — A QUARREL. — AN ACCIDENT. — GOES HOME TO HIS MOTHER.

THE years of 1844 and 1845 included a period of great uncertainty with James. His hard work and the needs of life, felt by him unusually early, had given to his mind a somewhat premature development. He possessed a tough, awkward body, and features which were not very prepossessing. But his mind was bright and mature. He labored very hard. For a few months he found employment in "boiling salts," which, in that early day, was made moderately profitable by the presence of immense quantities of ashes left in the clearings. The process of leaching the ashes and extracting the salts by boiling the liquid was a very dirty and unpleasant business.

The boy was often as black with soot as the followers of the kindred trade of charcoal burning, and his clothing was heavy with ashes and smoke. In this, as in every other undertaking, he was determined to excel, and began early in the morning and worked late at night. Another portion of that period he spent in chopping wood, being paid by the cord. In this he did a mature man's work, and received, for the first time, a man's wages. He also engaged himself in harvesting, and swung the scythe through the grass, the sickle in the grain, and the rake over the meadow, the equal of the eldest. But the work was so exhausting that he often heartily wished that he could see some other way of securing an honest living.

One day he saw a carpenter, with saw and chisel, at work framing a barn, and it occurred to him that the trade of a carpenter would suit him better than the ceaseless drudgery of a pioneer farmer's life. He had shown some adaptability for that trade in the repairs he had from time to time made on his mother's house and barn, and in the toys which he had ingeniously constructed. On consulting with his mother, he decided to learn the carpenter's trade. But no opportunity presented itself just at that time, and he worked on in his heavy labor, waiting for some way to open to the lighter occupation. Thus, at fifteen years of age, we find him an uncultured country boy, with no acquaintance with the world beyond the clearings and cabins of that new land. He appears to have had no thought or ambition above that of being able to earn a living. He had given up attending the school in his district, in which he had made good progress, and considered his education complete, as far as school-books were concerned. Certainly, his prospects for a place among the learned of the nation could scarcely have been more discouraging than it was then. What had chopping wood, boiling salts, digging ditches in the meadows, and milking cows, to do with refinement and intellectual cultivation ? However, the industry of the family was such that they began to accumulate a little fund, with which they purposed to purchase the materials to construct a frame house.

They began laying up pennies for that object, and to that small fund added dollars, and as the children grew older and earned more, the prospect grew brighter. At last, Thomas, whose fatherly interest in the family was truly heroic, secured a contract for clearing a large tract of land in Michigan, and chopping the wood. The profits of his labor in that undertaking were such that, after paying all his expenses. the overjoyed young man was able to come back to the home he had missed so much, and present to his mother the sum of eighty dollars. That amount having been added to the building fund, they felt able to undertake the enterprise, for which they had so long planned.

When they considered the matter of securing a carpenter, to make the frame for their new house, the opportunity for James to learn the trade seemed to present itself. It was in the construction of this little house of four rooms, near their log cabin, that James performed his first work at the carpenter's trade. The carpenter under whose tutelage James succeeded in obtaining a good practical knowledge, was Jedediah Hubbell of Chagrin Falls, and throughout a long life he was the staunch friend of his former apprentice.

The year 1846, when James was fifteen years old, was an eventful one in the life of the inexperienced boy. They had a new house and he had entered upon a new trade. Henceforth, he would be a carpenter, and his greatest pride was to be found in the drawing of the shave and pushing the plane. That was a step upward. He could earn higher wages, and it was less laborious than farming or clearing away timber. Yet, he never became such an expert at the trade as to deserve any especial praise. With the opportunities he had, with the few tools he could secure, and with employment only on the cheap farm houses and barns of that day, it is no surprise that he was an indifferent workman. His work was always carefully done, and gave the satisfaction that honest work gives to honest people. But in that trade he exhibited no striking genius, and constructed no buildings which would now be considered monuments of art or of remarkable skill.

He could not always find work as a carpenter, and was frequently, in the following years, compelled to leave the plane, and take up the hoe and shovel. Turning his hand to every kind of work that a young man could do, he found life rather hard, and his increase in knowledge and property very slow.

He had not found his level. He began to feel it severely when, after two years of toil, he found himself with but little money left with which to open another season. At one time he became utterly discouraged, and could see nothing before him but the same poverty and the same arduous toil. To be dissatisfied with one's trade or employment is not always an evidence of a fitness for any other station, although it often leads to the accomplishment of higher tasks. James, however, was not so much dissatisfied with his trade or work as he was with the unprofitableness of it, owing to the uncertainty of remunerative employment during the entire year.

At one of these seasons of uncertainty, the old longing to be a sailor returned with its pictures of the ocean's grandeur and sublimity; and for a time the old spirit of his early boyhood was upon him. Homesick for the sea! Yearning for adventure! Wishing to visit the strange lands of which the story books had told! In this restless mood, he determined to find some way in which to secure a place as a sailor on some Atlantic ship. But the offer of a job of chopping one hundred cords of wood made to him by his uncle, Thomas Garfield, called his attention away for a while, only to make it to return with greater determination.

The woodland where he worked for his Uncle Thomas, was situated near Newberg, and not very far from Lake Erie, and often, during his stay, he walked over to look out upon the changing hues of that ocean of fresh water. Once in a while he saw stately ships enter the harbor and furl their sails, and his heart beat fast with excited ambition. Yet he purposed not to be a sailor on so small a sea as Lake Erie. The mightiest oceans seemed none too large for him ; and the idea of sailing on the lake, was unworthy of his ambition.

Yet it occurred to him, as he chopped and pondered, — and chopping wood is a great promoter of thought, — that he could learn something of shipping by a trip on the lake and thus make more certain his employment in some Atlantic port. Hence, with a wisdom beyond his years, he resolved to try his hand at the business nearer home ; and if he liked the work, to seek some seaport as an experienced hand.

When the last stroke of the axe had been given, and the wood was all firmly and evenly piled for measurement, he started secretly and alone to Cleveland to see what chance he might find to ship as a deck-hand, or common sailor. He had heard that sailors were wanted, and had no doubt of his ability to find a place. Hence, with considerable confidence the awkward wood-chopper searched along the wharves for a vessel of such dimensions as would be suitable for his purpose. At last he found one large enough and with sails enough to be called a "stately, gallant ship," and he stepped on the deck from the wharf, alongside which the vessel was moored. Several rough-looking men were at work washing the deck and splicing the rigging.

"Where is the captain of this ship?" asked he of a sailor.

The sailor made no answer, but, with a queer expression of countenance, stared at the intruder.

"Can you tell me where I can see the captain?" asked he of another. The sailor with a motion of the hand indicated that the captain was below, and spoke not a word.

"Rather strict discipline I should say," thought James, as he approached the hatchway.

Suddenly the captain appeared at the hatches, who seemed at first astonished to see a stranger aboard his ship. He was almost too drunk to walk and James felt anxious lest the besotted, bloated wretch should fall backward into the hold.

"I would like to speak to the captain," said James to the drunken man.

For a stranger to board his ship without permission was evidently no light offense in the eyes of the captain. But to venture to speak to him, and especially to be ignorant of the fact that he was the captain, was too great an insult to be endured. The captain's wrath was uncontrollable.

"What in the —— are you here for?" yelled the inebriate. "Get out of this yeare craft, you sneakin' thief!"

There was not a fight, but if the captain had been sober and had indulged in such abuse, profanity and gesticulations, James would have picked up the rum-soaked tyrant and ducked him in the harbor. For James had inherited a powerful frame, and had increased his natural strength greatly by hard work.

But he swallowed his wrath, and, leaving the drunken wretch to vent his rage on some poor sailor, he walked away with nearly all the poetry of a sailor's life oozing swiftly out of his brain and heart. It was a great shock.   It made him feel as if he had met with a great loss.   For he never again encouraged the dreams of a sailor's happy life.   His longing for the sea was never wholly overcome, but his views of its hardships underwent an entire change.

In a discouraged mood he sought his uncle's house with a hope, perhaps, of securing another job of work in the woods.   There he learned that his cousins were soon to start out with a canal boat, owned by his uncle, to bring coal from the mines to Cleveland, on the Ohio Canal.   Hearing of no other employment, he asked the privilege of going with the boat in some capacity.   The only place they felt he was capable of filling was a driver boy to lead the horses along the bank of the canal, as they dragged the boat toward its destination.   It seems that it never occurred to James that, by taking such employment on the canal, he was throwing himself directly into the company and into the work which his father so much disliked, and to avoid which he had taken his children into the forest.

He soon found it a calling for which he was not fitted, or at least one which such a spirit as his could not long endure.

He never complained of his treatment by his employer or superiors.   The captain, Jonathan Myers, and his wife, were very favorably inclined toward him because of his strict adherence to the truth.   The canal boys were notorious for their long yarns, and often preferred to tell a lie when it was

Tow Boy.

much more for their interest to tell the truth.   Hence, his eccentric adherence to the facts made him unpopular with them.   He was clearly out of his place. He felt it, and told the kind captain that he should not stay long.   He had agreed to stay three months at ten dollars per month, and, as long as he could, he faithfully kept his contract.   But the long, monotonous tramps beside the horses, or the dull stops to await the passage of crowded locks gave him considerable time to think.   He knew that his mother had always desired to have him in some way obtain a liberal education.   He felt keenly the fact that he was engaged in a calling which had not her approval. The cursing, fighting and low conversation among the men were distasteful to him.   Once he was compelled to defend himself from an attack of an overbearing bully, and, it is said that James grappled with his opponent like a lion, and with dangerous precipitation sent the fellow rolling into the bottom of a flat boat.   Men and boys were respected there according to their strength of muscle and powers of endurance.   These he possessed in an eminent degree, and was seldom involved in any dispute.

Near the end of his term of three months, he was offered a position as steersman with an advance of wages.   He had often been called upon to relieve the steersman, and his judgment was so mature, and his skill so apparent, that the captain's wife advised him to make it his profession for life.   She urged the captain to secure the place for him, because she "felt much safer when Jim was at the helm."

But James could not be persuaded to make a new contract, nor did the large-hearted captain urge the matter. He said:

"Jim is too good a boy to stick to the canal. He loves his books too well to be confined to this hard life."

It was during this period that he met Dr. J. P. Robinson, a physician and preacher, who has been ever since that time a devoted friend. The doctor was an able and talkative man, whose good impulses were ever finding vent in some unexpected deed of kindness, and he had a great liking for James from the time of their first meeting. He advised him to find some place where he could work for his board and go to school, and told him of the great things he might do, and the great name he might gain by persevering in the attempt to obtain learning. The advice was not lost upon James, and he secretly resolved to find a place, if possible, where he could follow the doctor's advice.

Near the close of his three months' engagement, he began to be greatly afflicted with the fever and ague, which was a sad enemy of all the canal boatmen. The disease increased in virulence with alarming rapidity. His duties in caring for the careful passage of the boat, when meeting another, often required him to wade in the water, and sometimes he ventured in waist-deep. Such frequent baths, with the subsequent chill of the wet clothing which he wore until it was dry, greatly aggravated the disease.

One day after he became so weak that he could scarcely perform his work, while he was engaged in fastening a rope at the stern of the boat, he reached over the side to lift the rope from the water. He did not realize how weak he had become. He could not lift the rope. He tugged at it for a few moments, and then, while attempting to get a firmer hold, lost his balance and fell headlong into the water.

He had never learned to swim and he was in great danger of drowning. Fortunately, the rope which was the cause of the accident lay in the water within reach, and he had the presence of mind to clutch it, while the hands on the boat pulled him out. The shock and the chill of the cold water were more than his weak frame could endure. All the symptoms of a dangerous fever followed, and he determined to hasten home. In his journey he was assisted as far as Newberg by friends, but from that place, while burning with fever and dizzy with the ague, he walked determinedly home to his mother's cottage.

CHAPTER VI.

EFFORTS TO OBTAIN AN EDUCATION.

SLOW RECOVERY. — MEETING WITH MR. BATES. — A PRIVATE TUTOR. — DETERMINED BEGINNING. — THE GEAUGA SEMINARY. — ESTIMATES THE COST OF A TERM AT SCHOOL. — EARNS A SMALL SUM TO START WITH. — HIS MOTHER'S HELP. — BOARDING HIMSELF AT CHESTER. — PUDDING AND MOLASSES. — THE ADVANTAGES OF A HEALTHY BODY. — TEACHING SCHOOL. — VACATION WORK. — INTEREST IN RELIGION. — THE DISCIPLES OF CHRIST. — RELIGIOUS PERSECUTION. — TRUSTWORTHY WORK. — A GOOD NAME.

FOR weeks after his return to his home, he was confined to his bed by the fever. He was very sick. The disease was dangerous. The mercurial medicines prescribed appear to have been more dangerous. Yet after a few weeks he began slowly to recover, notwithstanding the depressing effects of exhaustion, ague and calomel. His mother's faithful nursing overcame both the disease and the prescription.

Again he was given an opportunity to think. He could not work, play or read. He was compelled by his inherited disposition to study, plan and dream of the future. He would never be a sailor. That was decided. He would never be a steersman on a canal. That, too, was settled. He could not content himself with the life of an indifferent carpenter, or even with that of a successful wood-chopper. What would he do after he had regained his strength?

This question was of untold importance to him and to others. Far greater than he then dreamed. The advice of Doctor Robinson, of the captain of the canal boat, and the prayers of his mother were not lost upon him.

His Uncle Amos, who frequently came to his bedside, added his precepts to the already strong evidence of the value of scholarship. Lying day after day, unable to move in his bed from one position owing to the ague cake which stubbornly refused to be reduced, he revolved in his mind various schemes for securing an education. He had nearly decided to try again the district school and swallow his pride, provided a teacher was engaged who could help him along, and had determined to seek the advice of some suitable person about the books he might need, when a most fortunate circumstance happened to give direction to his plans.

Samuel D. Bates, who has since been extensively known and revered as a Baptist preacher, was employed to teach school in Orange, and his attention was called to the studious and upright life which James was reputed to have led. He was especially impressed with the fact that it was said by all, that, through the poverty, wants and temptations of his life, James had not swerved from the honest truth. Neither wealth, nor fame, nor culture could have given the boy such a claim on the good man's heart. Mr. Bates sought the acquaintance of the Garfield family and was soon on intimate terms with James. His advice to him was clear and decided.

He told him that many boys as old and as ignorant as himself, had become great and good by perseverance and industry.   Mr. Bates advised him to fix his mind with unflinching determination on securing a college education.   Mrs. Garfield, with unmeasured joy, saw the influence which Mr. Bates was having upon James, and, with delight, saw in the behavior and plans of her son, that he had set his face resolutely toward learning and its accompanying responsibilities.

On his recovery, which was exceedingly slow, he abandoned the idea of attending further any public school, and began a course of private instruction, with Mr. Bates for his teacher.   Under the impetus of the fresh inspiration which James had obtained, his progress was surprising even to himself.   He had feared that he was too backward to enter any academy without being ashamed of himself, but with this assistant, he would soon take rank with the best.

It was a singular sight to see that awkward woodchopper, fresh from the timber lands and the canal boat, pouring over a grammar or an arithmetic. With features made coarse by exposure, and pallid with sickness, with his stiff hair, which the sun had made crisp and wiry, standing up in a great tuft from his forehead, and with hands grim and horny, he had a most unpromising appearance as a candidate for literature or scholarship.   There were those who regarded the attempt which James was making, as a very foolish effort of a country farm-hand " to

get above his business," and even said that it would
be better to advise the boy to lay up his money and
to help his mother, rather than waste his valuable
time in useless "book learning."   Even Uncle Amos,
with all his reverence for the ministry, and admira-
tion of able temperance lecturers, did not think it
worth while for any boy of such plebian stock as the
neighborhood of Orange was supposed to produce,
to spend his time in securing anything more than a
knowledge of the "common English branches."
But James had made an unchangeable resolution ;
and, with a keen love for books, and a heart greatly
moved by the religious interest which the Church of
the Disciples was awakening in that community, he
stubbornly compelled every hindering circumstance
to bend to his will.

At noon by his carpenter's bench, at evening after
his work on his mother's farm, he sought his books
and solved arithmetical problems.

At this time there stood on a beautiful eminence
about twelve miles from Orange, and in the town of
Chester, a commodious, three-story wooden building,
used for a school of a higher grade than the common
schools, and called the "Geauga Seminary."   It was
in one of the most charming localities in Ohio.
The school was then in a very prosperous condition,
and attracted students from distant parts of the State.
It was established by the Freewill Baptists as a
denominational school, and, but for the unfortunate
religious persecution in which that denomination in
Ohio was concerned with others, it would have con-

tinued, doubtless, in their hands, and might long ago have been a college. Its standard of education at that time was not higher than the lower classes in the high schools now. But that was a great advance upon the rudimentary knowledge imparted in the common schools.

Mr. Bates had been a student at the Geauga Seminary, and pointed out to James the great advantage it would be to him if he could manage to attend that school. At the time the suggestion was made to James, there did not appear to be any probability or possibility of his being able to attend the school. He could neither spare the time from work, nor get the money with which to pay his board. Yet his courage abated not at the prospect. His mother agreed with him that somehow and in some way he must go. All his family, including Thomas, now grown to manhood, and his sisters, Mehitable and Mary, now in the ranks of womanhood, were kindly disposed, but they were poor. If he attended the academy he must depend on himself and his mother.

When the advantages of the seminary at Chester began to be discussed in the community, Uncle Amos thought that it might be well to permit his sons to attend school there, provided they could earn the money, as James must do. Long and anxious discussions followed in both families, sometimes in a kind of joint convention, and sometimes in their separate circles, upon the ways and means for obtaining an academic education. They calculated the cost of the tuition, then estimated how much their food would cost if they had no luxuries at all and boarded themselves on the very cheapest food, such as hasty pudding, and corn bread. They were compelled to add the cost of some stout cloth for a suit of clothes, with a cap and a pair of boots for each. How provokingly it did count up! How great were the difficulties in the way of those young men!

If they boarded themselves, how many dishes would it take, how many knives and forks, how many towels, and how many kettles? All those must be borrowed from home to save the expense of purchasing new. Yes, that could be arranged; but yet the project seemed very distant.

It was not until some months after the matter was first talked of, that a way opened for James. He had an opportunity to earn a few dollars on an unusually profitable job of carpentering, and, although the sum seemed a mere pittance for one in his circumstances to begin such an undertaking, he resolved to make a beginning and trust the future to open the way to further advancement.

In 1849, that year made memorable by the discovery of gold in California, and which witnessed the departure of so many young men for the gold fields, James began his course of instruction at Chester. It was the humblest beginning that could be made, and it must have most severely wounded his pride to be associated with scholars more advanced and so much more favored in worldly possessions. He was too brave to exhibit any misgivings, or let people know that he noticed the distinctions which are always, but often unconsciously, made between the rich and poor by the best of men and women.

A description of their style of living at the Geauga Seminary has been given to the author by one of his room-mates who attended the school the second term of James's stay at Chester. There were three of them in one room — James, his cousin, Henry Boynton, and Orren Judd. The room was about ten feet wide and twelve feet long, and was in a small farm-house near the academy. They selected that room because it was cheaper than those which were let in the academy building, and for the same reason the three boys occupied but one room. With the two narrow beds, their cook-stove, boxes, and three chairs, there was but little room for themselves. They divided up the work, and each alternately prepared the meals for a day. When the fire was burning in the old box-stove, which had but one cover, the heat often drove out all but the cook.

Their meals, however, were often cold, and for many weeks their only diet consisted of mush and milk. When the bread from home gave out, the supply being renewed nearly every week, they returned invariably to their hasty pudding, or to their hot corn-cakes and molasses. They were at the academy to study, and not to cook. To keep alive was the only object in eating at all; and whenever they were compelled to eat, they did it with dispatch, and returned to their books. Near the end of their second term, the boys became very much dissatisfied with their board, and made up their minds that boarding themselves was not a successful enterprise. James is said to have thrown down his spoon one day as he finished his dish of pudding and molasses, saying, —

"I won't eat any more of that stuff, if I starve!"

But all their drawbacks did not appear to hinder their progress in their studies. James worked very hard, and made such masterly strides upward that he soon had reason to feel proud of his achievements. His hard fare, hard work, and close application made no impression upon the hardy constitution which had been disciplined by chopping wood, planting crops, and drawing the plane ; and while his classmates and room-mates faltered and weakened under the strain and the privations, he kept steadily pulling onward, with his health and strength unimpaired.

How few successful men have spent their entire youth in school. The keenest intellects and the greatest minds of earth have almost universally been found with those whose youth was inured to hardships, and whose early years were spent in physical hard work. With a healthy body, no man need despair of getting an education, even if he must begin in middle age. A college education is such a very small part of the learning necessary, in this day, to entitle a person to a position among scholars or men of letters, that it is universally regarded by cultivated men as only a beginning. No man with a rugged body and a thoughtful mind need lack a college education. The knowledge of mathematics, of science, of the languages, or of history is no more valuable because it has been learned inside the halls of a college building. They can all be learned elsewhere; and to be a leader among men, much that is more difficult and more profound must be acquired away from them. The boy who has graduated from a college has only just begun, if he really hopes for success; and this after-education cannot be acquired in the rough contact with the cares of life, without a sound body to draw upon. Many men who never heard a college lecture, and never darkened the doors of the humblest university, have started late in life, with vigorous health, and acquired a fund of learning beyond that of college professors, and performed great deeds, which precocious students had not the strength to execute. All schools and colleges are a help, but they are not an absolute necessity. Health is always a necessity. It gives the late scholar a strong advantage over an early one. It gives the power to become learned and great to him, who may have passed a score of years in ignorance. It is an inestimable blessing to any one, and worth the sacrifice of early school-days. Experience, as in the case of James, has taught that a neglected early education is no loss, if the young man possesses the moral courage to acknowledge his ignorance. and vigorously sets himself at the task of making up his deficiencies. It often requires more fortitude than to fight a battle. But he who wins in that contest will conquer in all others. James lost nothing in the end by being poor and out of school in his boyhood, and others need not.

Even the delay in his progress, caused by his absence for the purpose of earning money enough to pay his way, seems to have been easily made up. Having an opportunity to teach a school in his native town, he eagerly accepted the position, and was absent from the academy the entire winter.

That school was a difficult one to control, and was noted for its unruly boys. James was an enthusiast then, on the subject of learning, and took the most eager interest in all the lessons of the school. He was also a believer in good order, and in his ability to maintain it. It is told of him that several of the boys, led by a stubborn young giant, attempted to conduct themselves unseemly during the school hours, and engaged in open rebellion. When the rebellion was crushed, which was not long after the teacher set about it, there were several sore heads, a giant with a lame back, and the most perfect decorum throughout the school-room.

During these academic days, James took an active and permanent interest in religious matters. His free spirit and strong independence of character inclined him toward the Church of the Disciples, the creed of which, if it may be said to have had any in that day, was untrammeled by traditions and unfettered by any laws, save the words of the Bible, without change or comment. They formed a religious community, in which all were supposed to have an equal share, and in which every one could preach, if he so desired, without the usual ceremony of ordination or installation. It claimed then, as the large church does now, to follow the example of Jesus, as the disciples followed it, and to be as free from church organization and creeds, as were the apostles. Alexander Campbell, the founder of the sect, was long a member of the Baptist church, and claimed to differ from them only in his disbelief in the binding force of the church creed, and in the necessity of ministerial ordinations. Such, in the main, seems to be the faith of the church he founded.

In 1848 and 1849, the religious movement in favor of the Disciples was very strong in the northern part of Ohio, and Mrs. Garfield was one of its early converts. With her, were many members of the families in Orange, including "Uncle Amos." They were a sensible, devout, sincere and unobtrusive sect, and their belief and example naturally appealed to the large-hearted, plain people of Ohio.

It may be that the church would not have grown with such rapidity, had it not been for a most absurd persecution which sprung up among the Baptist and Freewill Baptist churches. Opposition and unjust persecution have ever been meat and drink for new religious movements. Churches thrive under opposition, and lag in profound peace. Many of the Freewill Baptists, having gained considerable strength themselves by the persecution they had endured, were foolish enough to repeat the everrecurring event of the past history, and in turn began the persecution of the Disciples. It was a movement discountenanced by many of the best members, and few churches, as a body, took a share in it. But the spirit of persecution showed itself in little acts of discourtesy, in refusing to speak when accosted, in shunning companionship, in refusing to allow the children to play together, in favoritism in school, and on public occasions, and sometimes in angry personal disputes.

James had no sympathy whatever with that spirit, and sympathized deeply with the inoffensive yet injured party. The Geauga Seminary at Chester felt the effects of public opinion, and became the scene of frequent disputes and of unpleasant religious controversy. The same feeling existed in other schools ; and as the " Disciples of Christ " grew stronger and bolder, the necessity for an institution of learning for their sons and daughters forced itself on their attention, and led to the foundation of an academy at Hiram, Portage county, of which we shall speak further in the next chapter.

In all the discussions on religious topics, James was the outspoken champion of entire religious freedom, and fought with all his heart against any ostracism or persecution because of religious opinions. He claimed the right to follow the faith the Bible appeared to him to teach, and stoutly maintained that every other person should be given the same sacred right. His Christian faith and his behavior were both open, courageous, generous and impartial, and his advocacy of the Disciples did much in that early day to strengthen the stakes of their tabernacle.

His life as a Christian young man did much to assist the creed to which he adhered. For no opposing politician has ever been found,—and they are the most merciless of critics,—who would venture to say that James led an inconsistent life. One old gentleman residing in Mayfield, who knew James in that early day, said of him afterwards, that,—

"His conscience kinder went ahead on him inter his work, an' ye could allers trust him to du any job, hoein', rakin,' hewin', planin', teachin', or any other thing, fur he'd feel much the wust ef he left any out as it had n't dorter be. He did n't cover up nothin' h'ed spiled, an' he'd work just as fast if the man who paid him warnt around. He was right-up-'n-down squar!"

Such is the universal testimony of those for whom he labored in field and shop, woodland and school-room during his vacations, and when the strongest temptations which ever beset a young man urged him to slight his work and obtain money without giving an honest equivalent. Such a name was of inestimable value to him in after years, and to the church whose cause he thus early espoused.

CHAPTER VII.

SCHOLAR AND TEACHER AT HIRAM.

LEAVING CHESTER. — DESCRIPTION OF HIRAM. — THE CROWN OF OHIO. — THE ECLECTIC INSTITUTE. — THE COURSE OF STUDY. — A LEADER AMONG THE STUDENTS. — JANITOR OF THE BUILDING. — URGED TO BECOME A PREACHER. — DETERMINED TO ATTEND COLLEGE. — THE DEBATING CLUB. — A REVOLT. — OUTSIDE STUDIES. — WORK AS A TEACHER. — WORKS ON ALONE INTO THE COLLEGE TEXT-BOOKS. — BORROWS MONEY OF HIS UNCLE THOMAS. — STARTS FOR WILLIAMS-TOWN COLLEGE.

NOTWITHSTANDING all his hardships and annoyances at Chester, James parted with the school and town, at the end of his last term there, with feelings of sincere regret. It had opened a new life to him, and he was profoundly grateful. It was an excellent school. Its teachers were faithful, kind and competent. The boys and girls who attended there went for the purpose of making themselves useful in the future, and they had been most congenial companions. The wide landscape, which stretched far away in every direction from the pleasant hill-top where the academy stood, was one he often loved to contemplate, and it had exercised its useful influence in shaping the course of his life. There, among other pleasant faces, he had been gratified to meet the modest, quiet girl they called

'Crete Rudolph, whose home was in Hiram, and who was to cross his path again. He had obtained in that recitation room, they called "the chapel," many new ideas, and a fund of encouragement. He came to it a coarse and awkward woodsman, and in portions of two years, it had lifted him into an aspiring scholar, with attainments worthy of any of his age. It had made the world more beautiful, more valuable, and life more earnest and sublime. It had revealed to him the latent power within himself. It had shown him the distant mountain-tops of fame and greatness, and set his feet in the path that led heavenward. It is said of him that he was wise enough to see and appreciate it all, and if he did, his heart throbbed sadly as he turned away from those beloved scenes.

His life at the Chester Academy had much of sunshine in it after all. He had not always worn the coarsest clothes, nor had he every term boarded himself. For to-day, teachers will show to the visitor the battered and narrow chamber in the third story of the academy, in which he slept during the two terms he boarded in the building, and the same old stove at which he warmed himself.

Thus, with feelings of gratitude for the past, and with high hopes of the future, James turned from Chester toward Hiram. He had no more capital then, than when he came to Chester, except the ability to command higher wages as a teacher, and the increased skill which a few months more of practice had given him as a carpenter.

HIRAM COLLEGE, HIRAM. OHIO.

The town of Hiram is in Portage county, and its situation is such that it might be styled "the crown of Ohio." It is located very close to that elevated line where the waters divide, one part flowing southward to the Ohio river, and the other portion northward to Lake Erie. From the commanding eminence where the college is located, the panorama is beautiful and extensive. The spectator looks down upon fields of grain and tracks of woodland, and away to hills and forests, with glimpses of the neatest of farm-houses in the country, and of clustered dwellings in the distant villages, adding the romance of art to the attractions of nature. So varied is the landscape and so serenely quiet seems everything in sight, that many beholders stand and gaze, and gaze again, with an inexhaustible satisfaction. It is one of those sweet and quiet retreats whose embowered walks and shady lawns seem most consistent with a thoughtful mood and a virtuous mind. Strikingly suggestive of the sylvan shades of antiquity, in the shape of the hills and the verdure of its trees, the college seems to be a part of the natural landscape.

There, in 1849, the leaders among the Churches of the Disciples decided to locate their academy; and March 1, 1850, the legislature of Ohio granted them a charter, under the name of "The Western Reserve Eclectic Institute." Among the founders of the institute was Mr. Zeb Rudolph, the father of Lucretia Rudolph, of whom mention was made in the last chapter. There was a flourishing church of their faith near the spot which they selected, and a neighborhood composed of very intelligent farmers, many of whom were born in New England. Professor B. A. Hinsdale, in writing for the "Centennial History of Education in Ohio," thus speaks of the aims which the founders had in establishing the school:

"The aims of the school were both general and special ; more narrowly they were· these :

(1) To provide a sound scientific. and literary education.

(2) To temper and sweeten such education with moral and scriptural knowledge.

(3) To educate young men for the ministry.

One peculiar tenet of the religious movement in which it originated, was impressed upon the Eclectic Institute at its organization. The Disciples believed that the Bible had been in a degree obscured by the theological speculations and ecclesiastical systems. Hence, their religious movement was a revolt from the theology of the schools, and an overture to men to come face to face with the Scriptures. They believed, also, that to the Holy Writings belonged a larger place in general culture than had yet been accorded to them. Accordingly, in all their educational institutions they have emphasized the Bible and its related branches of knowledge. This may be called the distinctive feature of their schools. The charter of the Eclectic Institute, therefore, declared the purpose of the institution to be : "The instruction of youth of both sexes in the various branches of literature and science, especially of moral science as based on the facts and precepts of the Holy Scriptures."

"The Institute rose at once to a high degree of popularity. On the opening day, eighty-four students were in attendance, and soon the number rose to two or three hundred per term. Students came from a wide region of country. Ohio furnished the larger number, but there was a liberal patronage from Canada, New York, and Pennsylvania ; a considerable number came from the Southern States, and a still larger from the Western. These students differed widely in age, ability, culture, and wants. Some received grammar school instruction; others high school instruction ; while others still pushed on far into the regular college course. Classes were organized and taught in the collegiate studies as they were called for ; Language, Mathematics, Literature, Science, Philosophy, and History. No degrees were conferred, and no students were graduated. After they had mastered the English studies, students were allowed a wide range of choice. The principle of election had free course. A course of study was published in the catalogue after the first year or two ; but it was rather a list of studies taught as they were called for than a *curriculum* that students pretended closely to follow."

The Institute had passed through one term when James appeared at Hiram ready for work. He was as courageous and as poor as ever. His cousins were with him, but they had abandoned the expectation of keeping pace with him. He carved his own way and was, at that time, a " law unto himself." He had won the battle for mental supremacy before he entered at Hiram, and ever after he was treated by the many students who came to Hiram from Chester, and soon by all at Hiram, as though he was of a different mould from the masses, and one who was expected to learn faster and know more than his class-mates.

Still the weights of poverty hung to his feet and the struggles for a livelihood were long, severe, bitter.

One of the first attempts he made to make sure of food while he studied, was to secure the place of janitor of the building, where he might build the fires, sweep the recitation rooms, and ring the bell for a small sum per month. He that afterwards became a professor in the same rooms he had swept as a young man ; he that was to be the President of that college, the bell of which he was glad of a chance to ring, began at the very lowest and stooped to conquer.

The good Christian people who took an active share in supporting the institute, noticed his meekness and recognized his superior abilities. They regarded him as providentially adapted to the work of preaching the gospel, and repeatedly urged him to follow that profession. They did not find in him any disinclination to do his duty; but there was at one time a hesitancy, on his part, about entering the ministry, owing to his distrust of his ability and fitness. He began, however, as early as his twenty-first year to fill the pulpits in various churches of his own denomination ; and before his graduation or departure from Hiram, he was in most flattering demand to supply vacant pastorates in the vicinity.

Some urged him to be satisfied with the instruction at the institute, which was not for many years after a college, and to abandon his plans for a collegiate course. But no offer, however large, and no place however high, could induce him to rest satisfied with anything less than the highest educational culture.

Living upon the simplest farmer's fare, and sleeping in the humblest and plainest of the basement rooms in the college, he kept steadily before him the hope of being able to stand among the highest and best in the land. He was a lover of college sports, and was eager to win the games in which he took part.

But the place he loved most to visit was the debating club which was to him both a recreation and a study. The debates were always vigorous and scholarly on the part of a portion of the students. and somewhat light and jocose on the part of others ; and it appears that the debating club to which James belonged had a serious division, owing to a difference in the tastes of the members. As is usually the case, those who enjoyed frivolity better than sound sense were in the majority and could carry by a preponderance of votes any measure which they brought before the club.

The contest over some matter concerning a public debate, become so serious and bitter that young Garfield arose, in considerable anger, and declared that sooner than be compelled to waste his time in such nonsense as the majority proposed, he would form another society, if he had to debate alone with himself. Believing the minority had rights which the majority were bound to respect, he demanded concessions from the party in power, or he would withdraw. The concessions were not made, and he set up the standard of revolt. To his colors the leading students flocked, and a second society was

7

formed with him for President which long outlived the one from which they withdrew.

It is said that he did not confine himself to the regular studies of the institute, but used his extra hours in reading history and theological works. The work which he accomplished must have been nearly double that of many students. Yet he found time for many vigorous games. He soon left many of the classes behind, and at the opening of his second year he was appointed as a teacher of some of the lower classes. In that way, by doubling his hours of work, and taking for study, many hours of the night, he was able to keep on in his recitations with the advanced classes, while he taught the lower grades. The way did not open for him to secure the funds with which to go to college, at the time when he had prepared himself for the Freshman classes, and so he kept on teaching, and preaching, and studying the text books of the regular college courses. It was for a long time in doubt whether he would be able to enter any college, his financial means were so limited. But he never abandoned the hope, sooner or later, in some way, to obtain the money. He was not one of those young men who wished to graduate from college for the social standing which it was supposed, through the ignorance of the public, to give a man, whether he had learned little or much. He desired the opportunities which colleges, libraries, and learned men could give to enlarge the field of his study. He knew that he could obtain elsewhere all that the colleges could give, and more, by persevering hard work over the books, and actually did secure for himself the first two years' course of college classes. Yet he saw that he could progress faster with congenial associates and among men more learned than he.

One day, he thought of his uncle, Thomas Garfield, whose various enterprises had been successful, and who had acquired a fortune. It occurred to him that his uncle might be willing to lend him enough to enable him to attend two years at Williams College in Massachusetts, where he heard that the expense was not great, and the standard of scholarship high. He had studied so faithfully that he felt very sure of entering two years in advance.

But he disliked very much to ask any person to lend him money. It was a most humiliating step to take. He sought advice from relatives, and they told him to try it. So he reluctantly went to his uncle, and asked for the use of five hundred dollars, until he could finish his college course, and earn that sum by teaching. His uncle had always been kind to him, and had seemed to take a friendly interest in his welfare ; but yet the nephew had the strongest doubt regarding the success of his petition for so large an amount of money. It was a large sum for a poor young man to borrow, but a very small sum on which to undertake two years of college life, five hundred miles from home.

His uncle met him in a generous manner, and saying that he felt sure of his pay, if his nephew lived, loaned young Garfield the sum for which he asked.

The young man, conscientiously desiring that his uncle should be secured in case of his death while in college, procured a policy on his life, in a Life Insurance company, for five hundred dollars, payable in case of his death to his uncle.

Thus the way opened to him, at last, for a collegiate education, and young Garfield, full of joy and ambition, took leave of his mother at Orange, and of his school-mate, Lucretia Rudolph, at Hiram, and with the sum his uncle had lent him, slightly augmented by a little sum he had saved, started on his long journey toward the classic Berkshire hills of the old Bay State.

Just before his departure for Williams he wrote a private letter to a friend, explaining his reasons for choosing Williams rather than the college of his denomination at Bethany. A part of it was as follows :

"After thinking it all over I have made up my mind to go to Williamstown, Massachusetts. * * * There are three reasons why I have decided not to go to Bethany. 1st. The course of study is not so extensive or thorough as in Eastern colleges. 2d. Bethany leans too heavily toward slavery. 3d. I am the son of Disciple parents, am one myself, and have had but little acquaintance with people of other views; and, having always lived in the West, I think it will make me more liberal, both in my religious and general views and sentiments, to go into a new circle, where I shall be under new influence. These considerations led me to conclude to go to some New England college. I therefore wrote to the President of Brown University, Yale and Williams, setting forth the amount of study I had done, and asking how long it would take me to finish their course.

"These answers are now before me. All tell me I can graduate in two years. They are all brief, business notes, but President Hopkins concludes with this sentence: 'If you come here we shall be glad to do what we can for you.' Other things being so nearly equal, this sentence, which seems to be a kind of friendly grasp of the hand, has settled that question for me. I shall start for Williams next week."

CHAPTER VIII.

LIFE AT WILLIAMS COLLEGE.

HIS HEALTH. — APPEARANCE OF THE HOOSAC VALLEY. — THE SCENERY ABOUT WILLIAMS COLLEGE. — THE GREAT NATURAL AMPHITHEATRE. — THE MOUNTAINS IN OCTOBER. — CHARACTER OF THE STUDENTS. — GARFIELD'S HABITS AS A STUDENT. — ENTERS THE JUNIOR CLASS. — HIS MODESTY. — THE FRIENDSHIP OF PRESIDENT HOPKINS AND PROFESSOR CHADBOURNE. — HIS TRUTHFULNESS AT COLLEGE. — HIS GRADUATION. — HIS CLASS-MATES.

THE three years of study at Hiram had not impaired young Garfield's health, and when, in September, 1854, at twenty-three years of age, he presented himself before the faculty at Williamstown College, for examination, he was a picture of health and strength. His broad shoulders, large face, bright blue eyes, high forehead, and brown hair were visible over the heads of many of his fellow students, and he was at once known among them as the "Ohio giant."

He appears to have been delighted with the professors, with the locality in which the college was situated, and with the extended mountain scenery. In his letters to his friends in Ohio, he was quite enthusiastic in his descriptions of the men and the landscapes. In fact he had been especially favored during his school days in the natural scenery which surrounded academies and college. Williamstown is situated on the Hoosac river, and among the most majestic of those mountains of which the term "Berkshire Hills" is both belittling and misleading. The college building stands on the top of a natural eminence, overlooking a wide plain, which all around it stretches away to the distant, towering mountains, and reminds the traveler somewhat of the situation of Jerusalem, where the city itself is on a hill, with higher mountains all around looking down upon it. But the great natural amphitheatre, in which the college hill at Williamstown stands, is far more attractive, more extensive, more majestic. The lofty mountains appear to enclose the plain, with no opening apparent anywhere for the egress of the streams whose clear waters unite below the town, to form the Hoosac river. Extensive forests of never-fading green crown the mountains, while woodlands of maple, birch, beach, poplar, and ash, adorn the mountain sides and checker the valley.

In October, and soon after the college term opened, the frost and sunlight combined to beautify the landscape, and nowhere in all the world can a more gorgeous scene be found than from the encircled plains of Williamstown, in the brilliant October days. The distant mountains, under their caps of green, are arrayed in all the varied hues and all the possible combinations and shades which the prism can show. A flowery landscape, as enchanting as the fabled beauty of the ancient vale of Cashmere. No one will obtain any idea of its autumn splendor unless he sees it for himself, nor believe the accurate descriptions of it until he visits the scene, and for himself

> "Sees old Hoosac on his throne,
>   With hills of beauty gathered round."

It is no overwrought figure which the Alumni of Williams use when they sing:

> " Dear Alma Mater, long as stand,
> Like pillars of our native land,
>   These everlasting hills,
> Thy grateful children shall proclaim
>   In every clime thy growing fame."

Aside from its scenery, Williams College possessed various attractions for the young Ohio student, which caused him to select that college as the most desirable place to pursue his studies.

The locality, the design of the founder and incorporators, the conservative character of the president, whose highest aim was to sustain a *safe* college, the class of students who frequented its halls, the absence of offensive, aristocratic and senseless snobs, and the quiet and honest habits of the little native community, made it a most appropriate and desirable institution for a self-made, country youth, like him. His modesty, his dislike for display, his indisposition to go anywhere or do anything for the name of it, and his desire to work undisturbed by outside attractions, as well as his limited means, combined to make congenial his opening days at Williams College.

He was admitted, without question, to the Junior

class, he having in three years' time, in the work
of preparing for college and in the studies of the
Freshman and Junior years, accomplished the usual
work of six years. The achievement is made more
astonishing by the large amount of other labor,
physical and mental, which he performed during that
period, in order to secure his board, clothing and
tuition.

He became at once a favorite of President Hopkins, and a close friend of Professor Chadbourne,
who had been elected a professor one year before.
It was a strong recommendation for young Garfield
to have the esteem and love of two such remarkable
men. Yet both those gifted scholars have kept him
fresh in their memories, and both have watched his
career with unabated interest. It was among such
men that he made his closest friendship. Only
thoughtful, studious, and earnest men would have
seen anything attractive in him. His class-mates
testify that his life was so retiring and his behavior
so unostentatious, that he made no especial impression on their memories. He studied hard, often
walked alone in the roads or fields, and attended to
all his duties with quiet promptness. It was understood that he was to enter the ministry, and in his
entire stay they saw nothing inconsistent with that
profession. He took an especial interest in metaphysical studies, rhetoric, and debate, and was a
leading mind among his class-mates on those topics.

During his collegiate course he tried to secure
small sums of money by teaching evening writing-

school, in the small towns around Williamstown, but was never so successful, in that scattered community, as to secure a very profitable number of scholars. He dressed very plainly and cheaply, and was compelled to economize, in every way, — in his board, his books, and in his traveling expenses, — in order to make the small sum he had secured to last until his graduation. He was the humblest of them all. He was very poor, and was brave enough to frankly acknowledge it. There is no more striking proof of the fact, so little understood, that college life is but a small part of the discipline and learning necessary to a liberal education than is found in the history of college classes. How often do we find that the honored, brilliant, and influential students sink almost immediately out of sight when they leave the college halls and enter the breakers of actual life; while the silent, thoughtful one, whose presence in the class is scarcely remembered, comes conspicuously to the surface, in civil or military life, and soon towers above all his acquaintances and school-day associates. Sometimes, in the annals of scientific discovery, or of national leadership, the popular and brilliant college student is found. Once in a while the valedictorian is again heard of in the vanguard of civilization, with the great and the good. But the rarity of it is a curious and sad feature connected with students' lives. It may be that the honors they received led them to the fatal conclusion that at their graduation they knew all that men need to learn, and stopping, they were soon left behind and beneath by the less successful candidates for class-day honors.

·Garfield's student days appear to have impressed him as but a portion of a whole life of study, and he conducted himself as if his graduation was to make no break in his pursuit of knowledge. Beginning it as if for a long journey, on which it would be unwise, at first, to hurry, he left the college as one who has passed the first mile, and looks back upon his progress with satisfaction, and forward with unflinching determination. He does not appear to have been actuated by any desire for fame, neither had he any confidence in his ability to acquire riches. He purposed to do quiet, solid work, either as a preacher, lawyer or teacher, and pictured to himself a life of studious quiet and religious peace.

In his college days, his characteristic simplicity and truthfulness were noticed and commended. He was determined to appear to possess no more than his actual acquirements would warrant. If he did not understand his lesson, or for some reason was behind in his studies, he manfully said so without reserve. His teachers never over-estimated him ; for his life was transparent, and his words bore the intangible but positive impress of truth. This noble trait of his character compelled him to make many sacrifices. If he neglected his study, there was no escape for him in manufactured excuses. If he was inferior to other students in certain branches of the college studies, he could not make up for it with "ponies," stolen translations, or borrowed keys. If he was late or absent at prayer-time, or at recitation, he could not feign sickness, nor evade the monitor's inquiries. Hence, he was forced, by his own rigid morality, to be thorough in his studies and obedient in his behavior. How much of human success and human greatness depends on the strictness and wisdom with which parents discipline and educate their children into that sublimest and most necessary of all acquirements, — invariable and unshaken adherence to the simple truth !

The two years of college life passed quickly with him, as they do with all, and the joyful day of graduation came to him as to thousands of others. But his joy was enhanced by the reflection that he should no longer be compelled to live on borrowed money. He is said to have longed, even at that early day, to be at work paying up his Uncle Thomas. With the success of his studies he must have been well satisfied. He had made solid progress. He had made many warm friends, especially among the faculty. He had secured the metaphysical honors of his class, and had the respect of all. Yet, to enable him to acquire this, he had drawn upon the future, and he longed to be at work. How the desire to see his mother, and that other lady at Hiram, may have influenced his joy on his graduation day, the historian at present can only surmise.

The class-mates of Mr. Garfield are now scattered through the different States of the Union, and are nearly all of that steady, sturdy character for which he was remarkable. William Rowe Baxter was a

captain in the regular service, and was killed in
Mississippi, June 1864; Stephen W. Bowles is a physician in Springfield, Massachusetts; Isaac Bronson
is a lawyer in New York; Elijah Cutler is a minister,
and agent of the Bible Society, Boston, Mass. ; Ham-
ilton N. Eldridge is a lawyer in Chicago, and was
brevetted a brigadier-general in the war of the rebellion ; James E. Fay is a lawyer in Chicago ; James
Gillfillan is a lawyer, and was for a time in the government service, at Washington ; Charles S. Halsey
lives at Canandaigua, New York ; James K. Hazen,
was a Presbyterian minister in Alabama; Clement
H. Hill is a lawyer, and clerk of the United States
Court, in Boston, Massachusetts ; Silas P. Hubbell is a lawyer at Champlain, New York ; Ferris
Jacobs is a lawyer at Delhi, New York, and was a
colonel in the war; Henry M. Jones is a Baptist
minister ; Henry E. Knox is a lawyer in New York ;
John E. D. Lamberton died in 1857 ; Charles W.
McArthur is a Presbyterian minister ; Elizur N. Man-
ley is a Presbyterian minister at Oakfield, New York ;
James McLean is a Congregational minister in Wisconsin ; Robert J. Mitchell is a lawyer in New York ;
George B. Newcomb is a Congregational minister in
Connecticut ; Joseph F. Noble is a Presbyterian
minister at Brooklyn, New York ; John T. Pingree
is a lawyer at Auburn, New York ; Andrew Potter
is a lawyer at Bennington, and was a colonel during
the war; Arnold G. Potter is a lawyer at North
Adams, Massachusetts ; Edwin H. Pound is a lawyer in Iowa ; Nathan B. Robbins was a lawyer, and
was drowned in 1859 ; Albion T. Rocwkell is a phy-

sician in Washington, and has long been in the government service; he was a lieutenant-colonel in the last war; Lester C. Rogers is a minister of the Reformed Dutch Church in New Jersey; Henry Root is a physician at Whitehall, New York; Frank Shepard is a teacher in Connecticut; Oren C. Sikes is a teacher at Lynn, Massachusetts; Edward C. Smith is a teacher in Philadelphia; John T. Stoneman is a lawyer in Iowa; John Tatlock is a Congregational minister at Troy, New York; Lemuel P. Webber is a Presbyterian minister; Charles Whittier is a Congregational minister in Maine; Charles D. Wilbur is a Professor of Geology in Illinois; John H. Wilhelm is a Baptist minister; Samuel Williams is a lawyer at St. Albans, Vermont, and Lavalette Wilson is a teacher in New York State.

CHAPTER IX.

A PREACHER AND PROFESSOR.

A PREACHER IN THE CHURCH OF THE DISCIPLES. — ESTIMATION OF HIS
ABILITIES AMONG HIS OLD NEIGHBORS. — RISE OF INFIDELITY AT
CHAGRIN FALLS. — SPIRITUALISM AND CHRISTIANITY. — EXCITING
PUBLIC DISCUSSION. — PROFESSOR DENTON VS. PROFESSOR GAR-
FIELD. — HOW THE VICTORY WAS WON. — MR. GARFIELD'S POPU-
LARITY AS A TEACHER. — TESTIMONY OF STUDENTS. — MARRIAGE
WITH MISS LUCRETIA RUDOLPH. — HIS SPEECH AT HIRAM.

ON his return home Mr. Garfield was received
with great joy by all his friends. The founders and
supporters of Hiram College had already laid their
plans to engage him sooner or later as a teacher.
While many of the congregations of the Disciples, to
whom he had preached, had equally confident hopes
of securing him for a permanent pastor. It is said
that he had not definitely marked out a course for
himself, but told his friends that he should probably
follow preaching as a profession. With a seeming
view to that calling, he supplied many pulpits and
attended many general meetings of his denomination. Among the people of the interior towns of
Ohio it was considered a very great achievement to
graduate from an Eastern college ; and Mr. Garfield
was at once received as a man of learning, and his
ideas on theological questions were accepted by the

lay members at least, as the authoritative exposition of scriptural truth.

He had ever been a close reasoner, and an enthusiastic admirer of the Bible from his early academic days. In some places he was looked upon with that awe and respect with which they might receive a prophet. In fact, it is seldom the lot of any man, in Church or State, to receive such devoted and loving expressions as those which were given to Mr. Garfield throughout his ministerial work.

An incident, illustrating both his ready wit, and ability to cope with difficult questions in science, philosophy and religion, and the respect in which he was held by his denomination, occurred at Chagrin Falls, near his old home.

Professor Denton, somewhat noted for his adherence to spiritualism, gave a series of lectures at Chagrin Falls, and attempted to prove by scientific discoveries that the Bible could not be true.

In the course of his discussion he had been able to convince quite a number of people, and it began to be boldly asserted, on the streets and in the factories, that the Bible was only an ingenious fable.

Professor Denton was a critical scholar and had a very plausible way of stating his theories ; and there was no one found to withstand his arguments. Ministers attacked him, but only with invectives, which did more harm than good. Teachers and public speakers often ridiculed him, but such things only avail against a shallow reasoner, or one manifestly unpopular. Professor Denton was gaining the thinking men and women, and felt sure, as his adherents boasted "of shutting up the churches and abolishing the Bible from Chagrin Falls." It was one of those strange, almost unaccountable freaks of public opinion, and men were drawn into it who, all their lives, had been the most orthodox believers in the Holy Bible.

The Churches of the Disciples viewed the success of Professor Denton with the deepest dismay. The church at Chagrin Falls seemed in danger of annihilation, and the whole denomination viewed its tottering condition with great alarm. It happened that the noted professor had one weak point illustrating the truth of that Book he was endeavoring to overturn, wherein it says that "great men are not always wise." He had a habit of boasting; and one evening he went so far as to challenge any and every believer of the Bible in Ohio to refute his statements. He offered the use of the hall and ample time to any person who dared to undertake the task.

At once, the listeners who adhered to the Bible thought of Mr. Garfield. They had heard him preach at Chagrin Falls and in the surrounding country towns, and they felt that if any man could cope with the learned professor, it would be he. They felt that some one must champion their cause or all would be lost. In a distress of mind not easily realized by people living in other portions of the religious world, these sincere and sorrowful Christians turned toward Mr. Garfield for help. At first he declined to meet the professor, thinking it unbecoming a Christian man to debate such questions in a public hall. But the continued petition of his friends and the alarm of the churches, caused him at last to consent, and a committee of citizens was appointed to arrange for the public discussion.

It was a great day at Chagrin Falls, and one which will not soon be forgotten, when these two champions met in the arena of serious, earnest, religious debate. Mr. Garfield had never heard Professor Denton and was consequently supposed to be ignorant of just the position which the professor would take.

But Mr. Garfield had been too wise to risk a cause which he believed so holy, to the impulses and guesses of an impromptu speech ; and, as soon as he knew that he was to meet the professor, he had taken steps to find out the arguments which the infidel used. Having ascertained privately that the professor was to lecture on the same topic in a distant part of the State before the date of the discussion, Mr. Garfield had sent a friend to hear these lectures, and write them out for his use.

Of course the professor knew nothing of this, and had no doubt of his ability to silence a man who had not made science a special study. When, however, Mr. Garfield had received the copies of the lectures, he had at once sent in various directions and procured the latest scientific books, together with those the professor had quoted as being against the Bible. He had also obtained learned opinions of distinguished scholars, and, before the day of the discussion, was thoroughly armed with arguments and authorities.

When the hour came for the discussion, the hall was crowded to suffocation by an eager, and on the part of the Disciples, an almost breathless audience. But they did not lose faith in Mr. Garfield. They thought that if any one could overcome the learned professor, then they had secured the right man.

The professor, amid the smiles of his followers and with a perfect confidence in his ability, opened the debate with his statements of scientific facts and their bearing on the accounts of creation and the miracles in the Bible. The professor did not try to be precise and accurate in all his statements, for he was sure that Mr. Garfield would not attack him on scientific ground, and, when he stated any difficult question, he explained it very kindly in "simple language" for Mr. Garfield's better understanding. He repeated, however, almost verbatim, the lecture of which Mr. Garfield had a copy.

Mr. Garfield said nothing until his turn came, and, when he arose, it was apparent to all that the professor had predisposed the audience in favor of infidelity.

When, however, Mr. Garfield coolly and with a readiness and knowledge which really astounded his hearers, took up the professor's arguments, one by one, and, quoting voluminously from books and history, using the professor's own authorities against him and piling up unanswerable names above them, there was such a sudden overturning as an earthquake might make. It seemed miraculous to the people, who very reasonably supposed that Mr. Garfield had not heard the professor's arguments before.

The professor had the closing speech to make, but he saw that he had lost the battle and that his forces were too thoroughly routed to be rallied again. So, while he claimed that with further research he could yet establish his theories, he manfully admitted that he was surprised and defeated for the time, by the apparently inexhaustible learning of his opponent. He said it was the first time he had met so gifted and learned an adversary. Of course the tide of unbelief in the Scriptures was stayed, and from that day to this, the community has not been again alarmed or disturbed by the popularity of any anti-scriptural lectures.

Mr. Garfield's return from college was in 1856; and from that time until 1861 he occupied the social position in the community, of a minister of the gospel, preaching nearly every Sunday, and delivering addresses at conferences and yearly meetings of the church.

The school at Hiram in which he was appointed a professor upon his return from college, was, as has already been stated, a denominational institution, and his position as a teacher in a school, a part of the purposes of which was to educate young men for the ministry, was a semi-pastoral one, and connected him closely with church work.

A year after his engagement as a teacher, Professor A. S. Hayden, the principal, resigned, and

Mr. Garfield was immediately elected to fill that important post.

Of Mr. Garfield's three years of labor as a principal of the school at Hiram, hundreds of students speak in terms of almost extravagant praise. He seems to have been loved as a father is loved, and the affection of his scholars was returned in large-hearted measure by him. He was remarkably successful in building up the school and in placing it on a footing where its transformation into a college was possible. He took an interest in the welfare of each student and stood on terms of familiar yet dignified acquaintance with them all. He taught them how to study. He played with them on the green.

An illustration of the character which has since made him famous is seen in an incident during his career as principal. His complete control of the school was the result of firmness and kindness. In the school-room he was obeyed with alacrity; on the play ground he was a kind playmate. One day, when he took his place in a game of ball, he chanced to see some small boys in a fence corner, close by, looking wistfully on. He said to the players:

"Are these boys not in the game?"

"Those little tads? Of course not. They'd spoil the game."

"But," said the principal, "they want to play just as much as we do. Let them come in."

"No," was the answer again, "it's no use to spoil the game; they can't play."

"Well," said he, laying down his bat, "if they can't play I won't."

"Well, well, let them come in," was the answer, and his kind heart had won the victory.

He lived in simple style as a boarder saving his money to repay his uncle, which, however, was soon accomplished. Frank, cheerful, honest and truth ful, he was honored by every one, and it is said with every appearance of truth that, in 1859, he had not an enemy in the world.

It was in 1858, during his successful administration of the institute at Hiram, that he married Miss Lucretia Rudolph, of that place. She had been his class-mate at Chester, ten years before, had attended the school at Hiram with him, and they had through the whole decade sustained a familiar acquaintance She was then, as now, a most remarkably sweet woman. She belonged to a most excellent family Her mother was the daughter of Elijah Mason of Lebanon, Connecticut, and a descendant, on her mother's side, of General Nathaniel Green. Mr Zeb Rudolph, the father of Mrs. Garfield, was a pros perous farmer at Garrettsville, at the time the insti tute at Hiram was established, and he was one of the most influential of its founders. He still lives in Hiram, his wife, Mrs. Garfield's mother, having died in 1879.

After his marriage he continued to board in a very plain style, his wife being one of those nota ble young women whose pretty face and social position in no way interfered with her common sense and her willingness to make her life conform to their financial circumstances. A kind Providence, which for his good had often left him to hardships and toil, most signally blessed his life through his mother and his wife. Both women had a great influence upon his later life. His wife, in her modesty, industry, economy and intellectual keenness, was a treasure of incalculable value to him in every walk of life, and on the day of their marriage the line can safely be drawn in his history, between the old, rough, self sacrificing struggle with adversity, and the new era of joy, prosperity and fame.

She was no less a favorite with the students than Mr. Garfield himself, and having been a teacher in the Cleveland schools, she understood well her husband's trials and needs. Many students came to them both for advice and help; and as one of the graduates afterwards wrote for publication: "There are men and women scattered over the United States holding positions of honor and wealth, who began the life which led them upward, by the advice and with the assistance of Mr. and Mrs. Garfield." Certainly it is no over-stated tribute when we say that the active, generous and pure life they led for two years at Hiram, was a blessing to the world through the influence of the students whose habits and ambitions were shaped by them.

In a speech delivered at Hiram years afterwards, Mr. Garfield thus spoke of his connection with the institution :

I said that there were two chapters in the history

of this institution. You have heard the one relating to the founders. They were all pioneers of this Western Reserve, or nearly all ; they were all men of knowledge and great force of character ; nearly all not men of means, but they planted this little institution. In 1850 it was a cornfield,with a solid, plain brick building in the center of it, and that was all. Almost all the rest has been done by the institution itself. That is the second chapter. Without a dollar of endowment, without a powerful friend anywhere, but with a corps of teachers, who were told to go on the ground and see what they could make out of it, to find their own pay out of the little tuition that they could receive. They invited students of their own spirit to come here on the ground and find out what they could make out of it, and the response has been that many have come, and the chief part of the respondents I see in the faces around and before me to-day. It was a simple question of sinking or swimming for themselves. And I know that we are all inclined to be a little clannish over our own. We have, perhaps, a right to be ; but I do not know of any place, I do not know of any institution, that has accomplished more with so little means as has this school on Hiram Hill. I know of no place where the doctrine of self-help has a fuller development, by necessity as well ns finally by choice, as here on this hill. The doctrine of self-help and of force has the chief place among these men and women around here. As I said a great many years ago about that, the act of Hiram was to throw its young men and women overboard and let them try it for themselves, and all those men able to get ashore got ashore, and I think we have few cases of drowning anywhere.

Now, I look over these faces and I mark the several geological changes remarked by Mr. Atwater so well in his address, but in the few cases of change of geological fact, there is, I find, no fossil. Some are dead and glorified in our memories, but those who are not, are alive — I think all

The teachers and the students of this school built it up in every sense. They made the cornfield into Hiram Campus. Those fine groves you see across the road, they planted. I well remember the day when they turned out into the woods to find beautiful maples and brought them in; when they raised a little purse to purchase evergreen; when each young man, for himself one, and perhaps a second for some young lady, if he was in love, planted two trees on the campus, and then named them after himself. There are several here to-day who remember Bolen. Bolen planted there a tree, and Bolen has planted a tree that has a luster — Bolen was shot through the heart at Winchester.

There are many here that can go and find the trees that you named after yourselves. They are great strong trees to-day, and your names, like your trees are, I hope, growing still.

I believe, outside of or beyond the physical features of the place, that there was a stronger pressure of work to the square inch in the boilers that run this establishment than any other that I know of; and, as has been so well said, that has told all the while with these young men and women. The struggle, whenever the uncouth and untutored farmer boys — farmers of course — that came here to try themselves and find what kind of people they were. They came here to go on a voyage of discovery. Your discovery was yourselves, in many cases. I hope the discovery was a fortune, and the friendships then formed out of that have bound this group of people longer and farther than most any other I have known in life. They are scattered all over the United States in every field of activity, and if I had time to name them the sun would go down before I had finished.

I believe the rules of this institution limit us to time—I think it is said, five minutes. I may have overgone it already. We have so many already that we want to hear from, we will all volunteer. We expect now to wrestle a while with the work before us. Some of these boys remember the time when I had an exercise that I remember with pleasure. I called a young lad out in class and said, in two minutes you are to speak to the best of your ability on the following subject, (naming it) and gave subject and let him wrestle with it. It was a trying theory, and I believe that wrestling was a good thing. I will not vary the performance save in this. I will call you and restrict you to five minutes, and let you select your theme about the old days of Hiram.

In another speech on the same subject he said:

It always has given me pleasure to come here and look upon these faces. It has always given me new courage and new friends. It has brought back a large share of that richness that belongs to those things out of which come the joys of life. While I have been sitting here this afternoon, watching your faces and listening to the very interesting address just delivered, it occurred to me that the best thing you have that all men envy—I mean all men who have reached the meridian of life—is, perhaps, the thing you care for least, and that is your leisure. The leisure you have to think in, the leisure you have to be let alone, the leisure you have to throw the plummet with your hands and sound the depths and find what is below, the leisure you have to walk about the towers of yourselves, and find how strong they are or how weak they are, and determine what needs building up, and determine how to shape them that you may be made the final being that you are to be. Oh, these hours of building ! If the superior Being of the universe would look down upon the world to find the most interesting object, it would be the unfinished and unformed character of young men, and of young women. Those behind me have, probably, in the main settled such questions. Those who have passed middle manhood and middle womanhood are about what they shall always be, and there is little left of interest or curiosity as to our development ; but to your young, unformed natures, no man knows the possibilities that lie treasured up in your hearts and intellects. While you are working up those possibilities with that splendid leisure, you are the most envied of all classes of men and women in the world. I congratulate you on your leisure.. I commend you to keep it as your gold, as your wealth, as your means, out of which you can demand all possible treasures that God laid down when he formed your nature, and unveiled and developed the possibility of your future. This place is too full of memories for me to trust myself to speak more, and I will not; but I draw again to-day, as I have for a quarter of a century, evidences of strength and affection from the people who gather in this place, and I thank you for the permission to see you and meet you and greet you as I have done to-day.

CHAPTER X.

POLITICIAN AND LAWYER.

POLITICAL SYMPATHIES. — HOPE OF MAKING THE LAW A PROFESSION. —
ENTERS HIS NAME AS A STUDENT. — YEARS OF HARD STUDY. —
PROFITABLE USE OF ALL HIS TIME. — HIS LEGAL RESEARCH. — IN-
TEREST IN LOCAL POLITICS. — THE STUMP-SPEAKER'S CHALLENGE.
— FIRST SPEECH. — NOMINATION FOR THE STATE SENATE. — IN THE
SERVICE OF THE STATE. — LEAVING THE GOSPEL FOR POLITICS. —
MRS. GARFIELD'S LOVE OF DOMESTIC LIFE.

AFTER Mr. Garfield's graduation from college, he found more time to interest himself in the current affairs of his time. Although his sympathies were with the Republican party, at its birth, yet he had been too much engaged in the arduous task of securing an education to give much attention to politics. But when he did have time to read and ponder upon national questions, he began to be a vigorous and persistent opponent of slavery, and often expressed his regret that Fremont and Dayton were not elected. Day by day, his interest in public affairs increased, until he began to feel a great indignation at the conduct of the Buchanan administration.

He also took a keen interest in local politics, and watched with anxiety the measures which were before the legislature of Ohio. This patriotic interest in the welfare of his State and nation naturally led his mind toward the laws which governed the country, and the methods of making· them. He was never satisfied with a superficial knowledge of anything in which he had an interest, and without any definite purpose, beyond a determination to understand the matter, he began to read such law books as he could readily borrow. Soon, however, he inclined to the hope of making the law his profession, and began a regular course of systematic and earnest study.

Soon after he was married, he entered his name, in the law office of Riddle & Williamson, attorneys, in Cleveland, Ohio, as a student of law. This he was required to do by the law, if he intended to be admitted to the bar. He did not, however, study in the office at all, and his purpose to become an attorney was kept a secret from all his relatives.

His ability to pursue hard study, day after day, served him well in his legal researches, for he kept evenly on with his teaching all the while, and was not absent from his work, or from the evening exercises connected with the institute, during the term.

He had formed a habit of studying at odd times and places, filling the entire day with some profitable occupation or healthy sport. It would astonish the great portion of mankind to reckon up the number of hours in a year which they lose, in waiting, traveling, or useless conversation. Thousands of men and women might have acquired a mastery of law, medicine, science, or theology, in the odd hours which they have thoughtlessly wasted. The busiest business life has its hours of waiting and delay, which could be profitably applied to acquiring knowledge from books.   Mr. Garfield's life clearly demonstrates this statement.   He acquired a habit, which may have been contracted under the influence of his mother's early example, of having a profitable book at hand for use, when his usual occupation was suspended or finished.   In that way he prosecuted his legal studies; and that industry, with his natural desire to be thorough, as far as he went, gave him a great advantage over young men of looser habits.

It is well known to attorneys how difficult it is for a young man to comprehend legal terms and expressions, without an actual contact with the practice, in the office and in the courts.   It requires much more study on the part of any person to obtain an understanding of law away from the practice, while the number is very limited who would succeed in obtaining any useful understanding of it.

The success of Mr. Garfield, therefore, as we shall see, was something so unusual and astonishing that it may be regarded as the greatest intellectual achievement of his life.   He understood the laws of his State and of the nation so well that, when he was admitted to the bar, he was capable of stepping from his little country home into the courts, of any grade, and trying the most difficult cases.

So improbable will this seem to attorneys, whose years of study and practice have left them none too well-furnished with legal acumen, that it would not be stated here, did not the most trustworthy of our law reports fully corroborate it.

During all this critical study of the most dry and difficult of all subjects, he neglected not his preaching, his public addresses, his private correspondence, or his family. It was all accomplished by the careful use of all his time.

His interest in political matters, however, did not lead him to take any public part in the campaigns, and his appearance in the political field was sudden and unexpected, both to the people and to him.

The story of his first political speech, and of his first nomination, have embodied themselves in the traditions of the neighborhood, and have thus been preserved for the historian.

A Democratic speaker, of considerable ability and notoriety, published a challenge for a political debate which any person in Portage county was at liberty to accept. In Ohio, they often used to engage in political disputes, with the different parties represented by speakers, in the same evening. Such was to be the proposed debate. The Republicans, who had heard Mr. Garfield speak on some minor political occasion, endeavored to persuade him to accept the challenge, and more to satisfy the urgent demands of his circle of acquaintances than for any other object, he consented to do so, and set the time. He had no such advantage of his opponent in this debate as that which he so shrewdly secured over Professor Denton, and had to rely more on the success of an independent speech, than on any hope of answering the precise arguments which his opponent might put forth. He seems to have approached that contest with many misgivings. He could preach a sermon worthy to be published, and that on a short notice; but a political stump speech was a much more difficult matter to him. His opponent had been in many campaigns, and had all the defects and short-comings of the new Republican party by heart.

The hall was again crowded, but there was not much confidence expressed in the success of Mr. Garfield, and some of the Republicans regretted, as did Mr. Garfield, that they had not selected some one else.

But his opponent was over-confident, and consequently said some things which he was sure this young debater could know nothing about, but which he stated in a way and with constructions to suit himself. Of course, where a disputant is allowed to manufacture his facts, and to base his arguments upon them undisturbed, he is certain of victory.

Near the close of his speech, which was able and convincing, the old politician read an extract from the *Congressional Globe*, giving the official report of some Abolitionist's speech, and it did put the Abolitionist in Congress, and his party, before that audience, in a very bad light. After reading the extract, with great show of indignant disapproval, the excited speaker threw the paper furiously down upon the platform near him, and within Mr. Garfield's easy reach. The latter had never before seen the official reports of congressional debates, and with a feeling of despair he took up the paper and glanced along its columns, with no purpose but that of curiosity.

He carelessly looked down the column from which the speaker had quoted, wondering all the while how any man in Congress could make such absurd remarks, when he noticed the name of a Democrat in the column. On looking closer the name of the Republican did not appear at all in that column, and the unprincipled politician had been quoting a Demcratic speech, and claiming it to be the official report of the Republican's words. Mr. Garfield placed the paper securely in his pocket, and, when his turn came to speak, arose and addressed the audience calmly and clearly, giving his views of the heinousness of slavery and the right inherent in every man to life, liberty and the pursuit of happiness. When he came to his opponent's arguments, he denied in toto all the statements of the first speaker to the great astonishment of the audience. Mr. Garfield said :

"So absurd and untrue are they that I need not spend your time and mine in discussing them. I will, however, say this much, that I thank him for saving me the trouble of criticizing the speech he has read from the *Congressional Globe*, for its foolishness, absurdity and unpatriotic sentiments deserve unqualified condemnation. The party, too, which would support such a man for office, or would endorse such sentiments should be crushed out of existence. But the difference between the previous speaker and myself is one of fact to be determined by you. He says it was a speech made by a Republican. I claim

9

it was a speech made by a Democrat. Here is the same paper. Here is the name of the speaker. This is the speech. Any one doubting my word will be kind enough to come to the platform and read for himself."

There was a shout of laughter, then cheers, and the "young preacher" bore off the honors of the occasion.

His nomination for the State Senate came about without the slightest effort on his part and against his expectations. The senatorial district in which he resided in 1859 was composed of two counties, viz: Summit and Portage. In that year by the system of rotation adopted by the party, Portage county had the right to name the candidate of the convention. A friend of Mr. Garfield's who was dissatisfied with the persons whose names were mentioned as the probable candidates, was elected a delegate. He thought of Mr. Garfield, and believed that the presentation of his name at the right time might secure success. But when the caucus met it was found that so many delegates had been pledged beforehand, that Mr. Garfield's name was not received with the acclaim his friend expected. Yet the first ballot, while there was no choice, showed that he had a strong support. The difficulty was that the politicians did not know him. His opponents also added that he was too young. The young professor was a delegate to the convention, but hardly knew what all the whispering and private discussion were about. After several ballots in which there was no choice, it became evident that on the next Mr. Garfield would be nominated. Whereupon the opposition determined to " bolt " and left the hall with boisterous demonstrations of displeasure. Mr. Garfield was nominated unanimously by those who remained; and, on presentation of his name to the joint convention, he was chosen as the candidate of the district, with but little opposition. He was elected by a sweeping majority and took his seat in the State Senate of the following Legislature — its youngest member.

His acceptance of the nomination and election was regarded quite unfavorably by many members of his denomination. Those who were his political opponents were especially loud in their expressions of disapproval. To the defeated ones there seemed to be an awful inconsistency in his conduct as a "Christian minister." How could a good man belong to any party but the one with which they affilliated?

Even his political friends and old neighbors could not avoid saying that "it was a sad day for 'the cause' when Mr. Garfield gave up the gospel for politics." Of course they knew nothing of his purpose to become a lawyer, and they had yet to learn, as he soon taught them, that a sincere, generous Christian may be a very successful and noble politician. Yet, there remain a few old and stubborn church members of his sect who felt his loss when he practically retired from the ministry, as they would have felt the loss of an inspired prophet, and cannot be reconciled to the idea that their great champion orator, and leader, should "descend so low," as to be a statesman.

To him the election was a piece of good fortune. It added something to the amount of his limited income, and it gave him a most valuable and agreeable acquaintance with the public men of Ohio. It gave him an opportunity to study in the law libraries of Columbus and gave him a deeper sense of the importance of legal studies. It gave him an opportunity to make practical use of the learning which had ad so assiduously accumulated. He was a decided enemy of slavery and made several most telling hits when a question of national jurisdiction over slaves, as property, incidentally arose. He was not distinguished however, so much for his speeches, as for his persevering hard work in the preparation of bills, reports and orders. "He had a genius for hard work," and physical constitution able to support it, for which he was much indebted to his severe hardships and toil when a boy.

He did not resign his position as principal of the Hiram school, nor did they secure a permanent teacher of Latin and Greek to take his place as a professor, for, neither he nor the managers of the school expected that he would continue in public life. His wife with her natural aversion to publicity and display, was quite anxious that he should return to his teaching, to his study of languages with her, and to the holy quiet and rest of their first years of married life. No honors, nor titles, nor wealth would have induced her to give up their simple and happy domestic life in Hiram. Nothing but some great duty, some imperative call to help the weak or free the enslaved was worth considering in the question of exchanging their simple life for one of excitement or parade.

But the home life so sweet and dear to them both was broken then, never again to be renewed in its holy retirement. A great duty called him; the weak and enslaved asked for help, and he promptly and cheerfully responded.

CHAPTER XI.

THE EVENTFUL YEAR OF 1861.

ADMISSION TO THE BAR. — WITHDRAWS FROM MINISTERIAL WORK. — OPPOSITION TO SLAVERY. — LEADERSHIP IN THE STATE SENATE. — THE GOVERNOR'S ASSISTANT. — PROVIDING FOR THE TROOPS. — THE REGIMENT OF HIRAM STUDENTS. — DEPLETION OF THE CLASSES. — APPOINTMENT AS LIEUTENANT-COLONEL. — PROMOTION. — DEPARTURE FOR THE FIELD. — CONSULTATION WITH GENERAL BUEL. — PLAN OF A CAMPAIGN. — MARCH AGAINST MARSHALL. — BATTLE OF PRESTONBURG. — THE ACCOUNT OF F. H. MASON. — PROMOTION.

THE eventful year of 1861 found Mr. Garfield, at its opening, ready to enter upon the practice of law, so far as a knowledge of its principles was concerned. But the announcement of his admission to the bar, at Cleveland, was a surprise to nearly all his acquaintances, and completely dashed the hopes of the anxious members of his denomination, who were hoping and praying for his active entry into the profession of the ministry. Occasionally he took a part in the services, on special occasions, such as Sabbath-school conventions, yearly meetings of the churches, or at dedications; but thinking that the belief, so prevalent then, that politics and religion were at variance, would injure his influence for good, he wisely withdrew from any active participation as a preacher or teacher in church services. He did not enter the practice of law at once after his admission to the bar, as he was actively engaged in the State Senate; and it appears that he was hesitating between opening an office in Cleveland and remaining as a teacher at Hiram, when the war broke out.

His studies and public duties had called his attention so much to the institutions of the nation, and his natural disposition was so inclined toward a sym-

STATE CAPITOL OF OHIO.

pathy with the oppressed, that his heart was fired with an almost uncontrollable patriotic fervor, at the first news of the purposed rebellion.

As early as January, 1861, he stood up in his place in the Ohio Senate and declared it to be his unalterable determination to oppose the institution of slavery, or any compromise with it. It was a heinous national sin, and he would not condescend to negotiate with it. Senators Monroe and Cox stood with him then, and later, Senators Morse, Glass, Buck, Parish and Smith voted with him. When the constitutional amendment was submitted to the Ohio Legislature, which would guarantee to the slave States the perpetuity of slavery, he led the uncompromising minority, and with a remarkable display of ability, opposed, with pointed speeches and his vote, every measure or resolution which could be construed into a concession to the party in favor of human bondage. He was in earnest. He had a ready command of language: He knew the laws and their purpose. He had been bred to hate every form of meanness, unkindness, and oppression. Hence, his speeches were eloquent, thoughtful, and sincere. He seemed to care nothing for popularity, and expected only to do his duty while there, and retire with a clear conscience to private life, when his term of office should close.

But the earthquake of the rebellion overturned many plans, and sent confusion and alarm into every household in the nation. While he was yet in the Senate, the attack on Fort Sumter, and the battle of Bull Run added dismay to the already over-excited public mind. Mr. Garfield, from the first, declared his intention of going to the war, should it last more than the "ninety days," and the regular militia of the State prove insufficient.

At the adjournment of the Legislature, he offered his services to Governor Dennison, to assist him in the difficult task of organizing and providing supplies

for the troops, then flocking toward the camps.   In
the multiplicity of duties, and the incessant annoyances which perplexed and harassed Governor Dennison, he appears to have overlooked Mr. Garfield's
ability and patriotism, and to have repeatedly promoted to high office, men of much inferior ability,
because, in some way, they were placed prominently
before the Governor's attention.   Mr. Garfield would
never ask for an office, and worked diligently on in
his unofficial relation to the Governor for some
weeks, going hither and thither for arms, clothing,
ammunition, and provisions, never appearing to have
had a thought that, amid all these army promotions
and profitable stations, he might have secured a valuable office for himself.   If a high official position
had been offered him in the army, he would have refused it, with his usual excuse that he did not feel
competent to undertake it.

But when the news came to the Governor that the
students of Hiram College, over which Mr. Garfield
was still the official head, purposed to organize a
regiment, it at last occurred to him that Mr. Garfield
could possibly be spared in such an emergency, and
he asked the latter to recruit and organize it.

Mr. Garfield would not at first take the office of
colonel, saying that he should need some military
training before he could handle a regiment.   He
seems to have forgotten that his less able colleagues
in the Legislature had taken commissions as briga-
dier-generals, without the slightest hesitation.   So
he was appointed, August 14, 1861, a lieutenant-

colonel, and entered upon the task of organizing his command.

One of the first meetings for raising volunteers for his regiment was held at Hiram, and the enthusiasm was intense. The institution was almost wholly depleted of its male students by the spontaneous enlistment of the scholars. Graduates of the school came from distant counties, and even from other States, moved by the popularity of Mr. Garfield, and the great enthusiasm of that early period of the war. Although the regiment was filled almost immediately, there were many delays, caused by the difficulty of securing arms and uniforms, and it did not leave for the South until September 14th. Meantime, the pressure upon the Governor, on the part of the regiment and its friends, for the promotion of Mr. Garfield to the head of the regiment, was so unanimous and persistent that both the Governor and Mr. Garfield were compelled to submit to the demand.

September 18th, Colonel Garfield's regiment, the 42d Ohio, arrived at Cattletsburg, Kentucky, which is close to the border of both Ohio and Virginia, the two rivers at the junction of which it was situated being the boundaries of the three States. Colonel Garfield was ordered to report, in person, to General Buel, at Louisville.

General Buel was a native of Ohio, as were also Generals Grant, Sherman, McPherson, Sheridan, McClellan, Rosecrans, Mitchel, Gilmore, McDowell, Schenck, Custer, Hazen, Cox, Steadman, Weitzel,

Stanley, Crook, Swain, McCook, and Leggett, surely a most astounding leadership to be obtained so honorably by a single State. General Buel was not ignorant of Colonel Garfield's ability, nor of his popularity in Ohio, and hoped to find in the new colonel a vigorous supporter. The campaign in West Virginia had succeeded passably well, and General Buel hoped to be able to be equally successful in clearing Kentucky of the rebels, and of capturing Nashville. The general was a rather harsh disciplinarian, and did many foolish things with his raw troops. His ideas of military discipline were better adapted to a military empire, or an established and unlimited monarchy, than to the assemblies of free men, who were fighting for themselves, and not for a king. However, he was earnest, patriotic, and brave, and recognizing those qualities in Colonel Garfield, he at once confided to him the plan of the Kentucky campaign. Colonel Garfield did not pretend to be a military strategist, but when he looked over the map with General Buel, and heard how many rebel forces were in Eastern Kentucky, and how many in Western Kentucky, he thought it was folly to attempt to march through the center of the State to Nashville, with such forces on both flanks. The general thought that some movement ought to be made at once, and if the colonel had any doubts about the proposed plan it would be well to think the matter over and consult again about it the next day.

The following morning Colonel Garfield brought in a draft of his plan, which was to move into the

State in three·columns, leaving no forces behind them, and if either column defeated its opponent, it could readily unite with the center and move on to Nashville. After some discussion, and after the general had asked the colonel if he would undertake the direction of the eastern column, the plan submitted was adopted so far as it could be without the co-operation of General Halleck's command in Missouri. The general plan was, however, somewhat modified by Zollicoffer's entrance into Kentucky at Cumberland Gap with a rebel army to co-operate with General Humphrey Marshall, who was already in Kentucky near Pound Gap. But General George H. Thomas was sent to drive back Zollicoffer, and Colonel Garfield's orders to attack Humphrey Marshall were not changed.

Thus we find him with a most important campaign on his hands before he had any useful experience in drilling a regiment in the manual of arms. The purposed movement was one of such importance, in view of the necessity of keeping Marshall from moving to Zollicoffer's aid and striking General Thomas's forces on the flank, that it is a little surprising that General Buel with his ideas of military manœuvers, should have intrusted it to a commander so fresh from civil life. Colonel Garfield had never seen a skirmish nor heard the crack of a single hostile rifle. It therefore seemed somewhat inconsistent with Colonel Garfield's well known character to assume the direction of so important a military movement. It seems probable that he did not know just how important it was, nor

"Give 'em Hail Columbia!"

appreciate how eagerly the whole field was being watched by President Lincoln and the authorities at Washington for some signs of ultimate victory. It was one of the gloomiest periods of the war; and when the news of the selection of Colonel Garfield for the expedition up the Big Sandy river to meet Marshall was announced to Mr. Lincoln, he sought Secretary Stanton, who was also a native of Ohio, and asked who the man was they were sending "into such dangerously close quarters." The President anxiously awaited General Buel's forward movement toward Bowling Green and Nashville; and seeing how important the defeat of the rebel's flank movements under Marshall and Zollicoffer had become, he followed the movements of Colonel Garfield and General Thomas with the deepest interest.

Colonel Garfield's orders to proceed up the Sandy Valley were delivered to him December 13th or 14th. A few days later, he collected the forces entrusted to him at the mouth of the Big Sandy river, and began his march up the valley. His command, which was called a brigade, did not number over twenty-three hundred available men, and consisted of the Fortieth and Forty-Second Ohio infantry, the Fourteenth and Twenty-Second Kentucky infantry, and eight companies of cavalry. To these he hoped to add a small force then stationed at Paris, and to which he sent orders directing its commander to join him near Paintville.

General Marshall had a force of five thousand men, and was in a country with which he was familiar, while Colonel Garfield was in a strange region with about one-half that number of troops. If there had been any hesitation or delay on the part of the union forces it would have encouraged Marshall to attack them on their march, for the rebel general was among his friends, and all the people acted as spies and couriers in communicating the advance and condition of the invading forces. But so determinedly and steadily did the troops march on, that it seem to have created a fear of them in advance which went far toward giving them the victory when the battle came.

All the information which Garfield could gain seemed to locate Marshall near Paintville, and hence, he expected a contest at that point. But Marshall retreated to Prestonburg before Garfield arrived, but left a company of cavalry to hold the place and delay the union troops. Garfield finding the enemy, and supposing that the rebel army was immediately in front, notwithstanding the fatigue of his troops, moved immediately forward to attack them.

Directing his cavalry to engage the enemy in front, Garfield made a circuit with his infantry, hoping to reach Marshall's rear.

It is said that when he had given his orders to the cavalry, and had started forward on foot with the infantry, he took off his coat and threw it into a tree, and shouted back to the horsemen so soon to charge, "Give 'em Hail Columbia, boys!"

But before his troops reached the road in the rear, the vigorous charge of the union cavalry had sent the enemy flying toward Prestonburg in such haste as to leave their canteens, haversacks, blankets and dead bodies strewing the highway.

This retreat was quite unexpected to General Garfield, and he had so confidently counted upon a battle at that point, that his brigade was not supplied with provisions for a march further into the interior. To supply the necessary provisions caused a day's delay, and compelled him to leave a portion of his troops at Paintville while, he pressed on after Marshall. At Paintville, however, he was joined by the troops from Paris, numbering about one thousand or twelve hundred.

On the following day, which was the 9th of January, Garfield followed Marshall to Prestonburg and found that the rebels were posted on a hill in a most advantageous position with their artillery in a most effective range. Garfield had been misinformed about Marshall's movements and was compelled to ascertain the enemy's position by skirmishing and feints. While awaiting the troops, which he decided to order up from Paintville, his troops were constantly engaged in skirmishing, and the whole command was under fire, many of the men for the first time.

It must have given a much more serious appearance to the art of war, to see the line of gray, and hear the shot and shell shriek over their heads. To the colonel, on whose word and judgment hung the lives of so many and, perhaps, the fate of a mighty nation, the feeling of responsibility must have been great, while the peculiar sense of danger and dread of the unforeseen which fills the heart at the opening of the first battle, must have been a trial in his inexperience.

It was nearly dark when the reinforcements arrived, and without delay, and amid the enthusiastic cheering of the men, he ordered an advance, to be followed by a charge upon the enemy's guns. There was a sharp musketry fire for a short time, as the enemy fell slowly back toward their guns, and the artillery of the rebels was handled most skillfully.

When, however, the lines of the union forces had secured the desired position from which to make their charge, Marshall suddenly sounded a retreat, and left the field under cover of the darkness.

The sudden disappearance of the enemy and the silence which prevailed, together with the uncertainty whether it was an actual retreat or a ruse, made the hour following the disappearance, one of great anxiety. The troops, fatigued and hungry, moving cautiously about in the dark woodland and fields, anxiously awaiting developments, were but a counterpart of that other historical picture of the great President at Washington, pacing his room at that very hour, and saying, "I cannot bear this dangerous delay. Have n't we any one who will fight?"

General Garfield's suspense was not long, however, for soon the clouds overhead began to assume an unusual color, and a little later were lit up with the lurid glare of distant fires. The distant mountains stood out prominent in the unnatural light, and pillars of illumined smoke arose along the road toward the gate to Virginia.   It was clear, then, that Marshall was retreating out of Kentucky, and was burning his immense military stores.

To pursue the rebels that night was impracticable, and after a short cavalry reconnoissance, the tired troops used the light of the enemy's burning camps to prepare their meager supper and hard beds. The time, the circumstances, and the fact that the enemy numbered forty-nine hundred, made the victory an important one, while Colonel Garfield's bravery and ability, displayed in the march and engagement, placed him at once among the experienced and trustworthy soldiers.

The next day the enemy was pursued to the Virginia line, and the order was then given to return to their camps near Piketon with their prisoners. They had killed two hundred and fifty of the enemy and taken forty prisoners, with a loss to the union troops of only thirty-two men.   Colonel Garfield's commission as a brigadier-general was dated so as to take effect from that battle at Prestonburg.

Mr. F. H. Mason, a private soldier connected with the 42d Ohio has written the following most excellent account of the battle.   He says:

"The advance column marched all day, but the roads were so wretched that it was night before it had reached the foot of a high hill, north of the mouth of Abbott's Creek, three miles below Prestonburg and on the west side of the Big Sandy.   Ascending this hill soon after dark, Colonel Garfield's advance encountered at the summit a cavalry picket, which fired a volley and retreated. Being evidently in the immediate presence of a large force of the enemy, Colonel Garfield brought his command to the top of the hill, and with strong guards thrown out to the front and rear, rested until morning. It was a bitter January night. The rain which had fallen all day turned to sleet, and a keen, biting gale from the north whistled through the mountain pines and stiffened the wet clothing of the soldiers with ice. No fire could be permitted in such a situation, and the men shivered and waited through the long, dreary night as best they could. When morning dawned, they found themselves on a high hill from which the road descended by a steep, zig-zag course to the valley of Abbott's Creek.

Immediately after encountering the cavalry the evening before, Colonel Garfield had sent back a message directing Colonel Cranor to put all the available men at Paintville in motion at once and march to his support. The order reached Cranor before daylight, and within an hour, twelve hundred men, made up from all the regiments in the brigade, were on the march.

The advance column, meanwhile, descended early on the morning of the 10th, to the valley of Abbott's Creek, and found that the enemy had retired up the stream and across the dividing ridge into the valley of Middle Creek, which comes down from the mountains parallel with Abbott's Creek, and flows into the

Big Sandy, about a mile further up than the mouth of the latter.

It was at once apparent that Colonel Garfield was in the presence of Marshall's entire force, and that the latter was disposed to fight. Marshall was known to have about thirty-five hundred men of all arms, infantry, cavalry and artillery, and had come into the Sandy Valley to spend the winter, and, by occupying the country, promote enlistments into the confederate service. This purpose he could not, of course, relinquish without a fight, and he chose his ground, for the encounter, deliberately and well.

Proceeding cautiously and deliberately, in order to allow the reinforcements under Lieut.-Col. Sheldon to come up, Colonel Garfield passed up the valley of Abbott's Creek, forded the stream, crossed the ridge and descended into the valley of Middle Creek. Here he found Marshall's cavalry drawn up in line across the valley, but a few shots from the advance drove them back. One cavalry man was cut off from the main body, and in attempting to swim the creek, was captured, the first prisoner of war taken by the Forty-Second on a battle-field. A heavy line of skirmishers was thrown across the valley, and the advance began. The enemy's cavalry made a formidable show in the broad meadows, but kept at a discreet distance. Once, they formed behind a small spur of hill that ran out into the valley, and from behind that cover charged down upon the advancing column. Throwing his troops into a hollow square, Colonel Garfield awaited the attack, and when the cavalry came within range, sent them a volley which broke and turned them back. The skirmish line, under command of Adjutant Olds, advanced again and drove the cavalry from a spur behind which it was attempting to rally. This little spur of high ground upon which stood a log church, surrounded by a few graves, was then occupied by the federal force as a base from which to attack or defend, as circumstances might require. Drawing up his little force on the slope, Colonel Garfield saw that Marshall had come to a stand. Across the valley half a mile distant was the confederate cavalry, and on the same line near the foot of the hills, to the right of the creek, a battery was in position, which, as the skirmishers advanced, opened fire and gave the line a momentary check. A few shells were also fired at the main force on Graveyard Point; but the guns were badly trained and the shells buried themselves harmlessly in the mud. The enemy's cavalry and artillery being thus accounted for, it remained for Colonel Garfield to discover the location of his infantry. On the south side of the creek to the right of the battery rose a high hill, heavily timbered and crowned with a ledge of rock. Around the foot of the hill wound the creek, and close beside this, but on the opposite side of the stream, lay the road. It was at once conjectured that Marshall's infantry had occupied the hill, and that the federal column, if it advanced round the curve, would be caught by an ambushed fire from the opposite bank. To verify this theory, Garfield sent his escort, a handful of Kentucky cavalry, to charge up the road and draw the fire of the main body. The ruse was boldly performed and was completely successful. As the little group of horsemen galloped up the creek and round the curve in the road, the battery fired harmlessly over their heads, and the whole infantry force, with the trepidation of new troops, opened fire at long range, and completely unmasked their position. They occupied the wooded hill from its base halfway to its summit. It was now time for real work.

About four hundred men of the Fortieth and Forty-Second Ohio were sent to ford the creek, climb the mountain and attack the rebel position in front. Major Pardee of the Forty-Second, who was practically in command of the fighting in that part of the field, threw forward as skirmishers his detachments of Companies "A" and "F" of the Forty-Second and Company "A" of the Fortieth, and began the ascent. The skirmish line was in command of Captain F. A. Williams, who, like Major Pardee, seemed to take naturally to the business of fighting. Two companies of the Fourteenth Kentucky, under Lieutenant-Colonel Monroe of that regiment, were sent to cross the creek lower down, gain a narrow ledge or crest of a ridge that ran up to the main hill, and by advancing along that ridge, attack the enemy in the flank and save Williams' little force from being overpowered. As Williams' line advanced up the hill it soon encountered heavy opposition. A sharp fire came from behind the trees, logs and rocks, and the rebels swarmed down the hill, shouting and firing as they came. Half of the remaining reserve on Graveyard Point was sent to Pardee's support, and thus strengthened, he pushed forward.

The firing now became as hot as a thousand men on one side and three thousand on the other could make it. Had the casualties been proportionate to the amount of powder burned, the union force, at least, would have been annihilated. But the rebels fired unaccountably wild. They were fighting down a steep hill, and, as is usual with raw troops in such a position, they overshot their mark, and their bullets, for the most part, merely barked and scarred the trees over their enemies' heads. They were, moreover, armed to a large extent with smooth-bore muskets and squirrel rifles of small calibre, and fought like a mob, without plan or unity of action.

The federal line, on the other hand, advanced steadily, kept well under cover, fired deliberately, and, as the result proved, with excellent effect. The rebels were so numerous that the trees and logs were insufficient to cover them. Four or five frequently fought behind one tree. Instead of rushing down upon Williams' line, and profiting by the weight of superior force, Marshall's men stood and skirmished with an enemy whose very disparity of numbers, by enabling every man to keep well under cover, became almost a positive advantage. Firing up hill with their heavy, long range Belgian rifles, the Ohio men delivered a steady and effective fire. Gradually they pushed the enemy up the hill. Reinforcements came up over the crest and down to the rebel line, which seemed to be preparing for a change down the slope, when, at the opportune moment, Colonel Monroe's Kentuckians appeared on the ridge to the left, and from the rocks on the flank and rear of the enemy's line, opened an enfilading fire.

At the moment of Colonel Monroe's appearance in the fight, Lieutenant-Colonel Sheldon, who, with twelve hundred men, had left Paintville that morning and marched through mud and water nearly twenty miles, appeared round a curve in the road, a few hundred yards in the rear of Garfield's little reserve on Graveyard Point. The advancing column sent up a cheer of encouragement, which was caught and repeated by the reserves, and re-echoed by their comrades fighting on the hill.

Dr. Pomerene, the kind-hearted, enthusiastic surgeon of the Forty-Second, who had grown anxious with the sight of this maiden battle, had discovered Monroe's line streaming over the hill, and fancied that Major Pardee's force was being surrounded. The Twenty-Second Kentucky men were uniformed in sky blue, the first we had seen, and through the foggy afternoon the good doctor mistook their clothing for gray. Mounting a horse, hatless and distressed, he came splashing through the mud to hurry up the reinforcements. Coming within hail of Colonel Sheldon, he begged him for God's sake to hurry, "or the boys on the other side would be captured." The men gave another cheer, tried hard to double-quick through the mud, and promptly formed a line across the road in the rear of the log church, where the ground was so soft that some of the men mired, and the line was moved up on Graveyard Point. The effect of this new show of force was decisive, if, indeed, there were needed anything more to decide the victory of that day.

Marshall, though far outnumbering his assailants, had been out-fought from the first, and his line, pressed hard by Pardee, began to retreat up the hill. Inspired by the cheers of their comrades from below, the gallant Ohioans — to whom that day's business was the first baptism of war — pushed stubbornly forward, driving the rebels into the ledge of broken rocks at the summit of the hill, which position they held until the already gathering night closed the fight.

Colonel Sheldon promptly, upon his arrival, forded the creek and began to climb the hill; but before Major Pardee's position could be reached, darkness had settled down upon the combatants, and the battle was over.

The position not being one that could be safely or advantageously held during the night, orders were sent directing Monroe and Pardee to retire. They came down the hill, carrying their wounded, crossed the creek, and the whole of Colonel Garfield's force was re-united for the night on Graveyard Point. Strong pickets were posted up the road and beyond the creek; and notwithstanding the belief that a still harder struggle would come on the morrow, the little army slept proudly upon its first victory.

Shortly after dark a brilliant light blazed up from behind the hill upon which the fighting had taken place during the afternoon. What it meant could only be guessed, until the next morning, when a reconnoissance at daylight showed the hill abandoned, and the enemy gone. The illumination of the night before had come from the funeral pile upon which Marshall had sacrificed his wagons and baggage — everything that could impede his retreat through the mountains to Pound Gap, the gateway of the Cumberlands into Southwestern Virginia. Pursuit was, of course, useless. With ten hours' start, a perfect knowledge of the country, and a competent rear guard of cavalry, the now unencumbered enemy could have safely retreated from any pursuers, however formidable.

Colonel Garfield's little force was weary and short of food. It had started with but two days' rations; the country afforded nothing, and it was necessary to return to the river, from which supplies could be received. It remained only, therefore, to look over the field of yesterday's fight, bury the dead, and carry the wounded as carefully as possible to the river. A careful survey of the ground upon which the fight had taken place showed a remarkable disparity in losses. On the federal side the entire loss was but one killed and eleven wounded — eight of the latter being members of the Forty-Second.

The enemy suffered far more severely. Nineteen dead were found on the hill-side, up which Marshall's men had been driven by Williams' men, and among the rocks at the summit of the hill. The heartless way in which the rebels disposed of their dead made a strong impression upon the not yet callous-hearted boys from Ohio. At one place eleven of the confederate dead had been tumbled down into a large fissure in the rocks. They were taken out by the reconnoitering party next day, and decently buried. A squad of the Fourteenth Kentucky still further violated the decencies of war by stripping the corpses of their buttons and trifling valuables. There was abundant evidence that the confederate loss was by no means limited to the nineteen dead soldiers found on the hill. Seven graves were found at the foot of the mountain, near where the baggage had been burned. A native, whose hut was near the scene of the burning, professed to have filled the graves during the night, and said that they contained the bodies of officers. From his account, not less than fifty wounded had been carried away in wagons by the retreating enemy.

The remarkable disparity in losses is explained by the facts already stated. The federals had the better weapons, they fired up hill from behind trees, and fought from first to last with remarkable coolness and skill. The scars made by their bullets on the trees were mainly less than five feet from the ground. The bullet marks of the rebels, on the other hand, were wild, being often ten and twenty feet above the ground.

On the federal side, the battle of Middle Creek was fought by less than a thousand men. The principal fighting detachment was led by Captain Frederick A. Williams, of Company " A," Forty-Second Ohio, who six months before had been a student at Hiram. If there was a single man in his command who had ever before been under fire, that fact was not known then and is not known to-day. Colonel Garfield accepted battle from an enemy whom he knew to out-number his own force by at least three to one, and the fight was won by simply attacking the foe promptly in his own position, making intelligent use of whatever advantages the ground offered, and fighting with steady courage and skill as long as daylight lasted.

The Forty-Second regiment was engaged in many bloodier and more renowned battles during its three years of service, but it may be fairly questioned whether the regiment ever performed a day's duty of more timely and permanent value to the country. The battle of Middle Creek, skirmish though it may be considered, in comparison with later contests, was the first substantial victory won for the union cause. At Big Bethel, Bull Run, in Missouri, and at various points at which the union and confederate forces had come in contact, the latter had been uniformly victorious. The people of the North, giving freely of their men and their substance, in response to each successive call of the Government, had long and anxiously watched and waited for a little gleam of victory to show that Northern valor was a match for Southern impetuosity in the field. They had waited in vain since the disaster at Bull Run, during the previous summer, and hope had almost yielded to despair. The story of Garfield's success at Middle Creek came, therefore, like a benediction to the union cause. Though won at a trifling cost, it was decisive, so far as concerned the purposes of that immediate campaign. Marshall's force was driven from Kentucky, and made no further attempt to occupy the Sandy Valley. The important victories at Mill Spring, Forts Donelson and Henry, and the repulse at Shiloh followed. The victory at Middle Creek proved the first wave of a returning tide."

CHAPTER XII.

CAMPAIGNS IN KENTUCKY AND TENNESSEE.

LACK OF PROVISIONS. — THE GREAT FLOOD. — DANGEROUS SITUATION OF THE TROOPS. — GENERAL GARFIELD GOES TO THE OHIO RIVER. — PERILOUS VOYAGE UP THE BIG SANDY. — RECEPTION BY THE HUNGRY TROOPS. — EXPEDITION AGAINST THE ENEMY AT POUND GAP. — GENERAL ORDERS CONNECTED WITH HIS CAMPAIGN. — HIS TRANSFER TO LOUISVILLE. — HIS NEW COMMAND. — FORCED MARCHES. — THE BATTLE OF CORINTH. — REFUSAL TO RETURN SLAVES TO THEIR MASTERS. — ELECTION TO CONGRESS. — APPOINT-MENT AS CHIEF OF GENERAL ROSECRANS' STAFF. — BATTLE OF CHICAMAUGA. — PROMOTION TO MAJOR-GENERAL. — RESIGNATION.

THE next day after establishing the brigade camp, a heavy rain storm came on which laid a large portion of Sandy Valley under water. It was impossible to march or to transport provisions over land. The river became so swollen that the steamboats were detained in the Ohio, and that source of supply was also closed. It was a most alarming condition of affairs, for it was impossible for the army to find sufficient food in the surrounding region, even if they transgressed the strict orders forbidding foraging. When they had rations for two days only the puzzled commander saw no way to save his little army from actual starvation. If the army had been able to march or wade through the mud, it would have been a disobedience of orders to leave the country to be again occupied by the enemy.

In his perplexity he decided to go for provisions himself, thinking that he might find some boat along the river which could be brought up in such an extremity.

But he went as far as the Ohio river before he found one. The great flood was so powerful that no one dared venture into its surges. He found two or three boatmen who said that a boat had once ascended the Big Sandy in a flood like that, but it was a miracle that it escaped destruction.

"Some boat *must* go up," said the general. "My men shall not starve!"

He found a rickety steamboat fastened to the bank of the stream awaiting a subsidence of the flood, and he ordered the captain to take a load of provisions up the river to the camp. The captain refused, saying that it would be as bad as suicide to undertake it. But Colonel Garfield insisted, and the captain and men, thinking they might as well be drowned as be shot for disobedience of military orders, allowed the boat, with themselves, to be taken by the general for the dangerous experiment. Finding no one he dared to trust to take the wheel or who was strong enough to manage it in the swift current, the general himself took the wheel, and for two days and the greater part of one night stood at his post. It required the most cautious steering to avoid the projecting banks and trees covered by the flood, and often the boat would graze an obstruction which would have sunk it, if it had struck near the prow.

Once the craft ran aground on a hard sandbank

and refused to back off when the wheel was reversed, and the general tried to induce some of the men to take the small boat and go on shore to fasten a rope so that they might pull the boat off the bank by the aid of the windlass. Not one dared tempt the terrific flood. So the general took the boat and the rope, and at a most hazardous risk of his life, especially so, as the river navigation was new to him, he crossed the stream and fastened the rope.

It was a triumphant hour for him, when he saw the crowd of his anxious troops on the river bank awaiting his coming, and one in which he blessed the day on which he learned to steer a canal boat.

The half-famished men, who had descended in despair to the river, believing that no boat could stem the flood, shouted themselves hoarse, and performed all kinds of childish antics, when they saw their general skillfully steering the frail and trembling river steamer. They could scarcely believe their own eyes; and many a night about the camp fires the soldiers afterwards told the story of the general's dangerous trip up the Sandy, with rations for his hungry men.

For three months the union troops remained at or near Piketon, often making short expeditions to drive out stray bands of rebel marauders.

In the month of March, General Garfield determined to drive out the rebels who were posted near Pound Gap, on the Virginia side of the Cumberland mountains; and with seven hundred men, including two hundred cavalry, he made a forced march of forty miles, and encamped secretly near the enemy's quarters. Early next morning, in a blinding snow storm, he sent the cavalry through the Gap, while the infantry clambered up by a difficult path to surprise the rebels in the rear. He was completely successful in surprising the post, but the rebels scattered so fast that he captured but few of them. They left valuable stores of amunition and provisions behind, of which he took possession. The next day he burned the camp and returned to his quarters. A few days later he was ordered to report with the greater part of his command at Louisville.

The order of General Buel, which he had thus obeyed so implicitly and fully, was dated December 17, 1861, and reads as follows :-

HEAD-QUARTERS DEPARTMENT OF THE OHIO,
LOUISVILLE, KY., December 17, 1861.

SIR :—The brigade, organized under your command, is intended to operate against the rebel force threatening, and, indeed, actually committing depredations in Kentucky, through the valley of the Big Sandy. The actual force of the enemy, from the best information I can gather, does not probably exceed two thousand, or two thousand five hundred, though rumor places it as high as seven thousand. I can better ascertain the true state of the case when you get on the ground.

You are apprised of the position of the troops under your command. Go first to Lexington and Paris, and place the 40th Ohio regiment in such position as will best give a moral support to the people in the counties on the route to Prestonburg and Piketon, and oppose any further advance of the enemy on that route. Then proceed with the least possible delay to the mouth of the Sandy, and move, with the force in that vicinity, up that river and drive the enemy back or cut him off. Having done that, Piketon will probably be in the best position for you to occupy to guard against future incursions. Artillery will be of little, if any, service to you in that country. If the enemy have any, it will encumber and weaken, rather than strengthen them.

Your supplies must mainly be taken up the river, and it ought to be done as soon as possible, while the navigation is open. Purchase what you can in the country through which you operate. Send your requisitions to these head-quarters for funds and advance stores, and to the Quartermasters and Commissary at Cincinnati for other supplies.

The conversation I have had with you will suggest more details than can be given here. Report frequently on all matters concerning your command.

Very respectfully,
Your obedient servant,
D. C. BUEL,
Brigadier-General Commanding.

The above order was followed by a congratulatory order, dated January 20, 1862, which reads as follows:

HEAD-QUARTERS DEPARTMENT OF THE OHIO,
LOUISVILLE, KY., January 20, 1862.

[General Orders No. 40.]

The general commanding takes occasion to thank General Garfield and his troops for their successful campaign against the rebel forces under General Marshall on the Big Sandy, and their gallant conduct in battle. They have overcome formidable difficulties in the character of the country, the condition of the roads, and the inclemency of the season ; and without artillery, have, in several engagements terminating in the battle on Middle Creek on the 10th inst., driven the enemy from his entrenched positions and forced him back into the mountains with the loss of a large amount of baggage and stores, and many of his men killed or captured. These services called into action the highest qualities of a soldier, — fortitude, perseverance, courage."

When General Garfield arrived at Louisville, he found that General Buel was far away in Tennessee, hurrying to the assistance of General Grant, at Pittsburg Landing. So General Garfield, obedient to fresh orders, bade a hasty farewell to his comrades, and hurried on after the army. He overtook General Buel at Columbia, Tennessee, and was at once assigned to the command of the 20th brigade, in the division of General T. J. Wood.

This change in his command was a great grief to General Garfield, who had hoped to keep the Fortieth Ohio in his brigade, and thus be with his old friends, scholars and neighbors throughout the war. But from that time their paths diverged, and never united again during the entire contest.

The army, of which his new command formed a part, made a forced march from Columbia to Savannah, on the Tennessee river, and from that point they were in great haste hurried on by boat to Pittsburg Landing. The battle of Shiloh had been raging for more than a day, when these reinforcements arrived. Without rest or time to enter camp they hurried on to the field of battle, and General Garfield's command was under fire during the final contest which gave the victory to the federal troops.

The next day his brigade, with other forces under General Sherman, was sent in pursuit of the retreating enemy, and a short but hotly contested battle was fought, in which General Garfield was conspicuously cool and brave.

During that tedious siege of Corinth, which followed, his brigade was nearly all the time at the outposts, and was engaged often in skirmishes with the rebels, and were with the first column that was ordered forward when the town was evacuated by Beauregard.

In June, 1862, his brigade was sent to repair and protect the Memphis and Charleston railroad, between Corinth and Decatur, after which he advanced to Huntsville, Alabama, and gained no little credit for his skill in military engineering, connected with the fortifications.

It has been often related of him that while in command of this brigade, a fugitive slave came rushing into his camp, with a bloody head, and apparently frightened almost to death. He had scarcely passed the head-quarters, when a regular bully of a fellow came riding up, and with a volley of oaths began to ask after his "nigger." General Garfield was not present, and he passed on to the division commander. The division commander was a sympathizer with the theory that fugitive slaves should be returned to their masters, and that the union soldiers should be made the instruments for returning them. He accordingly wrote a mandatory order to General Garfield, in whose command the darkey was supposed to be hiding, telling him to hunt out and deliver over the property of the outraged citizen. He took the order and deliberately wrote on it the following indorsement : —

" I respectively but positively decline to allow my command to search for or deliver up any fugitive slaves. I conceive that they are here for quite another purpose. The command is open, and no obstacles will be placed in the way of search."

The indorsement frightened his staff officers, and they expected that, if returned, the result would be that the general would be court-martialed. He simply replied, "The matter may as well be tested first as last. Right is right, and I do not propose to mince matters at all. My soldiers are here for other purposes than hunting and returning fugitive slaves. My people, on the Western Reserve of Ohio, did not send my boys and myself down here to do that kind of business, and they will back me up in my action." He would not alter the indorsement, and the order was returned. Nothing ever came of the matter further.

June 15th, General Garfield was detailed to sit in a trial by court-martial of a lieutenant of the Fifty-Eighth Indiana volunteers. His skill in that case, combined with his memory of judicial decisions, caused the officers, sitting with him in the court, to commend him for his signal ability in such matters. On July 5th, he was again detailed to act as president of the important court-martial detailed to try Colonel Turchin, of the Nineteenth Illinois. Of that court, General Garfield's adjutant-general, Captain P. T. Swain, acted as judge advocate.

July 30th, he was given a leave of absence, owing to the return of the fever and ague, which had not disturbed him until that season, from the spring when he left the canal. For two months he lay at Hiram, dangerously sick, and several important commands were offered him, which his illness compelled him to decline. It was during this summer that he paid for the small wooden dwelling in Hiram, which was afterwards his home.

As soon as he was able to travel he was ordered by the Secretary of War to report to the War Department, at Washington. This he did about the 25th of September. His fame as a jurist in martial trials had reached Washington, and he was ordered to sit on the court of inquiry in the case of General McDowell. At one time he was ordered to proceed to South Carolina, with General Hunter, but circumstances intervened to keep them in Washington.

November 25, 1862, he was made a member of the court in the celebrated trial of General Fitz-John Porter for the failure to co-operate with General Pope, at the battle of Bull Run. At that trial he had a delicate and important duty to perform, and did his work with such wisdom as to secure the unsolicited compliment from its president that "he must have been a great lawyer in Ohio."

During his engagements at Washington, he was called home by the illness and death of his only child. It was a sad blow to a heart so tender as his; and it is said of him that while he held the body of the sweet little child in his arms, after its death, he remarked how inappropriate to everything about him was his military uniform, and of how little consequence, compared with the love and peace of a happy home, were the honors which men could bestow.

While he was at home, in the months of August and September, as already stated, and confined to his bed, there was no little agitation going on in that congressional district, over a successor to the renowned anti-slavery champion, Joshua R. Giddings. The excitement was caused by the fact that Mr. Giddings had been defeated in the nominating convention, two years before, by some means, and his friends laid all the blame on the successful candidate. They therefore determined upon preventing the renomination of Mr. Giddings' successor. In their canvas for a candidate who would be sure to carry the convention, as there was no hope that the health of Mr. Giddings would admit of his return to Congress, even if he could have left his post as consul-general of Canada, they hit upon General Garfield, who at that time was recovering, but whose return to the malarial districts was considered dangerous. His name was one which was sure to overcome any combination or opposition. It does not appear that they consulted with General Garfield at all, but very carefully concealed their design, both from him and the opposition.   On the presentation of his name to the Republican congressional convention, in September, it was received with all the enthusiasm that the friends of the measure had expected.   He was the single man on the "Western Reserve" against whom it would be a farce to make any opposition.

The movement did not at first meet with General Garfield's approval, and he reserved his decision whether he should refuse the honor, until he could confer with President Lincoln.   His pay as a general was much larger than that of a congressman; he had entered the war to stay, and he disliked to leave it.

On the other hand, his health might break down if he returned to the South, and it was probable that the war would be closed in the year which would intervene between his election and the opening of the Congress to which he would be chosen.

When he visited the President, and told him the circumstances, Mr. Lincoln bluntly remarked that there were generals enough already and plenty more to be had, but the number of congressmen who understood the needs of the country were few, and if the rebellion continued, it was likely to be lessened by the death or enlistment of good men.   Other members of the Cabinet giving him the same advice, he silently acquiesced in the nomination, and was elected with unheard of unanimity.

In January he had so far recovered that he was

ordered into thefield, and directed to report to General Rosecrans, at Murfreesboro'. Immediately after his arrival he was appointed chief of staff to General Rosecrans, then commanding the army of the Cumberland.

The writer of the history of the Forty-Second Ohio regiment, whose sources of information were so trustworthy, and whose gifts as a writer were so apparent as to lead to his selection, by that regiment of students, as their historian, wrote, in 1875, of General Garfield's share in the campaigns of the army of the Cumberland, as follows:

"He was assigned to duty as chief of staff of the army of the Cumberland, in place of the lamented Colonel Garesche, who had been killed in the battle of Stone river. Early in the spring of that year Captain D. G. Swain, his adjutant-general since the previous April, was directed to organize a Bureau of Military Information. By a system of police and scout reports, very full and trustworthy information was obtained of the organization, strength, and position of the enemy's forces.

Early in June the general commanding required each general of a corps and division of the army of the Cumberland, to report his opinions, in writing, in reference to an early or immediate advance against the forces of General Bragg. Seventeen general officers submitted written opinions on that subject. Most of them were adverse to any early movement, and nearly all advised against an immediate advance. General Garfield presented to the commanding general an analysis and review of these opinions, and urged an immediate movement against the enemy. For more than five months the army of Rosecrans had lain inactive at Murfreesboro', while the commanding general had haggled and bandied words with the War Department. As chief of staff, General Garfield did all that adroit diplomacy could do to soften these asperities, and meanwhile give all his energy to the work of preparing the army for an advance, and ascertaining the strength of the enemy.

His Bureau of Military Information was the most perfect machine of the kind organized in the field during the war. When at last June came, the Government and the people demanding an advance, and the seventeen subordinate generals of Rosecrans advising against it, the analysis of the situation drawn up and submitted by General Garfield, met and overthrew them all. Speaking of this letter, Mr. Whitelaw Reid in his 'Ohio in the War,' says : 'This report we venture to pronounce the ablest military document known to have been submitted by a chief of staff to his superior during the war.' This is high praise, but it is history.

Twelve days after it was submitted, the army moved, — against the will and opinion of Gene. 'l Crittenden and nearly all Rosecrans' leading officers. It marched into the Tullahoma campaign, one of the most perfectly planned and ably executed movements of the war. The lateness of the start, caused by the objections which General Garfield's letter finally overcame, alone saved Bragg's army from destruction.

There was a certain work to do, which might as well have been begun on the 1st of June as the 24th. Had it been begun on the first of these dates, Bragg's army might, in all probability, have been destroyed. As it was, the heavy rains intervened and saved him from pursuit.

With his military reputation thus strengthened, General Garfield went with his chief into the battle of Chickamauga. His influence over Rosecrans had by this time become almost supreme. His clear and comprehensive mind grasped every detail, and his opinions were invariably consulted on all important questions. He wrote many orders upon his own judgment, submitting them to Rosecrans for approval or alteration. On the field of Chickamauga, he wrote every order except one, and that one was the fatal order to General Wood which ruined Rosecrans' right wing and lost the battle. The order from Rosecrans to Wood, as the latter interpreted it, required him to move his command behind another division, leaving a wide gap in the line of McCook's corps, which held the right. Wood says that he knew this move would be fatal, but it was ordered and he felt impelled to execute it. Longstreet saw the blunder, hurled Hood's division into the gap, and within an hour McCook's corps was broken and streaming, a disorganized mob of men, back to Chattanooga. Trying vainly to check the tide of retreat, General Garfield was swept with his chief back beyond Rossville. But the chief of staff could not concede that defeat had been entire. He heard the

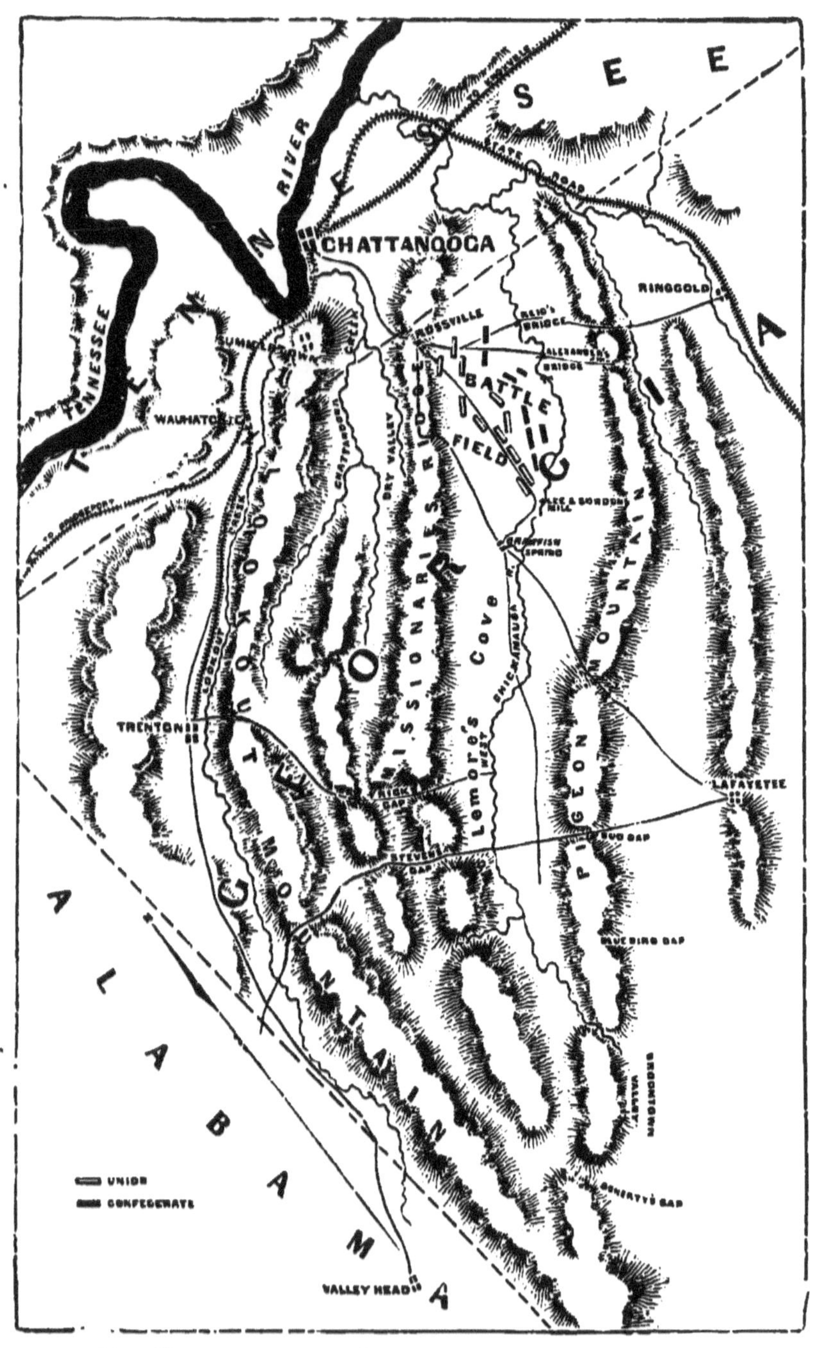

THE BATTLEFIELD OF CHICKAMAUGA AND ITS VICINITY.

roar of Thomas' guns on the left, and gained permission of Rosecrans to go round to that quarter and find the army of the Cumberland. While the commander busied himself with preparing a refuge at Chattanooga for his routed army, his chief of staff went back, accompanied only by a staff officer and a few orderlies, to find whatever part of the army still held its ground, and save what there was left. It was a perilous ride. Long before he reached Thomas one of his orderlies was killèd. Almost alone he pushed on over the obstructed road, through pursuers and pursued, found the heroic Thomas encircled by fire, but still firm, told him of the disaster on the right, and explained how he could withdraw his right wing and fix it upon a new line to meet Longstreet's column, which had turned the right of Thomas' position and was marching in heavy column upon his rear. The movement was made just in time; but Thomas' line was too short, it would not reach to the base of the mountain. Longstreet saw the gap, drove his column into it and would have struck Thomas' line fatally in the rear, but in that critical moment General Gordon Granger came up with Steadman's division, which moved in heavy column, threw itself upon Longstreet, and after a terrific struggle, drove him back. The dead and wounded lay in heaps where those two columns met, but the army of General Thomas was saved. As night closed in upon the heroic army of the Cumberland, Generals Garfield and Granger, on foot and enveloped in smoke, directed the loading and pointing of a battery of Napoleon guns, whose flash, as they thundered after the retreating column of the assailants, was the last light that shown upon the battle field of Chickamauga. The struggle was over, and the rebels retired repulsed. Had the two shattered corps of McCook and Crittenden that night been brought upon the field and enabled Thomas to hold his ground, there might have been a second day to that battle which would have changed its complexion in history.

The battle of Chickamauga practically closed General Garfield's military career. About four weeks after the engagement he was sent by Rosecrans to Washington to report minutely to the President and the War Department the position, deeds, resources, and capabilities of the army at Chattanooga. He went, had frequent lengthy interviews with the President and Secretary Stanton, and thus, point by point, made a most thorough and satisfactory report. Meanwhile, General Garfield had been promoted to a major-generalship of volunteers 'for gallant and meritorious services at the battle of Chickamauga,' to take rank from the 19th of September, 1863. Rosecrans had been removed from the command of the army at Chattanooga and General Grant appointed to his place.

General Garfield was now called to a new field of duty. In October of the year previous, while the Forty-Second was retreating from Cumberland Gap, the people of the Nineteenth Congressional District of Ohio had elected him as their representative to the Thirty-Eighth Congress.

He was a major-general, young, popular in the army, and in high favor at Washington ; he was poor, and his army pay was double the slender salary of a Congressman, but he had been chosen by the people of his district as their representative under circumstances which in his judgment would not permit him to decline the trust. General Thomas offered him the command of a corps; but Lincoln urged him to resign his commission and come to Congress. The President was strenuous, and his advice prevailed. There was no want of major-generals, but there was need of all the zeal, courage and ability that could be assembled in Congress. So his friends argued, and the sequel proved the wisdom of their demand upon him. Yielding to this, he resigned his commission on the 5th of December, 1863, having served in the army more than a year after his election to Congress, and took his seat on the same day in the House of Representatives, where he has been in continuous service since that day.

The influence of General Garfield upon the Forty-Second regiment was unbounded. As colonel, not less than as professor and principal of a collegiate school, he evinced a rare and extraordinary power in controlling, interesting and inspiring young men. It was due largely to his enthusiastic efforts that the regiment was made up of some of the best material that Ohio sent into the field. The careful, laborious education, the discipline, the quickening of individual self-respect that the regiment underwent at his hands while in Camp Chase, were never lost upon its men.   Long after he had gone to other duties, the recollection of his words was a source of inspiration to the men ; and as they went into their first fight at Middle Creek, against overwhelming numbers, with serene confidence, because their trusted colonel had sent them, so afterwards they fought and marched as though conscious that the eye of their first commander was still upon them."

CHAPTER XIII.

REVIEW OF HIS MILITARY CAREER.

FITNESS FOR MILITARY AFFAIRS. — HOW HE BECAME FAMILIAR WITH INFANTRY TACTICS. — CARRIES THE CHIEF CHARACTERISTICS OF HIS BOYHOOD INTO ARMY LIFE. — HIS KNOWLEDGE OF LAW. — MILITARY TRIALS. — THE TULLAHOMA CAMPAIGN. — HIS ABILITY AS AN ENGINEER. — HIS GREAT PLAN FOR AN ONWARD MOVEMENT FROM MURFREESBORO'. — HIS OFFICIAL REPORT. — COMPLIMENT FROM GENERAL ROSECRANS. — HIS RESIGNATION.

GLANCING back upon General Garfield's military career, with the accumulated facts of history adding their testimony to the high estimate made of him in 1863, the most conservative writer must be astonished at the ability displayed by him. It will also appear, that while the fact that the Secretary of War was from Ohio, and might be predisposed to observe the merits of a soldier from the same State, yet all the promotions which came to him were clearly and undisputedly deserved by him, and for the national good. He had a natural fitness, in some way, for military affairs. He seemed to be experienced in all the emergencies that met him; and everywhere acted, as his associates testify, "like an old soldier."

It is interesting to note how much of this success and appearance of familiarity was due to his early habits. He had accustomed himself to occupy all his time in some profitable work or study. He had, from the time he possessed but one book to study, schooled himself to thoroughly understand whatever he was given to learn.

Place these two characteristics together, and notice its bearing on his military usefulness. A scrutiny of the history of those early days of the war shows that he began to study military works as early as his days in the Senate of Ohio; and that from the day that Governor Dennison notified him of his appointment as a lieutenant-colonel, he bent his whole energy toward gaining an understanding of the art and rules of war. He applied himself closely to the practice of infantry tactics, and studied intently the directions for movements in regimental, battalion, and brigade drill. When his regiment began to assemble at Camp Chase, near Columbus, he was able to establish an officer's school, and to teach the most important matters himself. His confidence in himself came from his consciousness of having thoroughly mastered the subject. He studied military engineering in the same manner; and from that went to the plans of successful campaigns made by great soldiers of the past.

To those must be added the other prominent marks in his character, and a solution of his sudden rise is explained. The same active and obedient imagination, which in his boyhood turned the orchard trees into Indian chiefs, made the fields of wheat a host of buccaneers, and the bowing young maples an attentive audience, served him in his study of military movements, by supplying him with squads and regiments to drill, which were invisible to the natural eye and even to the imagination of many persons in his situation. He could give the orders and see the evolutions, and this mental practice made his appearance on his first trial seem like that of a veteran.

But combined with all the traits already mentioned was that sterling truthfulness, which has been mentioned as a characteristic of his boyhood. It won for him the respect of his superiors and the love of his inferiors. His word was implicitly trusted. To this known characteristic was due, in a great measure, the confidence which was placed in the Bureau of Information, which was managed by Major Swain, under General Garfield's direction. He misrepresented nothing. He over-estimated nothing. Before him the lying scouts, spies, fugitives, slaves and captives seemed to be in awe of his integrity; and, as one of his staff has said, "he impelled them to tell the truth by the very force of his presence and example." The information he obtained of the enemy's movements and numbers was so correct that great armies moved on to victories, led by his directions.

His thorough knowledge of law and his administrative ability, combined with the traits already mentioned, caused his words and decisions to be respected in martial courts. He had been thorough and honest with himself in his studies, and one who is honest and sincere with himself is honest and sin-

12

cere with all the world. It is a rule that works both ways.

But the crown of all his military achievements, and one which our successful general have all pronounced to be a masterly stroke of military genius, is found in his plan of the Tullahoma campaign, from Murfreesboro', by the army of the Cumberland. All testify that, had General Rosecrans moved at once, instead of hesitating to hear the advice of other generals, who opposed it, General Bragg's command must have been captured, and the rebellion cut in twain, a year before Sherman marched to the sea.

As it was, the campaign was an important and successful movement, and gave our armies many advantages in the movements which Grant afterwards made.

Whitelaw Reid, in his great work on "Ohio in the War," has printed entire the paper submitted by General Garfield to the commanding general, at that time, and it deserves a place in every biography of General Garfield.

General Rosecrans had been waiting five months for a favorable opportunity to attack General Bragg, and had many foolish quarrels with the War Department on account of his delay and strenuous demands for cavalry and stores. But, at last, under the urgent advice of General Garfield, his chief of staff, he asked the advice of the generals in command of divisions in the army of the Cumberland, about an advance. All advised against it. General Garfield was in favor of an immediate' move, and gave his reasons for it. His advice was taken, with the good results already mentioned. The document gives such an insight into the condition of affairs, and exhibits so strikingly General Garfield's customary caution, foresight, and logical arrangement, that it is given entire.

HEAD-QUARTERS DEPARTMENT OF THE CUMBERLAND.

MURFREESBORO', June 12, 1864.

General : — In your confidential letter of the 8th inst., to the corps and division commanders and generals of cavalry, of this army, there were substantially five questions propounded, for their consideration and answer, viz. :

1. Has the enemy of our front been materially weakened by detachments to Johnston, or elsewhere ?

2. Can this army advance on him at this time, with strong, reasonable chances of fighting a great and successful battle ?

3. Do you think an advance of our army at present likely to prevent additional reinforcements being sent against General Grant by the enemy in our front ?

4. Do you think an *immediate* advance of the army advisable ?

5. Do you think an early advance advisable ?

Many of the answers to these questions are not categorical, and cannot be clearly set down either as affirmative or negative. Especially in answer to the first question there is much indefiniteness, resulting from the difference of judgment as to how great a detachment could be considered a " material reduction of Bragg's strength." For example, one officer thinks it has been reduced ten thousand, and not " materially weakened."

The answers to the second question are modified, in some instances, by the opinion that the rebels will fall back behind the Tennessee river, and thus no battle can be fought, either successful or unsuccessful.

So far as these opinions can be stated, in tabular form, they will stand thus : —

					Yes.	No.
Answer to first question,	.	.	.	.	6	11
Answer to second question,	.	.	.	.	2	11
Answer to third question,	.	.	.	.	4	10
Answer to fourth question,	.	.	.	.		15
Answer to fifth question,	.	.	.	.		2

On the fifth question, three gave it as their opinion that this army ought to advance as soon as Vicksburg falls, should that event happen. The following is a summary of the reasons assigned why we should not, at this time, advance upon the enemy : —

1. With Hooker's army defeated, and Grant's bending all its energies in a yet undecided struggle, it is bad policy to risk our only reserve army to the chances of a general engagement. A failure here would have most disastrous effect on our lines of communication, and on politics in the loyal States.

2. We should be compelled to fight the enemy on his own ground, or follow him in a fruitless chase; or, if we attempted to out-flank him and turn his position, we should expose our line of communication, and run the risk of being pushed back into a rough country, well-known to the enemy and little to ourselves.

3. In case the enemy should fall back without accepting battle, he could make our advance very slow, and with a comparatively small force posted in the gaps of the mountains, could hold us back while he crossed the Tennessee river, where he would be measurably secure, and free to send reinforcements to Johnston.

His forces in East Tennessee could seriously harrass our left flank and constantly disturb our communications.

4. The withdrawal of Burnside's ninth army corps deprives us of an important reserve and flank protection, thus increasing the difficulty of an advance.

5. General Hurlburt has sent the most of his force away to General Grant, thus leaving West Tennessee uncovered, and laying our right flank and rear open to raids of the enemy.

The following incidental opinions are expressed : —

1. One officer thinks it probable that the enemy has been strengthened, rather than weakened, and that *he* (the enemy) would have reasonable prospect of victory in a general battle.

2. One officer believes the result of a general battle would be doubtful, a victory barren, and a defeat most disastrous.

3. Three officers believe that an advance would bring on a general engagement. Three others believe it would not.

4. Two officers express the opinion that the chances of success in a general battle are nearly equal.

5. One officer expresses the belief that our army has reached its maximum strength and efficiency, and that inactivity will seriously impair its effectiveness.

6. Two officers say that an increase of our cavalry, by about six thousand men, would materially change the aspect of our affairs, and give us a decided advantage.

In addition to the above summary, I have the honor to submit an estimate of the strength of Bragg's army, gathered from all the data I have been able to obtain, including the estimate of the general commanding, in his official report of the battle of Stone river, and facts gathered from prisoners, deserters and refugees, and from rebel newspapers. After the battle, Bragg consolidated many of his decimated regiments and irregular organizations ; and at the time of his sending reinforcements to Johnston, his army had reached the greatest effective strength. It consisted of five divisions of infantry, composed of ninety-four regiments, and two independent battalions of sharp-shooters, —say ninety regiments. By a law of the confederate Congress, regiments are consolidated when their effective strength falls below two hundred and fifty men. Even the regiments formed by such consolidation (which may reasonably be regarded as the fullest) must fall below five hundred. I am satisfied that four hundred is a large estimate of the average strength.

The force, then, would be : —

Infantry, 95 regiments, 400 each,	. . .	38,000
Cavalry, 35 regiments, say, 500 each,	. . .	17,500
Artillery, 26 batteries, say 100 each,	. . .	2,600
Total,	. . . .	58,600

This force has been reduced by detachments to Johnston. It is as well known as we can ever expect to ascertain such facts, that three brigades have gone from McConn's division, and two or three from Breckinridge's, — say two It is clear that there are now but four infantry divisions in Bragg's army, the fourth being composed of fragments of McConn's and Breckinridge's divisions, and must be much smaller than the average. Deducting the five brigades, and supposing them composed of only four regiments each, which is below the general average, it gives an infantry reduction of twenty regiments, four hundred each — eight thousand — leaving a remainder of thirty thousand.   It is clearly ascertained that at least two brigades of cavalry have been sent from Van Dorn's command to the Mississippi, and it is asserted in the *Chattanooga Rebel*, of June 11th, that General Morgan's command has been permanently detached and sent to Eastern Kentucky.   It is not certainly known how large his division is, but it is known to contain at least two brigades.   Taking this minimum as the fact, we have a cavalry reduction of four brigades.

Taking the lowest estimate, four regiments to the brigade, we have a reduction, by detachment, of sixteen regiments, five hundred each, leaving his present effective cavalry force nine thousand five hundred. With the nine brigades of the two arms thus detached, it will be safe to say there have gone, —

Six batteries, 80 men each, ...	480
Leaving him 20 batteries, ...	2,120
Making a total reduction of	16,480
Leaving, of the three arms, ...	41,680

In this estimate of Bragg's strength, I have placed all doubts in his favor, and I have no question that my estimate is considerably beyond the truth   General Sheridan, who has taken great pains to collect evidence on this point, places it considerably below these figures.   But assuming these to be correct, and granting what is still more improbable, that Bragg would abandon all his rear posts, and entirely neglect his communications, and could bring his last man into battle, I next ask : What have we with which to oppose him ?

The last official report of effective strength, now on file in the office of the assistant adjutant general, is dated from June 11th, and shows that we have in this department, omitting all officers and enlisted men attached to department, corps, division and brigade head-quarters : —

1.   Infantry — One hundred and seventy-three regiments ; ten battalions sharp-shooters ; four battalions pioneers ; and one regiment of engineers and mechanics, with a total effective strength of seventy thousand nine hundred and eighteen.

2.   Cavalry — Twenty-seven regiments and one unattachee company, eleven thousand, eight hundred and thirteen.

3.   Artillery — Forty-seven and a half batteries field artillery, con-

sisting of two hundred and ninety-two guns and five hundred and sixty-nine men, making a general total of eighty-seven thousand eight hundred.

Leaving out all commissioned officers, this army represents eighty-two thousand seven hundred and sixty-seven bayonets and sabers. This report does not include the Fifth Iowa cavalry, six hundred strong, lately armed ; nor the First Wisconsin cavalry : nor Coburn's brigade of infantry, now arriving; nor the two thousand three hundred and ninety-four convalescents, now on light duty in "Fortress Monroe."

There are detached from this force as follows : —

At Galatin,	969
At Carthage,	1,149
At Fort Donelson,	1,485
At Clarkesville,	1,138
At Nashville,	7,292
At Franklin,	900
At Lavergne,	2,117
Total,	15,130

With these posts as they are, and leaving two thousand five hundred efficient men, in addition to the two thousand three hundred and ninety-four convalescents, to hold the works at this place, there will be left sixty-five thousand one hundred and thirty-seven bayonets and sabers to show, against Bragg's forty-one thousand six hundred and eighty.

I beg leave, also, to submit the following considerations : —

·1. Bragg's army is weaker now than it has been since the battle of Stone river, or is likely to be, at present, while our army has reached its maximum strength, and we have no right to expect reinforcements for several months, if at all.

2. Whatever be the result at Vicksburg, the determination of its fate will give large reinforcements to Bragg. If Grant is successful, his army will require many weeks to recover from the shock and strain of his late campaign, while Johnston will send back to Bragg a force sufficient to insure the safety of Tennessee. If Grant fails, the same result will inevitably follow, so far as Bragg's army is concerned.

3.   No man can predict, with a certainty, the results of any battle, however great the disparity in numbers.   Such results are in the hand of God.   But, reviewing the question in the light of human calculation, I refuse to entertain a doubt that this army, which in January last defeated Bragg's superior numbers, cannot overwhelm his present greatly inferior forces.

4.   The most unfavorable course for us that Bragg could take, would be to fall back without giving us battle ; but this would be very disastrous to him.   Besides the loss of material of war, and the abandonment of the rich and abundant harvest, now nearly ripe in Central Tennessee, he would lose heavily by desertion.   It is well known that a wide-spread dissatisfaction exists among his Kentucky and Tennessee troops.   They are already deserting in large numbers.   A retreat would greatly increase both the desire and the opportunity for desertion, and would very materially reduce his physical and moral strength. While it would lengthen our communication, it would give us possession of McMinnville, and enable us to threaten Chattanooga and East Tennessee ; and it would not be unreasonable to expect an early occupation of the former place.

5.   But the chances are more than even that a sudden and rapid movement would compel a general engagement, and the defeat of Bragg would be, in the highest degree, disastrous to the rebellion.

6.   The turbulent aspect of politics in the loyal States renders a decisive blow against the enemy, at this time, of the highest importance to the success of the government at the polls, and in the enforcement of the Conscript Act.

7.   The government and the War Department believe that this army ought to move upon the enemy.   The army desire it, and the country is anxiously hoping for it.

8.   Our true objective point is the rebel army, whose last reserves are substantially in the field, and an effective blow will crush the shell, and soon be followed by the collapse of the rebel government.

9.   You have, in my judgment, wisely delayed a general movement hitherto, till your army could be massed, and your cavalry could be mounted.   Your mobile force can now be concentrated in twenty-four hours, and your cavalry, if not equal in numerical strength to that of the enemy, is greatly superior in efficiency and morale.   For this rea-

son I believe an immediate advance of all our available forces is advisable, and, under the providence of God, will be successful.

Very respectfully, your obedient servant,

J. A. GARFIELD,

Brigadier-General, Chief of Staff.

Major-General ROSECRANS,
    Commanding Dep't. Cumberland.

That the estimate which this biography has placed upon the character of General Garfield may not seem to be overdrawn, the following testimony given by a writer at Zenia, Ohio, in the autumn of 1862, is inserted in these pages:

"We have known General James A. Garfield for several years, and entertain for him the highest personal regard. He is one of the most eloquent men in Ohio, as well as one of the ripest scholars. Socially and morally he has no superior. He is popular with all, as the attachment of his scholars, as well as his soldiers, for him demonstrates.

In respect to abilities, nature has by no means been unfriendly to him; and he has neither despised nor slighted her gifts. A severe course of mental training, combined with the mental practice obtained by presiding over one of the colleges of Ohio, has fully developed his natural endowments.

Above all these considerations, everyone respects General Garfield for his stern, unyielding, uncompromising patriotism. The permanent good of his country, the restoration of its unity, and the perpetuation of the national power and glory through all coming time, are the objects which he keeps steadily in view."

For more than a year after his election to Congress, General Garfield kept the field, and without flinching endured the severest tests which come to the soldier in war.   He lost no time and shirked no hardships. He bravely entered the most dangerous lines of battle when his duty called him there, and the number of men killed at his side, and horses wounded or killed under him, attest his proximity to the enemy.

In General Rosecran's official report of the battle of Chickamauga he bears testimony to General Garfield's soldierly qualities and said :

"To Brigadier-General James A. Garfièld, chief of staff.   I am especially indebted for the clear and ready manner in which he seized the points of action and movement, and expressed in orders the ideas of the general commanding."

To this testimony the War Department put its seal by issuing to him a commission as major-general dated the day of that great battle.

On December 5th, a few weeks after the battle and after General Rosecrans was relieved, General Garfield resigned his commission and immediately took his seat in Congress.   At the time he resigned, he felt that he was needed in Congress ; yet, his unwillingness to leave the service, nearly overcome his resolution to take his seat in the House of Representatives, and in November, before he left the army, he wrote to the President that were it not for the strong belief he had that the war would close within a few months, he should remain with the army.

CHAPTER XIV.

SERVICE AS A LEGISLATOR.

A NEW FIELD. — THE HIGHEST TEST OF HUMAN GREATNESS. — THE
AMERICAN CONGRESS. — FREQUENT FAILURES OF NOTED MEN. —
THE TRIALS OF THAT CRISIS. — PLACED ON THE MILITARY COMMIT-
TEE. — THE STYLE OF HIS SPEECHES. — HIS INDUSTRY. — HIS REPLY
TO MR. LONG. — AN IMPROMPTU SPEECH. — THE COMPLIMENTS OF
OLD MEMBERS.

HITHERTO we have noted the career of a man who, notwithstanding his surprising success, was nevertheless a man among men, finding often his equal in the work which he had chosen. His childhood, youth, and army experience were such as to entitle him to the praise and thanks of the people, but thus far in common with many others.

Thousands of boys have chopped wood, boiled salts, and drove canal horses and mules, and have succeeded in life, notwithstanding such humble beginnings. If it were not so, the history of his career would be a drawback rather than an encouragement to American youths.

But now our record enters upon a higher plain, where the number of remarkable successes is far less and where many prosperous lives find their final level. In the legislative halls of a mighty nation the ability and integrity of men find their severest tests. They may have enjoyed unlimited success from their cradle to the oath of office, but it is no guarantee of usefulness or fame in such a body as the American Congress. Great soldiers, with the scars of many battles and the fame of mighty conquerors, have entered the doors of the Capitol amid the applause of an idolizing constituency, and have been immediately lost from sight, and soon from notice. Distinguished lawyers whose acquaintances regarded them as giants in the intellectual world, seem to become helpless and worthless as soon as they are lost in the crowd of talented men who gather at the Capitol. Scholars, poets, mathematicians, professors, preachers, railroad presidents, bankers, merchants, discoverers, inventors and millionaires, enter the legislative chambers with brilliant reputations and under the impetus of some great deed, only to be hid in a political fog, where they sit for a while in silent helplessness, and go home without a sign of welcome or approval.

The story of Gen. Garfield's success in the legislative department of the American nation, is the most interesting and the most remarkable part of the history of his life. We have already seen how his qualities as a young man commended him to the respect and attention of the Senate of Ohio, and we shall see how quickly those same qualities lifted him above the mass of congressmen, and brought him into the notice of the nation.

It must not be considered by the reader that, because General Garfield was known to the President, and to some of the great captains of our army, and was loved and honored by the people of the Western Reserve, that he was known in the House of Representatives. There were hundreds of generals in the field whose names were far better known than that of Rosecrans' chief of staff. There were generals in the House of Representatives who had seen severer service, and whose deeds had been far wider proclaimed. There were old statesmen there whose hairs had grown white in the service of the nation. There were scholars of the highest reputation, and orators whose words had become classic. Not a score of the whole assembly knew him by sight, or could recall his place of residence or past services when his name was called.

It was a new start in life. In Congress, as in the back woods, he must overcome difficulties and fight his way alone. To win distinction there he must be something more than daring, truthful, and industrious; he must possess that peculiar combination of strong talents and intellectual acuteness to which men somewhat vaguely apply the term, "greatness." To be eminently great in a nation of great men, and in a time when especial circumstances combined to develop and disclose human nobility, required masterly talents and incessant watchfulness. To be of unusual service to humanity and of exceptional value to a nation, when twenty-five millions of people were striving, at a fever heat, to do the same thing, is something of which a man has reason to be proud. Such is General Garfield's record. He entered upon his duties in Congress at a time when there were foes within and foes without; when a strong army threatened the nation in the Southern States, and Great Britain menaced it from the ocean ; when the finances of the government were getting into an almost inextricable snarl ; when the people were searching for their greatest men, for councillors in the nation's peril and distress; and when it required fortitude, wisdom and patriotism above the common order, to provide securely for the nation's future.

For this work, General Garfield was well endowed by nature and education. He was a ready speaker, — apt, elegant, pointed, vehement. He had all the scholarship of the colleges, and more to draw upon. He had the practice of cultured public speaking. He had the experience of war, and a course of extensive reading from which to draw forcible and illuminating illustrations. He had all the physical characteristics of dignity, strength, countenance and voice, which are so useful in the public forum. Thus he was well equipped for a place in a deliberate assembly. But the growth of a member's influence, under the most favorable circumstances, is slow. He could not be a leader there until he had again and again displayed his ability for the post. He does not appear to have aspired to leadership ; but, from the first day of the session, set himself with stubborn purpose at the task of securing a complete knowledge of the rules and history of Congress.

Then followed a study of the resources of the nation in men and money, and of the history of other countries, whose experience could throw any light, or give any suggestion to statesmen, in the complicated and perplexing trials of the union. His habits of incessant study served him well, and he always had a book in his hand or in his pocket, for use in any spare moment. His astonishing readiness in congressional debates upon any question of commerce, manufactures, finance, revenue, international law, or whatever came up, can be accounted for by this industrious habit. Never idle himself,

CAPITOL AT WASHINGTON.

and assisted by his wife, as only a talented, patient and affectionate woman of her unusual gifts can assist a man of letters, he steadily and heartily assisted the measures he thought were wise and good, and earnestly, and sometimes excitedly, opposed those actions which he deemed to be pernicious and wrong.

He was given a place at once, upon his entry into Congress, on the very important committee on military affairs. His colleagues bear testimony to his activity, industry and efficiency, from the very beginning of his term. His speeches were often models of graceful oratory, and yet have about them none of that objectional air of conceit which would suggest that the speaker delivered them for any other purpose but to convince.

Early in the Thirty-eighth Congress, in which Mr. Garfield first made his appearance as a congressman, Mr. Alexander Long of Ohio, made a long and labored argument, to show that it was useless to try further to coerce the South. The tendency of Mr. Long's speech was to encourage the rebellion and censure the patriots who attempted to preserve the union. To that speech General Garfield replied, without preparation, having taken the floor immediately upon the completion of Mr. Long's address.

"Mr. Chairman," said he, " I should be obliged to you if you would direct the sergeant-at-arms to bring a white flag and plant it in the aisle between myself and my colleague who has just addressed you.

I recollect on one occasion when two great armies stood face to face, that under a white flag just planted I approached a company of men dressed in the uniform of the rebel confederacy and reached out my hand to one of the number and told him I respected him as a brave man. Though he wore the emblems of disloyalty and treason, still, underneath his vestments, I beheld a brave and honest soul.

I would reproduce that scene here this afternoon, I say, were there such a flag of truce,—but God forgive me if I should do it under any other circumstances! I would reach out this right hand and ask that gentleman to take it, because I honor his bravery and his honesty. I believe what has just fallen from his lips is the honest sentiment of his heart; and, in uttering it he has made a new epoch in the history of this war; he has done a new thing under the sun; he has done a brave thing. It is braver than to face cannon and musketry, and I honor him for his candor and frankness.

But now I ask you to take away the flag of truce, and I will go back inside the union lines and speak of what he has done. I am reminded by it of a distinguished character in 'Paradise Lost.' When he had rebelled against the glory of God and 'led away a third part of heaven's sons, conjured against the Highest,' when after terrible battles in which mountains and hills were hurled by each contending host 'with 'jaculations dire'; when at last the leader and his hosts were hurled down 'nine times the space that measures day and night,' and after the terrible fall lay stretched prone on the burning lake, Satan lifted up his shattered bulk, crossed the abyss, looked down into Paradise, and, soliloquizing, said:

'Which way I fly is hell, myself am hell.'

It seems to me in that utterance he expressed the very sentiment to which you have just listened; uttered by one no less brave, malign and fallen. This man gathers up the meaning of this great contest, the philosophy of the moment, the prophecies of the hour, and, in sight of the paradise of victory and peace, utters them all in this wail of terrible despair, 'Which way I fly is hell.' He ought to add, 'Myself am hell.'

Mr. Chairman, I am reminded of two characters in the war of the revolution as compared with two others in the war of to-day.

The first was Lord Fairfax who dwelt near the Potomac, a few miles from us. When the great contest was opened between the mother country and the colonies, Lord Fairfax, after a protracted struggle with his own heart, decided that he must go with the mother country. He gathered his mantle about him and went over, grandly, solemnly and impressively and joined the fortunes of Great Britain against the home of his adoption.

But there was another man who cast in his lot with the struggling colonies, and continued with them till the war was well-nigh ended. But in a day of darkness, which just preceded the glory of the morning, that other man, deep down in the damned pits of his black heart, hatched the treason to surrender forever all that had been gained to the enemies of his country. *Benedict Arnold* was that man.

Fairfax and Arnold find their parallel in the struggle of to-day.

When this war began, many good men stood hesitating and doubting what they ought to do. Their doctrine of State rights, their sympathies, all they had ever loved and longed for, were in the South ; and after long and painful hesitation, some of them at last went with the enemies of the nation. At that time Robert E. Lee sat in his home across the river here doubting and delaying, and going off at last almost tearfully, to join the enemies of his country. He reminds me in some respects of Lord Fairfax, the stately royalist of the revolution. But now, when hundreds of thousands of brave souls have gone up to God under the shadow of the flag, and when thousands more, maimed and shattered in the contest, are sadly awaiting the deliverance of death; now, when three years of terrific warfare have raged over us, when our armies have pushed the rebellion back over mountains and rivers, and crowded it back into narrow limits, until a wall of fire girds it; now, when the uplifted hand of a majestic people is about to let fall the lightning of its conquering power upon the rebellion; now, in the quiet of this hall, hatched in the lowest depths of a similar dark treason, there rises a Benedict Arnold and proposes to surrender us all up, body and spirit, the nation and the flag, its genius and its honor, now and forever, to the accursed traitors to our country. And that proposition comes — God forgive and pity my beloved State! — it comes from a citizen of the honored and loyal Commonwealth of Ohio.

I implore you, brethren, in this House, not to believe that many such births ever gave pangs to my mother State such as she suffered when that traitor was born.

[Suppressed applause and sensation.] I beg you

not to believe that on the soil of that State another such growth has ever deformed the face of nature and darkened the light of God's day. [An audible whisper, 'Vallandigham.'] But ah! I am reminded there are other such. My zeal and love for Ohio have carried me too far. I retract. I remember that only a few days since a political convention met at the capital of my State, and *almost* decided to select from just such material a Representative for the Democratic party in the coming contest; and, to-day, what claim to be a majority of the Democracy of that State say that they have been cheated or they would have made that choice. I therefore sadly take back the boast in behalf of my native State.

But, sir, I will forget States. We have something greater than States and State pride to be talked of here to-day. I will, if I can, dismiss feeling from my heart, and try to consider only what bears upon the logic of the speech to which we have just listened.

First of all, the gentleman tells us that the right of secession is a constitutional right. I do not propose to enter into the argument. I have expressed myself hitherto on State sovereignty and State rights, of which this proposition of his is the legitimate child.

But the gentleman takes higher ground, and in that I agree with him, namely, that five million or eight million people possess the right of revolution. Grant it ; we agree there.

If fifty-nine men can make revolution successful,

hey have the right of revolution. If one State vishes to break its connection with the federal gov-:rnment, and does it by force, maintaining itself, it s an independent State. If the eleven Southern States are determined and resolved to leave the inion, to secede, to revolutionize, and can maintain hat revolution by force, they have the revolutionary ight to do so. Grant it. I stand on that platform vith the gentleman. And now the question comes, s it our constitutional duty to let them do it? That s the question; and in order to reach it, I beg to :all your attention not to an argument, but to the :ondition of affairs which would result from such .ction, the mere statement of which becomes the trongest possible argument. What does this gen-leman propose? Where will he draw the line of livision? If the rebels carry into successful seces-ion what they desire to carry; if their revolution :nvelops as many States as they intend it shall :nvelop; if they draw the line where Isham G. Harris, the rebel governor of Tennessee, in the ebel camp near our lines, told Mr. Vallandigham hey would draw it, — along the line of the Ohio and if the Potomac; if they make good their statement o him, that they will never consent to any other ine, then, I ask, what is the thing that the gentle-nan proposes to do?

He proposes to leave to the United States a terri-ory reaching from the Atlantic to the Pacific, and ine hundred miles wide in the center! From Wells-ille, on the Ohio river, to Cleveland on the lakes, is one hundred miles. I ask you, Mr. Chairman, if there be a man here so insane as to suppose that the American people will allow their magnificent national proportions to be shorn to so deformed a shape as this ?

I tell you — and I confess it here — that while I hope I have something of human courage, I have not enough to contemplate such a result. I am not brave enough to go to the brink of the precipice of successful secession, and look down into its damned abyss. If my vision were keen enough to pierce to its bottom, I would not dare to look. If there be a man here who dare contemplate such a scene, I look upon him either as the bravest of the sons of women, or as a downright madman. Secession to gain peace ! Secession is the tocsin of eternal war. There can be no end to such a war as will be inaugurated if this thing be done.

Suppose the policy of the gentleman were adopted to-day. Let the order go forth ; sound the ' recall ' on your bugles, and let it ring from Texas to the far Atlantic, and tell the armies to come back. Call the victorious legions back over the battle-fields of blood, forever now disgraced. Call them back, over the territory which they have conquered. Call them back, and let the minions of secession chase them with derision and jeers as they come. And then tell them that that man across the aisle, from the free State of Ohio, gave birth to the monstrous proposition. Mr. Chairman, if such a word should be sent forth through the armies of the union, the wave of terrible vengeance that would sweep back over this land could never find a parallel in the records of history. Almost in the moment of final victory, the 'recall' is sounded by a craven people not deserving freedom. We ought every man to be made a slave, should we sanction such a sentiment.

The gentleman has told us there is no such thing as coercion justifiable under the constitution. I ask him for one moment to reflect that no statute ever was enforced without coercion.

It is the basis of every law in the universe, — God's law as well as man's. A law is no law without coercion behind it. When a man has murdered his brother, coercion takes the murderer, tries him and hangs him. When you levy your taxes, coercion secures their collection; it follows the shadow of the thief, and brings him to justice; it accompanies your diplomacy to foreign courts, and backs the declaration of the nation's rights by a pledge of the nation's power. But when the life of that nation is imperiled, we are told that it has no coercive power against the parricides in its own bosom. Again, he tells us that oaths taken under the amnesty proclamation are good for nothing.

The oath of Galileo, he says, was not binding upon him. I am reminded of another oath that was taken; but perhaps it, too, was an oath on the lips alone, to which the heart made no response.

I remember to have stood in a line of nineteen men from Ohio, on that carpet yonder, on the first day of the session; and I remember that, with uplifted hands before God, those nineteen took an oath to support and maintain the constitution of the United States ; and I remember that another oath was passed around, and each member signed it as provided by law, utterly repudiating the rebellion and its pretenses. Does the gentleman not blush to speak of Galileo's oath? Was not his own its counterpart?

He says the union can never be restored because of the terrible hatred engendered by the war. To prove it, he quotes what some Southern man said a few years ago, that he knew no hatred between peoples in the world like that between the North and the South. And yet that North and South have been one nation for more than eighty years !

Have we seen in this contest anything more bitter than the wars of the Scottish border? Have we seen anything bitterer than those terrible feuds in the days of Edward, when England and Scotland were the deadliest foes on earth? And yet for centuries, those countries have been cemented in an indissoluble union that has made the British nation one of the proudest of the earth.

I said a little while ago that I accepted the proposition of the gentleman that the rebels had the right of revolution ; and the decisive issue between us and the rebellion is, whether they shall revolutionize and destroy, or we shall subdue and preserve.

We take the latter ground. We take the common weapons of war to meet them ; and if these be not sufficient, I would take any element which will overwhelm and destroy ; I would sacrifice the dearest

ind best beloved ; I would take all the old sanctions
if law and the constitution and fling them to the
winds, if necessary, rather than let the nation be
iroken in pieces and its people destroyed with end-
ess ruin.

What is the constitution that these gentlemen are
ierpetually flinging in our faces, whenever we desire
o strike hard blows against the rebellion ?   It is the
iroduction of the American people.   They made it,
ind the Creator is mightier than the creature.   The
iower which made the constitution can also make
ither instruments to do its great work in the day of
ts dire necessity."

This speech was so eloquently spoken, and was
itamped with such sincerity, that old members of the
House of Representatives gathered about him during
ts delivery, and greeted him with most flattering
lemonstrations of approval at its close.

CHAPTER XV.

EARLY SPEECHES.

HIS POSITION CONCERNING THE DRAFT FOR THE ARMY. — DIFFERS WITH HIS OWN PARTY. — CONTENDS FOR FRANKNESS AND TRUTH. — HOPEFUL VIEW OF THE NATION'S SUCCESS.— NATIONAL CONSCIENCE AND SLAVERY. — EMANCIPATION THE REMEDY FOR NATIONAL EVILS. — DEFENCE OF GENERAL ROSECRANS. — TRIBUTE TO GENERAL THOMAS. — HIS ACCOUNT OF THE BATTLE OF CHICKAMAUGA. — THE DOCTRINE OF STATE RIGHTS. — CAMDEN AND AMBOY RAILROAD VS. THE UNITED STATES. — WHAT IS THE POWER AND PREROGATIVE OF THE NATION.

DURING General Garfield's first session, there was much contention over the draft for the army, and the clause in the law which allowed persons who were drawn to commute their service by the payment of three hundred dollars. The speech which General Garfield made illustrates, better than any description could do, certain phases of his character and his manner as a public speaker. In this he was not contending so much with the Democratic party, as with those of his own party with whom he differed in regard to the wisdom o. the laws regulating the draft. He said :

"Mr. Speaker, it has never been my policy to conceal a truth, merely because it is unpleasant. It may be well to smile in the face of danger, but it is neither

well nor wise to let danger approach unchallenged
and unannounced.   A brave nation, like a brave man,
desires to see and measure the perils which threaten
it.   It is the right of the American people to know
the necessities of the republic, when they are called
upon to make sacrifices for it.   It is this lack of confidence in ourselves and the people, this timid waiting
for events to control us, when they should obey us,
that makes men oscillate between hope and fear,—
now in the sunshine of the hill-tops, and now in the
gloom and shadows of the valley.   To such men, the
morning bulletin, which heralds success in the army,
gives exultation and high hope; the evening dispatch, announcing some slight disaster to our advancing columns, brings gloom and depression.   Hope
rises and falls by the accidents of war, as the mercury
of the thermometer changes by the accidents of heat
and cold.   Let us rather take for our symbol the
sailor's barometer, which faithfully forwarns him of
the tempest, and gives him unerring promise of serene skies and peaceful seas.   No man can deny that
we have grounds for apprehension and anxiety.   The
unexampled magnitude of the contest, the enormous
expenditures of the war, the unprecedented waste of
battle, bringing sorrow to every loyal fireside, the
courage, endurance and desperation of our enemy,
the sympathy given him by the monarchies of the
Old World, as they wait and hope or our destruction,
all these considerations should make us anxious and
earnest ; but they should not add one hue of despair
to the face of an American citizen ; they should not

abate a tittle of his heart and hope. The specters
of defeat, bankruptcy and repudiation have stalked
through this Chamber, evoked by those gentlemen
who see no hope for the republic, in the arbitrament
of war, no power in the justice of our cause, no peace
made secure by the triumph of freedom and truth.
Mr. Speaker, even at this late day of the session, I
will beg the indulgence of the House, while I point
out some of the grounds of our confidence in the final
success of our cause, while I endeavor to show that,
though beset with dangers, we still stand on firm
earth ; and though the heavens are clouded, yet above
storm and cloud the sun of our national hope shines
with steady and undimmed splendor. History is
constantly repeating itself, making only such changes
of programme as the growth of nations and centuries
requires. Such struggles as ours, and far greater
ones, have occurred in other ages, and their records
are written for us. I desire to refer to the example
of our ancestors across the sea, in their great struggles at the close of the last and the beginning of the
present century, to show what a brave nation can do
when their liberties are in danger, and their national
existence is at stake.

*   *   *   *   *   *

And can we, the descendants of such a people,
with such a history and such an example before us,
can we, dare we falter in a day like this ? Dare we
doubt ? Should we not rather say, as Bolingbroke
said to his people, in their hour of peril : ' Oh, woe
to thee when doubt comes ; it blows like a wind from

the north, and makes all thy joints to quake. Woe, indeed, be the statesmen who doubt the strength of their country, and stand in awe of the enemy with whom it is engaged.' At that same period, one of the greatest minds of England declared the three things necessary to her success : —

1. To listen to no terms of peace till freedom and order were established in Europe.

2. To fill up her army and perfect its organization.

3. To secure the favor of Heaven, by putting away forever the crime of slavery and the slave trade.

Can we learn a better lesson? Great Britain, in that same period, began the work which ended in breaking the fetters of all her bondsmen. She did maintain her armies and her finances, and she did triumph. We have begun to secure the approval of Heaven by doing justice, though long delayed, and securing to every human being in this republic freedom, henceforth and forever.

Mr. Speaker, it has long been my settled conviction that it was a part of the divine purpose to keep us under the pressure and grief of this war, until the conscience of the nation should be aroused to the enormity of its great crime against the black man, and full reparation should be made. We entered the struggle, a large majority insisting that slavery should be let alone, with a defiance almost blasphemous. Every movement toward the recognition of the negro's manhood was resisted. Slowly, and at a frightful cost of human lives, the nation has yielded its wicked and stubborn prejudices against him, till at last the blue coats cover more than one hundred thousand swarthy breasts, and the national banner is born in the smoke of battle by men lately loaded with chains, but now bearing the honors and emoluments of American soldiers. Dare we hope for final success till we give them the full protection of soldiers? Like the sins of mankind against God, the sin of slavery was so great that 'without the shedding of blood there was no remission.' Shall we not secure the favor of Heaven by putting it completely away? Shall we not fill up our armies? Shall we not also triumph? Was there, in the condition of England in 1812, a single element essential to success which we do not possess to-day?

*   *   *   *   *   *

If we will not learn a lesson, either from England or our revolutionary fathers, let us at least learn from our enemies. I have seen their gallantry in battle, their hoping against hope amid increasing disaster; and, traitors though they are, I am proud of their splendid courage, when I remember that they are Americans. Our army is equally brave, but our government and Congress are far behind them in earnestness and energy.

Until we go into the war with the same desperation and abandonment which mark their course, we do not deserve to succeed, and we shall not succeed. What have they done? What has their government done, — a government based, in the first place, on extreme State rights and State sovereignty, but which has become more centralized and despotic than the monarchies of Europe? They have not only called for volunteers, but they have drafted. They have not only drafted, but cut off both commutation and substitution. They have gone further. They have adopted conscription proper — the old French conscription of 1797 — and have declared that every man between sixteen and sixty years of age is a soldier. But we stand here bartering blood for money, debating whether we will fight the enemies of the nation, or pay $300 into its treasury. Mr. Speaker, with this brief review of the grounds of our hope, I now ask your attention to the main proposition in the bill before the House, — the repeal of the commutation clause. Going back to the primary question of the power to raise armies, I lay it down as a fundamental proposition, as an inherent and necessary element of sovereignty, that a nation has a right to the personal service of its citizens. The stability and power of every sovereignty rest upon that basis."

His fidelity to his friends and comrades led him to make another speech during his first session, which gives his opinion of his old chief, General Rosecrans, and also of General Thomas, and deserves a place in history. It was made upon a resolution of thanks to General Thomas, for his generalship in the battle of Chickamauga.

"This resolution proposes to thank Major-General George H. Thomas and the officers and men under his command for gallant services in the battle of Chickamauga. It meets my hearty approval for what it contains, but my protest for what it does not contain. I should be recreant to my own sense of justice did I allow this omission to pass without notice. No man here is ready to say, — and if there be such a man I am ready to meet him, — that the thanks of this Congress are not due to Major-General W. S. Rosecrans, for the campaign which culminated in the battle of Chickamauga. It is not uncommon throughout the press of the country, and many people, to speak of that battle as a disaster to the army of the United States, and to treat it as a defeat. If that battle was a defeat, we may welcome a hundred such defeats. I should be glad if each of our armies would repeat Chickamauga. Twenty such would destroy the rebel army and the confederacy, utterly and forever. What was that battle, terminating as it did a great campaign, whose object was to drive the rebel army beyond the Tennessee, and to obtain a foothold on the south bank of that river, which should form the basis of future operations in the Gulf States? We had never yet crossed that river, except far below, in the neighborhood of Corinth. Chattanooga was a gateway of the Cumberland mountains, and until we crossed the river and held the gateway, we could not commence operations in Georgia. The army was ordered to cross the river, to grasp and hold the key of the Cumberland mountains. It did cross, in the face of superior numbers; and after two days of fighting, more terrible, I believe, than any since this war began, the army of the Cumberland hurled back, discomfited and repulsed, the combined power of three rebel armies, gained the key to the Cumberland mountains, gained Chattanooga, and held it against every assault. If there has been a more substantial success against overwhelming odds, since this war began, I have not heard of it. We have had victories — God be thanked — all along the line, but in the history of this war I know of no such battle against such numbers; forty thousand against an army of not less by a man than seventy-five thousand. After the disaster to the right wing, in the last bloody afternoon of September 20th, twenty-five thousand men of the army of the Cumberland stood and met seventy-five thousand hurled against them. And they stood in their bloody tracks, immovable and victorious, when night threw its mantle around them. They had repelled the last assault of the rebel army. Who commanded the army of the Cumberland? Who organized, disciplined and led it? Who planned its campaigns? The general whose name is omitted in this resolution — Major-General W. S. Rosecrans.

And who is this General Rosecrans? The history of the country tells you, and your children know it by heart. It is he who fought battles and won victories in Western Virginia, under the shadow of another's name. When the poetic pretender claimed the honor and received the reward as the author of Virgil's stanza in praise of Cæsar, the great Mantuan wrote on the walls of the imperial palace:

'Hoc ego versiculos feci, tulit alter honores.'

So might the hero of Rich mountain say, 'I won this battle, but another has worn the laurels.'

' From Western Virginia he went to Mississippi, and there won the battles of Iuka and Corinth, which have aided materially to exalt the fame of that general, upon whom this House has been in such haste to confer the proud rank of lieutenant-general of the army of the United States, but who was not upon either of these battle-fields.

Who took command of the army of the Cumberland, found that army at Bowling Green, in November, 1862, as it lay disorganized, disheartened, driven back from Alabama and Tennessee, and led it across the Cumberland, planted it in Nashville, and thence, on the first day of the new year, planted his banners at Murfreesboro', in torrents of blood, and at the moment of our extremest peril, throwing himself into the breech, saved by his personal valor the army of the Cumberland and the hopes of the republic? It was General Rosecrans. From the day he assumed the command at Bowling Green, the history of that army may be written in one sentence, — it has advanced, and maintained its advanced position, and its last campaign, under the general it loved, was the bloodiest and most brilliant. The fruits of Chickamauga were gathered in November, on the hights of Mission Ridge and among the clouds of Lookout mountain. That battle at Chattanooga was a glorious one, and every loyal heart is proud of it. But, sir, it was won when we had nearly three times the number of the enemy. It ought to have been won. Thank

God that it was won. I would take no laurel from the brow of the man who won it ; but I would remind gentlemen here that while the battle of Chattanooga was fought with vastly superior numbers on our part, the battle of Chickamauga was fought with still vaster superiority against us.

If there is any man upon earth whom I honor, it is the man who is named in this resolution, General George H. Thomas. I had occasion, in my remarks on the conscription bill, a few days ago, to refer to him in such terms as I delighted to use ; and I say to gentlemen here that if there is any man whose heart would be hurt by the passage of this resolution as it now stands, that man is General George H. Thomas. I know, and all know, that he deserves well of his country, and his name ought to be recorded in letters of gold; but I know equally well that General Rosecrans deserves well of his country. I ask you, then, not to pain the heart of a noble man, who will be burdened with the weight of these thanks, that wrong his brother officer and his superior in command. All I ask is that you will put both names into the resolution, and let them stand side by side."

When the important question arose in Congress concerning a through line of railroad from Washington to New York, there was considerable opposition from the Camden and Amboy railroad, and from the officials of the New Jersey State government, and the question whether the State of New Jersey had the right to prohibit the construction of a national railroad, became somewhat interesting. Upon that question he said :

"Mr. Speaker, this lifts our subject above corporations and monopolies to the full hight of a national question ; I might almost call it a question of loyalty or disloyalty. I have only to say in regard to the language of this proclamation that if his Excellency had consulted Calhoun and his resolution of 1833, he would have its doctrines stated much more ably and elegantly. He calls upon the Legislature of New Jersey to inquire whether this bill will take away any of the revenue of the State, and how it will affect the sovereign rights of New Jersey. He says *New Jersey is a sovereign State.* I pause there for a moment. Mr. Coleridge somewhere says that abstract definitions have done more harm in the world than plague and famine and war. I believe it. I believe that no man will ever be able to chronicle all the evils that have resulted to this nation from the abuse of the words 'sovereign' and 'sovereignty.' What is this thing called State 'sovereignty?' Nothing more false was ever uttered in the halls of legislation than that any State of this union is sovereign. Consult the elementary text-books of law and refresh your recollection of the definition of 'sovereignty.' Speaking of the sovereignty of nations Blackstone says :

'However they began, by what right soever they subsist, there is and must be in all of them a supreme irresistible, absolute uncontrolled authority in which the *jura summi imperii* or *rights of sovereignty resisted.'*

Do these elements belong to *any* State of this republic? Sovereignty has the right to declare war. Can New Jersey declare war? It has the right to conclude peace. Can New Jersey conclude peace? Sovereignty has the right to coin money. If the Legislature of New Jersey should authorize and command one of its citizens to coin a half dollar, that man if he made it, though it should be of solid silver, would be locked up in a felon's cell for the crime of counterfeiting the coin of the real sovereign. A sovereign has the right to make treaties with foreign nations. Has New Jersey the right to make treaties? Sovereignty is clothed with the right to regulate commerce with foreign States. New Jersey has no such right. Sovereignty has the right to put ships in commission upon the high seas. Should a ship set sail under the authority of New Jersey it would be seized as a smuggler, forfeited and sold. Sovereignty has a flag. But, thank God, New Jersey has no flag ; Ohio has no flag. No loyal State fights under the 'lone star,' the 'rattlesnake,' or the 'palmetto tree.' No loyal State of this union has any flag but 'the banner of beauty and glory,' the flag of the union.

These are the indispensable elements of sovereignty. New Jersey has not one of them. The term cannot be applied to the separate States, only in a very limited and restricted sense, referring mainly to municipal and police re ulations. The ri hts of the

States should be jealously guarded and defended. But to claim that sovereignty, in its full sense and meaning, belongs to the States, is nothing better than rankest treason. Look again at this document of the governor of New Jersey. He tells you that the States entered into the 'national compact.' National compact! I had supposed that no governor of a loyal State would parade this dogma of nullification and secession, which was killed and buried by Webster on the 16th of February, 1833. There was no such thing as a sovereign State making a compact called a constitution. The very language of the constitution is decisive: 'We, the people of the United States, do ordain and establish this constitution.' The States did not make a compact to be broken when any one pleased, but the people *ordained* and *established* the constitution of a sovereign republic; and woe be to any corporation or State that raises its hand against the majesty and power of this great nation."

This proclamation closes with a determination to resist this legislation of Congress. This itself is another reason why I ask this Congress to exercise its right to rebuke this resurrected spirit of nullification. The gentleman from Pennsylviania (Mr. Broomall) tells us that New Jersey is a loyal State, and her citizens are in the army. I am proud of all the citizens of New Jersey who are fighting in our army. They are not fighting for New Jersey, but for the union ; and when it is once restored, I do not believe these men will fight for the Camden and Amboy

monopoly.   Their hearts have been enlarged, and
there are patriotic men in New Jersey in the army
and at home, who are groaning under this tyrannical
monopoly, and they come up here and ask to strike off
the shackles that bind them ; and I hold it to be
right and duty of this body to strike off their fetters,
let them go free.

CHAPTER XVI.

EULOGIES OF NOTED MEN.

TO ABRAHAM LINCOLN. — THE ANNIVERSARY OF MR. LINCOLN'S DEATH.
— THE CAUSE OF THE ASSASSINATION. — THE EFFECT OF HIS DEATH.
— A BEAUTIFUL TRIBUTE. — ORATION ON CARPENTER'S PAINTING.
— SIGNING THE EMANCIPATION PROCLAMATION. — ITS PLACE IN
HISTORY. — JOHN WINTHROP AND SAMUEL ADAMS. — THE GIFT OF
MASSACHUSETTS. — GENERAL GARFIELD'S TRIBUTE TO NEW ENG-
LAND. — THE LESSON OF SELF-RESTRAINT. — REMARKS UPON THE
DEATH OF SENATOR MORTON.

ON the first anniversary of the death of Abraham
Lincoln, and during General Garfield's third year of
service in the House of Representatives, Congress
adjourned for the day as a mark of respect for the
martyr President's memory. General Garfield was
selected to make the motion to adjourn, and in so
doing, was selected to make a short address. It was
one of the most cultured, thoughtful and appropriate
addresses to be found in the vast collection of patriotic speeches, which remain to this generation from
the days of war and reconstruction.

"I desire" said he, "to move that this House do
now adjourn. And before the vote upon that motion
is taken I desire to say a few words. This day, Mr.
Speaker, will be sadly memorable so long as this
nation shall endure, which God grant may be 'till

the last syllable of recorded time,' when the volume of human history shall be sealed up and delivered to the omnipotent Judge. In all future time, on the recurrence of this day, I doubt not that the citizens of this republic will meet in solemn assembly to reflect on the life and character of Abraham Lincoln, and the awful tragic event of April 14, 1865, —an event unparalleled in the history of nations, certainly unparalleled in our own. It is eminently proper that this House should this day place upon its records a memorial of that event. The last five years have been marked by wonderful developments of individual character. Thousands of our people, before unknown to fame, have taken their places in history, crowned with immortal honors. In thousands of humble homes are dwelling heroes and patriots whose names shall never die. But greatest among all these great developments were the character and fame of Abraham Lincoln whose loss the nation still deplores. His character is aptly described in the words of England's great laureate—written thirty years ago —in which he traces the upward steps of some

> ' Divinely gifted man,
> Whose life in low estate began,
> And on a simple village green ;

> ' Who breaks his birth's invidious bar,
> And grasps the skirts of happy chance,
> And breasts the blow of circumstance,
> And grapples with his evil star ;

> ' Who makes by force his merit known,
> And lives to clutch the golden keys,

> To mold a mighty State's decrees,
> And shape the whisper of the throne ;
>
> ' And moving up from high to higher,
> Becomes on Fortune's crowning slope,
> The pillar of a People's hope,
> The center of a world's desire.'

Such a life and character will be treasured forever as the sacred possession of the American people and of mankind. In the great drama of the rebellion there were two acts. The first was the war with its battles and sieges, victories and defeats, its sufferings and tears.

That act was closing one year ago to-night, and just as the curtain was lifting on the second and final act, — the restoration of peace and liberty, — just as the curtain was rising upon new characters and new events, the evil spirit of the rebellion, in the fury of despair, nerved and directed the hand of the assassin to strike down the chief character in both. It was no one man who killed Abraham Lincoln ; it was the embodied spirit of treason and slavery, inspired with fearful, despairing hate, that struck him down in the moment of the nation's supremest joy.

Ah, sir, there are times in the history of men and nations, when they stand so near the veil that separates mortals from the immortals, time from eternity, and men from their God, that they can almost hear the beatings, and feel the pulsations of the heart of the Infinite. Through such a time has this nation passed. When two hundred and fifty thousand brave spirits passed from the field of honor, through that thin veil, to the presence of God ; and when at last its parting folds admitted the martyr President to the company of the dead heroes of the republic, the nation stood so near the veil, that the whispers of God were heard by the children of men. Awe-stricken by his voice, the American people knelt in tearful reverence, and made a solemn covenant with Him, and with each other, that their nation should be saved from its enemies, that all its glories should be restored, and on the ruins of slavery and treason, the temple of freedom and justice should be built, and should survive forever. It remains for us, consecrated by that great event, and under a covenant with God, to keep that faith, to go forward in the great work until it shall be completed. Following the lead of that great man, and obeying the high behests of God, let us remember that, —

> ' He that sounded forth a trumpet that shall never call retreat;
> He is sifting out the hearts of men before his judgment seat ;
> Be swift my soul to answer him ; be jubilant my feet ;
> For God is marching on.' "

To the eulogy of 1866, he added another in 1878, which should be preserved for future generations to read.

On the 16th of January, 1878, he introduced into the House of Representatives the following joint resolution, which was adopted without a division. It was subsequently adopted by the Senate, and was approved by the President, February 1, 1878 :

Whereas, Mrs. Elizabeth Thompson of New York

city has tendered to Congress Carpenter's painting of President Lincoln and his Cabinet, at the time of his first reading of the Proclamation of Emancipation : Therefore,

Resolved by the Senate and House of Representatives of the United States of America in Congress assembled, That said painting is hereby accepted in the name of the people of the United States ; and the thanks of Congress are tendered to the donor for her generous and patriotic gift.

And be it further resolved, That the Joint Committee on the Library are hereby instructed to make arrangements for the formal presentation of said painting to Congress, on Tuesday, the twelfth of February next ; and said committee shall cause said painting to be placed in an appropriate and conspicuous place in the Capitol, and shall carefully provide for its preservation.

And be it further resolved, That the President is requested to cause a copy of these resolutions to be forwarded to Mrs. Thompson.

In pursuance of its provisions, the hour of two o'clock, P. M., Tuesday, February 12th, was fixed for the formal presentation and acceptance of the painting, and Mr. Garfield said : —

"Mr. President: By the order of the Senate and the House, and on behalf of the donor, Mrs. Elizabeth Thompson, it is made my pleasant duty to deliver to Congress the painting which is now unveiled. It is the patriotic gift of an American woman whose years have been devoted to gentle and generous charities, and to the instruction and elevation of the laboring poor.

Believing that the perpetuity and glory of her country depend upon the dignity of labor and the equal freedom of all its people, she has come to the Capitol, to place in the perpetual custody of the nation, as the symbol of her faith, the representation of that great act which proclaimed 'liberty throughout all the land unto all the inhabitants thereof.'

Inspired by the same sentiment, the representatives of the nation have opened the doors of this Chamber to receive at her hands the sacred trust. In coming hither, these living representatives have passed under the dome and through that beautiful and venerable hall which, on another occasion, I have ventured to call the third House of American representatives, that silent assembly whose members have received their high credentials at the impartial hand of history. Year by year, we see the circle of its immortal membership enlarging; year by year, we see the elect of their country, in eloquent silence, taking their places in this American pantheon, bringing within its sacred precincts the wealth of those immortal memories which made their lives illustrious; and year by year, that august assembly is teaching deeper and grander lessons to those who serve in these more ephemeral Houses of Congress.

Among the paintings, hitherto assigned to places within the Capitol, are two which mark events forever memorable in the history of mankind; thrice memorable in the history of America.

The first is the painting by Vanderlyn, which represents, though with inadequate force, the great discovery which gave to the civilized world a new hemisphere.

The second, by Trumbull, represents that great Declaration which banished forever from our shores the crown and scepter of imperial power, and proposed to found a new nation upon the broad and enduring basis of liberty.

To-day, we place upon our walls this votive tablet, which commemorates the third great act in the history of America — the fulfillment of the promises of the Declaration.

Concerning the causes which led to that act, the motives which inspired it, the necessities which compelled it, and the consequences which followed and are yet to follow it, there have been, there are, and still will be great and honest differences of opinion. Perhaps we are yet too near the great events of which this act formed so conspicuous a part, to understand its deep significance and to foresee its far-off consequences.

The lesson of history is rarely learned by the actors themselves, especially when they read it by the fierce and dusky light of war, or amid the deeper shadows of those sorrows which war brings to both. But the unanimous voice of this House in favor of accepting the gift, and the impressive scenes we here witness, bear eloquent testimony to the transcendent importance of the event portrayed on yonder canvas.

Let us pause to consider the actors in that scene.

In force of character, in thoroughness and breadth of culture, in experience of public affairs, and in national reputation, the Cabinet that sat around that council-board has had no superior, perhaps no equal, in our history. Seward, the finished . scholar, the consummate orator, the great leader of the Senate, had come to crown his career with those achievements which placed him in the first rank of modern diplomatists. Chase, with a culture and a frame of massive grandeur, stood as the rock and pillar of the public credit, the noble embodiment of the public faith. Stanton was there, a very Titan of strength, the great organizer of victory. Eminent lawyers, men of business, leaders of States and leaders of men completed the group.

But the man who presided over that council, who inspired and guided its deliberations, was a character so unique that he stood alone, without a model in history or a parallel among men. Born on this day, sixty-nine years ago, to an inheritance of extremest poverty; surrounded by the rude forces of the wilderness; wholly unaided by parents; only one year in any school; never, for a day, master of his own time, until he reached his majority; making his way to the profession of law by the hardest and roughest road; yet by force of unconquerable will and persistent, patient work, he attained a foremost place in his profession

> And, moving up from high to higher,
> Became, on fortune's crowning slope,
> The pillar of a people's hope,
> The center of a world's desire.

At first, it was the prevailing belief that he would be only the nominal head of his administration ; that its policy would be directed by the eminent statesmen he had called to his council. How erroneous this opinion was, may be seen from a single incident :

Among the earliest, most difficult, and most delicate duties of his administration, was the adjustment of our relations with Great Britain. Serious complications, even hostilities, were apprehended. On the 21st of May, 1861, the Secretary of State presented to the President his draught of a letter of instructions to Minister Adams, in which the position of the United States and the attitude of Great Britain were set forth with the clearness and force, which long experience and great ability had placed at the command of the secretary.

Upon almost every page of that original draught are erasures, additions and marginal notes, in the hand-writing of Abraham Lincoln, which exhibit a sagacity, a breadth of wisdom, and a comprehension of the whole subject, impossible to be found except in a man of the very first order. And these modifications of a great State paper were made by a man who, but three months before, had entered, for the first time, the wide theatre of executive action.

Gifted with an insight and a foresight which the ancients would have called divinition, he saw, in the midst of darkness and obscurity, the logic of events, and forecasted the result. From the first, in his own quaint, original way, without ostentation or offense to his associates, he was pilot and commander of his administration. He was one of the few great rulers whose wisdom increased with his power, and whose spirit grew gentler and tenderer as his triumphs were multiplied.

This was the man, and those his associates, who look down upon us from the canvas.

The present is not a fitting occasion to examine, with any completeness, the causes that led to the proclamation of emancipation ; but the peculiar relation of that act to the character of Abraham Lincoln cannot be understood, without considering one remarkable fact in his history.

His earlier years were passed in a region remote from the centers of political thought, and without access to the great world of books. But the few books that came within his reach, he devoured with the divine hunger of genius. One paper, above all others, led him captive, and filled his spirit with the majesty of its truth and the sublimity of its eloquence. It was the Declaration of American Independence — the liberty and equality of all men. Long before his fame had become national, he said :

That is the electric cord in the Declaration, that links the hearts of patriotic and liberty-loving men together, and that will link such hearts as long as the love of liberty exists in the minds of men throughout the world.

That truth runs, like a thread of gold, through the whole web of his political life. It was the spearpoint of his logic, in his debates with Douglas. It was the inspiring theme of his remarkable speech at the Cooper Institute, which gave him the nomination to the presidency. It filled him with reverent awe when, on his way to the capital, to enter the shadows of the terrible conflict then impending, he uttered, in Carpenter's Hall, at Philadelphia, these remarkable words, which were prophecy then, but are history now:

I have never had a feeling, politically, that did not spring from the sentiments embodied in the Declaration of Independence. I have often pondered over the dangers which were incurred by the men who assembled here and framed and adopted that Declaration. I have pondered over the toils that were endured by the officers and soldiers of the army who achieved that independence. I have often inquired of myself what great principle or idea it was that kept this confederacy so long together. It was not the mere matter of the separation of the colonies from the mother land, but that sentiment in the Declaration of Independence, which gave liberty, not alone to the people of this country, but, I hope, to the world, for all future time. It was that which gave promise that, in due time, the weight would be lifted from the shoulders of all men. This is the sentiment embodied in the Declaration of Independence. Now, my friends, can this country be saved on that basis? If it can, I shall consider myself one of the happiest men in the world if I can help to save it. If it cannot be saved upon that principle, it will be truly awful. But if this country cannot be saved without giving up that principle, I was about to say, *I would rather be assassinated on this spot than surrender it.*

Deep and strong was his devotion to liberty; yet deeper and stronger still was his devotion to the union, for he believed that without the union, permanent liberty for either race on this continent would be impossible. And because of this belief, he was reluctant, perhaps more reluctant than most of his associates, to strike slavery with the sword. For many months, the passionate appeals of millions of his associates seemed not to move him. He listened to all the phases of the discussion, and stated, in language clearer and stronger than any opponent had used, the dangers, the difficulties and the possible futility of the act.

In reference to its practical wisdom, Congress, the Cabinet and the country were divided. Several of his generals had proclaimed the freedom of slaves within the limits of their commands. The President revoked their proclamations. His first Secretary of War had inserted a paragraph in his annual report, advocating a similar policy. The President suppressed it.

On the 19th of August, 1862, Horace Greeley published a letter, addressed to the President, entitled 'The Prayer of Twenty Millions,' in which he said:

On the face of this wide earth, Mr. President, there is not one disinterested, determined, intelligent champion of the union cause who does not feel that all attempts to put down the rebellion, and at the same time uphold its inciting cause, are preposterous and futile.

To this the President responded in that ever-memorable dispatch of August 22, in which he said :

If there be those who would not save the union

unless they could at the same time save slavery, I do not agree with them.

If there be those who would not save the union unless they could at the same time destroy slavery, I do not agree with them.

My paramount object is to save the union, and not either to save or destroy slavery.

If I could save the union without freeing any slave, I would do it, if I could save it by freeing all the slaves, I would do it; and if I could do it by freeing some and leaving others alone, I would also do that.

What I do about slavery and the colored race, I do because I believe it helps to save the union; and what I forbear, I forbear because I do not believe it helps to save the union. I shall do less whenever I believe that what I am doing hurts the cause; and I shall do more whenever I believe doing more will help the cause.

Thus, against all importunities on the one hand, and remonstrances on the other, he took the mighty question to his own heart, and, during the long months of that terrible battle-summer, wrestled with it alone.

But at length, he realized the saving truth, that great, unsettled questions have no pity for the repose of nations.

On the 22d of September, he summoned his Cabinet to announce his conclusion. It was my good fortune, on that same day, and a few hours after the meeting, to hear, from the lips of one who participated, the story of the scene.

As the chiefs of the executive departments came in one by one, they found the President reading a favorite chapter from a popular humorist. He was lightening the weight of the great burden which rested upon his spirit. He finished the chapter, reading it aloud. And here I quote from the published journal of the late chief-justice, an entry, written immediately after the meeting, and bearing unmistakable evidence that it is almost a literal transcript of Lincoln's words :

The President then took a graver tone, and said : "Gentlemen, I have, as you are aware, thought a great deal about the relation of this war to slavery ; and you all remember that, several weeks ago, I read to you an order I had prepared upon the subject, which, on account of objections made by some of you, was not issued. Ever since then, my mind has been much occupied with this subject, and I have thought all along that the time for acting upon it might probably come. I think the time has come now. I wish it was a better time. I wish that we were in a better condition. The action of the army against the rebels has not been quite what I should have best liked, but they have been driven out of Maryland, and Pennsylvania is no longer in danger of invasion.

When the rebel army was at Frederick, I determined, as soon as it should be driven out of Maryland, to issue a proclamation of emancipation, such as I thought most likely to be useful. I said nothing to any one, but I made a promise to myself and (hesitating a little) to my Maker. The rebel army is now driven out, and I am going to fulfill that promise. I have got you together to hear what I have written down. I do not wish your advice about the main matter, for that I have determined for myself. This I say, without intending anything but respect for any one of you. But I already know the views of each upon this question. They have been heretofore expressed, and I have considered them as thoroughly and carefully as I can. What I have written is that which my reflections have determined me to say. If there is anything in the expressions I use, or in any minor matter which any one of you think had best be changed, I shall be glad to receive your suggestions. One other observation I will make. I know very well that many others might, in this matter as in others, do better than I can ; and if I was satisfied that the public confidence was more fully possessed by any one of them than by me, and knew of any constitutional way in which he could be put in my place, he should have it. I would gladly yield to him. But though I believe I have not so much of the confidence of the people as I had some time since, I do not know that, all things considered, any other person has more ; and, however this may be, there is no way in which I can have any other man put where I am. I am here ; I must do the best I can, and bear the responsibility of taking the course which I feel I ought to take."

The President then proceeded to read his Emancipation Proclamation, making remarks on the several parts as he went on, and showing that he had fully considered the subject in all the lights under which it had been presented to him.

The proclamation was amended in a few matters of detail. It was signed and published that day. The world knows the rest, and will not forget it till ' the last syllable of recorded time.'

In the painting before us, the artist has chosen the moment when the reading of the proclamation was finished, and the Secretary of State was offering his first suggestion. I profess no skill in the subtle mysteries of art criticism. I can only say of a painting, what the painting says to me. I know not what this may say to others; but to me, it tells the whole story of the scene, in the silent and pathetic language of art.

We value the Trumbull picture of the Declaration, — that promise and prophecy of which this act was the fulfillment, — because many of its portraits were taken from actual life. This picture is a faithful reproduction, not only of the scene, but its accessories. It was painted at the executive mansion, under the eye of Mr. Lincoln, who sat with the artist during many days of genial companionship, and aided him in arranging the many details of the picture.

The severely plain chamber, not now used for cabinet councils; the plain marble mantel, with the portrait of a hero president above it; the council-table, at which Jackson and his successor had presided; the old-fashioned chairs; the books and maps; the captured sword, with its pathetic history; — all are there, as they were, in fact, fifteen years ago. But what is of more consequence, the portraits are true to the life. Mr. Seward said of the painting, 'It is a vivid representation of the scene, with portraits of rare fidelity;' and so said all his associates.

Without this painting, the scene could not even now be reproduced. The room has been remodeled; its furniture is gone; and death has been sitting in that council, calling the roll of its members in quick succession. Yesterday, he added another name to his fatal list; and to-day, he has left upon the earth but a single witness of the signing of the proclamation of emancipation.

With reverence and patriotic love, the artist accomplished his work; with patriotic love and reverent faith, the donor presents it to the nation. In the spirit of both, let the re-united nation receive it and cherish it forever."

One of the most popular of General Garfield's eulogies, was upon John Winthrop and Samuel Adams, and was delivered December 19, 1876, the House then having under consideration the following resolution : —

IN THE SENATE OF THE UNITED STATES.

December 19, 1876.

Resolved by the Senate, (*the House of Representatives concurring,*) 1. That the statues of John Winthrop and Samuel Adams are accepted in the name of the United States, and that the thanks of Congress are given to the State of Massachusetts for these memorials of two of her eminent citizens, whose names are indissolubly associated with the foundation of the republic.

2. That a copy of these resolutions, engrossed upon parchment and duly authenticated, be transmitted to the governor of Massachusetts.

Attest: GEO. C. GORHAM,

By W. J. McDONALD, *Chief Clerk.*

He said : — " Mr. Speaker, I regret that illness has made it impossible for me to keep the promise, which I made a few days since, to offer some reflections appropriate to this very interesting occasion. But I cannot let the moment pass without expressing my great satisfaction with the fitting and instructive choice which the State of Massachusetts has made, and the manner in which her Representatives have discharged their duty in presenting these beautiful works of art to the Congress of the nation.

As, from time to time, our venerable and beautiful Hall has been peopled with statues of the elect of the States, it has seemed to me that a third House was being organized within the walls of the Capitol —a House whose members have received their high credentials at the hands of history, and whose term of office will outlast the ages. Year by year, we see the circle of its immortal membership enlarging; year by year, we see the elect of their country, in eloquent silence, taking their places in this American pantheon, bringing within its sacred circle the wealth of those immortal memories, which made their lives illustrious ; and, year by year, that august assembly is teaching a deeper and grander lesson to all who serve their brief hour in these more ephemeral Houses of Congress. And now, two places of great honor have just been most nobly filled.

I can well understand that the State of Massachusetts, embarrassed by her wealth of historic glory, found it difficult to make the selection. And while the distinguished gentleman from Massachusetts (Mr. Hoar) was so fittingly honoring his State, by portraying that happy embarrassment, I was reflecting that the sister State of Virginia will encounter, if possible, a still greater difficulty when she comes to make the selection of her immortals. One name I venture to hope she will not select,—a name too great for the glory of any one State. I trust she will allow us to claim Washington as belonging to all the States, for all time. If she shall pass over the great distance that separates Washington from all others, I can hardly imagine how she will make the choice from her crowded roll. But I have no doubt that she will be able to select two who will represent the great phases of her history, as happily and worthily as Massachusetts is represented, in the choice she has to-day announced. It is difficult to imagine a happier combination of great and beneficent forces, than will be presented by the representative heroes of these two great States.

Virginia and Massachusetts were the two focal centers from which sprang the life-forces of this republic. There were, in many ways, complements of each other, each supplying what the other lacked, and both uniting to endow the republic with its noblest and most enduring qualities.

To-day, the House has listened with the deepest interest to the statement of those elements of priceless value contributed by the State of Massachusetts. We have been instructed by the clear and masterly analysis of the spirit and character of that Puritan civilization, so fully embodied in the lives of Winthrop and Adams. I will venture to add, that, notwithstanding all the neglect and contempt with which England regarded her Puritans, two hundred years ago, the tendency of thought in modern England is to do justice to that great force which created the the Commonwealth, and finally made the British Islands a land of liberty and law. Even the great historian Hume was compelled reluctantly to declare that—

The precious spark of liberty had been kindled and was preserved by the Puritans alone ; and it was to this sect that the English owe the whole freedom of their constitution.

What higher praise can posterity bestow upon any people than to make such a confession? Having done so much to save liberty alive in the mother country, the Puritans planted, upon the shores of this New World, that remarkable civilization whose growth is the greatness and glory of our republic.

Indeed, before Winthrop and his company landed at Salem, the Pilgrims were laying the foundation of civil liberty. While the Mayflower was passing Cape Cod, and seeking an anchorage, in the midst of the storm, her brave passengers sat down in the little cabin, and drafted and signed a covenant which contains the germ of American liberty. How familiar to the American habit of mind are these declarations of the Pilgrim covenant of 1620,—

That no act, imposition, law, or ordinance be made or imposed upon us at present, or to come, but such as has been or shall be enacted by the consent of the body of free men or associates, or their representatives, legally assembled.

The New England town was the model, the primary cell, from which our republic was evolved. The town meeting was the germ of all the parliamentary life and habits of Americans.

John Winthrop brought with him the more formal organization of New England society; and, in his long and useful life, did more than perhaps any other to direct and strengthen its growth.

Nothing, therefore, could be more fitting, than for Massachusetts to place in our Memorial Hall the statue of the first of the Puritans, representing him at the moment when he was stepping on shore from the ship that brought him from England, and bearing with him the charter of that first political society which laid the foundations of our country; and that near him should stand that Puritan embodiment of the logic of the revolution, Samuel Adams. I am glad to see this decisive, though tardy, acknowledgment of his great and signal services to America. I doubt if any man equaled Samuel Adams in formulating and uttering the fierce, clear and inexorable logic of the revolution. With our present habits of thought, we can hardly realize how great were the obstacles to overcome. Not the least was the religious belief of the fathers — that allegiance to rulers was obedience to God. The thirteenth chapter of Romans was to many minds a barrier against revolution stronger than the battalions of George III., —

Let every soul be subject unto the higher powers. For there is no power but of God; the powers that be are ordained of God. Whosoever therefore resisteth the power, resisteth the ordinance of God.

And it was not until the people of that religious

age were led to see that they might obey God and still establish liberty, in spite of kingly despotism, that they were willing to engage in war against one who called himself 'king by the grace of God.' The men who pointed out the pathway to freedom by the light of religion as well as of law, were the foremost promoters of American independence. And of these, Adams was unquestionably chief.

It must not be forgotten that, while Samuel Adams was writing the great argument of liberty in Boston, almost at the same time, Patrick Henry was formulating the same doctrines in Virginia. It is one of the grandest facts of that grand time that the colonies were thus brought, by an almost universal consent, to tread the same pathway, and reach the same great conclusions.

But most remarkable of all is the fact that, throughout all that period, filled as it is was with the revolutionary spirit, the great men who guided the storm, exhibited the most wonderful power of self-restraint. If I were to-day to state the single quality that appears to me most admirable among the fathers of the revolution, I should say it was this : that amidst all the passions of war, waged against a perfidious enemy from beyond the sea, aided by a savage enemy on our own shores, our fathers exhibited so wonderful a restraint, so great a care to observe the forms of law, to protect the rights of the minority, to preserve all those great rights that had come down to them from the common law, so that when they had achieved their independence, they were still a law-abiding people.

In that fiery meeting in the old South church, after the Boston massacre, when, as the gentleman from Massachusetts has said, three thousand voices almost lifted the roof from the church, in demanding the removal of the regiments, it is noted by the historian that there was one, solitary, sturdy 'nay' in the vast assemblage; and Samuel Adams scrupulously recorded the fact that there was one dissentient. It would have been a mortal offense against his notions of justice and good order, if that one dissentient had not had his place in the record. And, after the regiments had been removed, and after the demand had been acceded to that the soldiers who had fired upon citizens should be delivered over to the civil authorities, to be dealt with according to law, Adams was the first to insist and demand that the best legal talent in the colony should be put forward to defend those murderers; and John Adams and Josiah Quincy were detailed for the purpose of defending them. Men were detailed whose hearts and souls were on fire with the love of the popular cause; but the men of Massachusetts would have despised the two advocates, if they had not given their whole strength to the defense of the soldiers.

Mr. Speaker, this great lesson of self-restraint is taught in the whole history of the revolution; and it is this lesson that to-day, more perhaps, than any other we have seen, we ought to take most to heart. Let us seek liberty and peace, under the law; and, following the pathway of our fathers, preserve the great legacy they have committed to our keeping."

Among other addresses made in Congress, upon the death of Senator Morton of Indiana, General Garfield delivered the following :

"For all the great professions known among Americans, special training-schools have been established and encouraged by law, except that of statesmanship. And yet no profession requires for its successful pursuit a wider range of general and special knowledge, or a more thorough and varied culture.

Probably no American youth, unless we except John Quincy Adams, was ever trained with special reference to the political service of his country. In monarchial governments, not only wealth and rank, but political authority descends, by inheritance, from father to son. The eldest son of an English peer knows from his earliest childhood that a seat awaits him in the House of Lords. If he be capable and ambitious, the dreams of his boyhood and the studies of his youth are directed toward the great field of statesmanship. To the favored few, this system affords many and great advantages, and upon the untitled many, whom 'birth's invidious bar' shuts out from the highest places of power, it must rest with discouraging weight.

Our institutions confer special privileges upon no citizen, and, we may now say, they erect no barrier in the honorable career of the humblest American. They open an equal pathway for all, and invite the worthiest to the highest seats. The fountains of our strength, as a nation, spring from the private life and the voluntary efforts of forty-five millions of people. Each for himself confronts the problem of life, and amid its varied conditions develops the forces with which God has endowed him. Meantime, the nation moves on in its great orbit, with a life and destiny of its own, each year calling to its aid those qualities and forces which are needed for its preservation and its glory. Now, it needs the prudence of the counselor, now, the wisdom of the law-giver, and now, the shield of the warrior to cover its heart in the day of battle. And when the hour and the man have met, and the needed work has been done, the nation crowns her heroes, and makes them her own forever. Such hours we have often seen during the last seventeen years, — hours which have called forth the great elements of manhood and strength from the ranks of our people, and crowded our pantheon with new accessions of glory. Seventeen years ago, at a moment of supreme peril, the nation called upon the people of twenty-two States to meet around her altar and defend her life. Of all the noble men who responded to that call, no voice rang out with more clearness than that of Oliver P. Morton, the young governor of Indiana. He was then but thirty-seven years of age. Self-made, as all men are who are worth the making, he had risen from a hard life of narrow conditions by fighting his own way, thinking his own thoughts, and uttering them without fear, until, by the fortune of political life, he had become the chief executive of his State. He saw at once, and declared the terrible significance of the impending struggle, and threw his whole weight into the conflict. His State and my own marched abreast in generous emulation.

But he was surrounded by difficulties and dangers which hardly found a parallel in any other State. With unconquerable will, and the energy of a Titan, he encountered and overcame them all; and keeping Indiana in line with the foremost, he justly earned the title of one of the greatest war governors of that heroic period. Thus, the great need of the nation called forth and fixed in the enduring colors of fame those high qualities which those thirty-seven years of private life had been preparing. To learn the lesson of his great life, let us recall briefly its leading characteristics.

He was a great organizer. He knew how to evoke and direct the enthusiasm of his people. He knew how to combine and marshall his forces, political or military, so as to concentrate them all upon a single object, and inspire them with his own ardor. I have often compared him with Stanton, our great War Secretary, whose windows at the war office, for many years, far into the night, shone out 'like battle-lanterns lit,' while he mustered great armies and launched them into the tempest of war, and 'organized victory.' In the whole circle of the States, no organizer stood nearer to him in character and qualities and friendship, than Oliver P. Morton.

His force of will was most masterful. It was not mere stubbornness, or pride of opinion, which weak and narrow men mistake for firmness. But it was

16

that stout-hearted persistency which, having once in-
telligently chosen an object, pursues it through sunshine and storm, undaunted by difficulties, and unter-
rified by danger.

He possessed an intellect of remarkable clearness
and force. With keen analysis, he found the core of
a question, and worked from the center outward.
He cared little for the mere graces of speech; but
few men have been so greatly endowed with the
power of clear statement and unassailable argument.
The path of his thought was straight —

> Like that of the swift cannon ball,
> Shattering that it may reach, and
> Shattering what it reaches.

When he had hit the mark, he used no additional
words, and sought for no decoration. These qualities, joined to his power of thinking quickly, placed
him in the front rank of debaters, and every year increased his power. It has been said that Senator
Morton was a partisan, a strong partisan, and this is
true. In the estimation of some, this detracts from
his fame. That evils arise from extreme partisanship,
there can be no doubt. But it should not be forgotten that all free governments are party governments.
Our great Americans have been great partisans.
Senator Morton was not more partisan than Adams,
Jefferson, Jackson, Clay, Calhoun, Benton, Marshall,
Taney and Chase. Strong men must have strong
convictions, and 'one man with a belief is a greater
power than a thousand that have only interests.'

Partisanship is opinion crystallizéd, and party organizations are the scaffoldings whereon citizens stand while they build up the walls of their national temple. Organizations may change or dissolve, but when parties cease to exist, liberty will perish. In conclusion, let me say, the memory of Governor Morton will be forever cherished and honored by the soldiers of my State. They fought side by side with the soldiers of Indiana, and in a hundred glorious fields his name was the battle-cry of the noble regiments which he had organized and inspired with his own lofty spirit.

To the nation he has left the legacy of his patriotism, and the example of a great eventful life."

CHAPTER XVII.

PERIOD OF UNPOPULARITY.

HIS PRACTICE OF LAW. — HIS FIRST CASE IN THE SUPREME COURT. — HIS SUCCESS AS A LAWYER. — UNPOPULARITY OF HIS DEFENSE OF REBELS IN COURT. — HIS CONNECTION WITH A MATTER CALLED THE DE GOLYER PAVEMENT CASE. — HOW HE WAS MALIGNED. — PERSISTENCY OF ENEMIES. — THE GREAT CREDIT MOBILIER CASE. — VINDICATION OF GENERAL GARFIELD. — HIS STORY OF HIS DEALINGS WITH OAKES AMES. — HIS OPPOSITION TO THE INCREASE OF SALARIES IN CONGRESS. — THE CENSURE OF HIS CONSTITUENTS. — HIS EXPLANATION. — RESTORATION TO PUBLIC FAVOR.

No great or good man ever served a capricious public without disheartening trials, and periods of unpopularity. Such experiences are often the test of a man's ability and integrity. In the history of General Garfield's Congressional career, however, his loss of public favor was due, in each instance, to a misunderstanding of the facts, on the part of the people. When his actions and positions on public measure were fully understood by the people, he was at once restored to favor and applause.

One cause of the first noticeable ebb in the public regard, which the student of his life observes, was the natural result of his practice of law.

He was a Congressman before he ever tried a case in court ; and his experience as an attorney is perhaps an exception to that of any other lawyer, inasmuch as his first case was in the Supreme Court of the United States. He never had a case in any other court.

His first appearance in the Supreme Court was in behalf of some conspirators who had been tried by court-martial, and condemned t death, for engaging in a movement to assist the rebellion. They were tried by martial law in a State, in time of peace *de facto* in the State, and in a section of State not under martial law. The legal question was, whether any military body had such power under the circumstances. Should the civil power be ignored in time of peace, or in sections of the country where martial law had not been proclaimed? It was a case for which he received no pay, and was undertaken as a test of this important principle.

He was sustained by the Court and complimented by the presiding justice for his able presentation of the case and the law, while the criminals were set at liberty. No sooner had the news of his interference in behalf of condemned rebels reached his district in Ohio, than the indignant voters loudly proclaimed his "treachery to his party and to the nation." In the following election, the great majority, with which he had always been elected, fell off more than a thousand votes, because of his supposed espousal of the cause of rebellious criminals.

Other cases followed with occasionally a like result, from which he easily recovered, but which, for the time, annoyed him and disturbed his district.

His practice in the Supreme Court increased very rapidly, and there was a time when he could have left his seat in Congress and entered upon a practice which would soon have made him rich. As it was, the income he thus derived was of great use to him, for his great generosity and thoughtlessness of self kept him almost incessantly in financial straits. He wasted no money on himself or his family; but he had rather pay a bill himself, than to ask another person, who owed it, for the money; and he gave to almost every good enterprise that came to his notice. He was often called upon to act as attorney for corporations and contractors, whose applications for money or privileges were to come before Congress; and though it was considered honorable by many Congressmen to act in such cases, provided the attorney refused to vote when the measure came before Congress, yet invariably, did General Garfield refuse such applications, and rejected the large fees which many statesmen thought it perfectly honorable for him to receive.

In 1873, General Garfield was called upon, by an attorney in Washington, to appear for him in a matter which the attorney (Mr. Parsons) said would not require much attention. The attorney being retained in the case, and being obliged to be absent when the matter was to come up, naturally sought some other attorney to temporarily take his place.

The matter to be attended to, in this instance, was a hearing before the Board of public works in Washington, concerning the durability of a wooden pavement, on which Messrs. De Golyer and McLellan held a patent.

General Garfield knew nothing about the pavement, and but little about the men; and knowing that he was to appear, as a matter of form, for another, he attended one hearing, where the questions of durability and material were the only ones discussed. Having performed this act of courtesy he dismissed the matter wholly from his mind. Some months afterwards, to his great surprise, the contract which was made between the patentees and the city, after the hearing upon the durability of the pavement, and with which he had nothing to do, came up in Congress, with the charge and appearance that the contract — not the pavement — was a great swindle. Immediately, the fact that he had, at one time, in some way, and somewhere, appeared as attorney for the patentees was noticed in the public press, and became the cause of a great uproar, and of much disgraceful abuse.

The charges that he was connected with the fraud were, for several years, proclaimed by some of the newspapers of the Democratic party, notwithstanding his complete vindication by the committee of investigation.

So much was said about it, that the Hon. J. M. 'Wilson, chairman of the Congressional committee of investigation, felt called upon to publish the following letter:

There was not in my opinion, any evidence that

would have warranted any unfavorable criticism upon his conduct.

The facts disclosed by the evidence, so far as he was concerned, are briefly these :

The Board of public works was considering the question, as to the kind of pavements that should be laid. There was a contest as to the respective merits of various wooden pavements. Mr. Parsons represented, as attorney, the De Golyer & McLellan patent, and being called away from Washington about the time the hearing was to be had before the Board of public works, on this subject, procured General Garfield to appear before the Board in his stead, and argue the merits of this patent. This he did ; and this was the whole of his connection in the matter. It was not a question as to the kind of contract that should be made, but as to whether this particular kind of pavement should be laid. The criticism of the committee was not upon the *pavement*, in favor of which General Garfield argued, but was upon the *contract* made with reference to it ; and there was no evidence which would warrant the conclusion that he had anything to do with the latter.

Very respectfully,

J. M. WILSON.

But the matter which made the greatest public scandal was the mention of his name, at one time, in connection with the great Credit Mobilier fraud in the construction of the Union Pacific railroad.

So completely was the scandal silenced, and so straightforward and open was General Garfield's course, that the re-action soon came in his favor, and that which, for a time, threatened to ruin him, fell harmless at his feet. His life of truthfulness and his unstained reputation for integrity and honor were of great value to him, when all his political opponents, with great glee, paraded his connection with the Credit Mobilier, derisively shouting, "Christian Statesman!" "moral patriot!" &c.   So clearly did he show the innocence of his dealings with Mr. Oakes Ames, and so clearly show that he could have had no connection with the schemes, that the record of the matter has now no historical value, except as showing how curiously public men may be beset, and how strangely misunderstood.   General Garfield has given an account of the whole case, and it shows a most interesting chapter of our national history.   This he made voluntarily, and to it always adhere.

General Garfield's history of the case is as follows:

"In the autumn of 1872, during the excitement of the Presidential campaign, charges of the most serious character were made against ten or twelve persons who were then, or had recently been, Senators and Representatives in Congress, to the effect that, five years ago, they had sold themselves for sundry amounts of stock of the Credit Mobilier company, and bonds of the Pacific railroad company.   The price at which different members were alleged to have bartered away their personal honor and their official influence was definitely set down in the newspapers; their guilt was assumed, and the public vengeance was invoked not only upon them, but also upon the party to which most of them belonged.

By a resolution of the House, introduced by one of the members, and adopted on the first day of the session, an investigation of these charges was ordered. The parties themselves and many other witnesses were examined; the records of the Credit Mobilier company and of the Pacific railroad company were produced; and the results of the investigation were reported to the House on the 18th of February. The report, with the accompanying testimony, was brought up in the House for consideration on the 25th of February, and the discussion was continued until the subject was finally disposed of, three days before the close of the session. The investigation was scarcely begun, before it was manifest that the original charge, that stock was given to members as a consideration for their votes, was wholly abandoned, there being no proof whatever to support it.

But the charge assumed a new form, namely: That the stock had been sold to members at a price known to be greatly below its actual value, for the purpose of securing their legislative influence in favor of those who were managing and manipulating the Pacific railroad for their own private advantage and to the injury both of the trust and of the United States. Eight of those against whom charges had been made in the public press, myself among the number, were still members of the House of Representatives, and were specially mentioned in the report. The committee recommended the adoption of resolutions for the expulsion of Messrs. Ames and Brooks, the latter on charges in no way connected with Mr. Ames or the other members mentioned. They recommended the expulsion of Mr. Ames for an attempt to influence the votes and decisions of members of Congress, by interesting them in the stock of the Credit Mobilier, and through it, in the stock of the Union Pacific railroad. They found that though Mr. Ames in no case disclosed his purpose to these members, yet he hoped so to enlist their interest that they would be inclined to favor any legislation in aid of the Pacific railroad and its interest, and that he declared to the managers of the Credit Mobilier company at the time, that he was thus using the stock which had been placed in his hands by the company.

Concerning the members to whom he had sold, or offered to sell, the stock, the committee say that they 'do not find that Mr. Ames, in his negotiations with the persons above named, entered into any detail of the relations between the Credit Mobilier company and the Union Pacific company, or gave them any specific information, as to the amount of dividends they would be likely to receive, further than has been already stated, [viz., that in some cases he had guaranteed a profit of ten per cent.] * * * They do not find, as to the members of the present House above named, that they were aware of the object of Mr. Ames, or that they had any other purpose in taking this stock than to make a profitable investment. * * * They have not been able to find that any of these members of Congress have been affected in their official action in consequence of interest in the Credit Mobilier stock. * * * They do not find that either of the above named gentlemen in contracting with Mr. Ames had any corrupt motive himself, or was aware Mr. Ames had any. Nor did either of them suppose he was guilty of any impropriety, or even indelicacy, in becoming a purchaser of this stock.' And finally, that ' the committee find nothing in the conduct or motives of either of these members in taking this stock, that calls for any recommendation by the committee of the House.'

In the case of each of the six members just referred to, the committee sum up the results of the testimony, and from that summary the conclusions above quoted are drawn. In regard to me, the committee find, that in December, 1867, or January, 1868, I agreed to purchase ten shares of Credit Mobilier stock of Mr. Ames, for $1,000, and the accrued interest from the previous July; that in June, 1868, Mr. Ames paid me a check on the Sergeant-at-Arms of the House for $329, as a balance of dividends on the stock, above the purchase price and accrued interest ; and that thereafter, there were no payments or other transactions between us, or any communication on the subject until the investigation began in December last.

I took the first opportunity offered by the completion of public business to call the attention of the House to the above summary of the testimony in reference to me. On the 3d of March I made the following remarks, in the House of Representatives, as recorded in the *Congressional Globe* for that day:

I rise to a personal explanation. During the late investigation by the committee, of which the gentleman from Vermont was chairman, I pursued what seemed to be the plain path of duty, to keep silence except when I was called upon to testify before the committee. When testimony was given which appeared to be in conflict with mine, I waited, expecting to be called again, if anything was needed from me in reference to these discrepancies. I was not recalled; and when the committee submitted their report to the House, a considerable portion of the testimony relating to me had not been printed.

In the discussion which followed here, I was prepared to submit some additional facts and considerations, in case my own conduct came up for consideration in the House; but the whole subject was concluded without any direct reference to myself, and since then the whole time of the House has been occupied with the public business. I now desire to make a single remark on this subject in the hearing of the House. Though the committee acquitted me of all charges of corruption in action or intent, yet there is in the report a summing up of the facts in relation to me which I respectfully protest is not warranted by the testimony. I say this with the utmost respect for the committee, and without intending any reflection upon them.

I cannot now enter upon the discussion; but I propose, before long, to make a statement to the public, setting forth more fully the grounds of my dissent from the summing up to which I have referred. I will only say now that the testimony which I gave before the committee is a statement of the facts in the case as I have understood them from the beginning. More than three years ago, on at least two occasions, I stated the case to two personal friends, substantially as I stated it before the committee; and I here add that nothing in my conduct or conversation has at any time been in conflict with my testimony. For the present I desire only to place on record this declaration and notice.

In pursuance of this notice, I shall consider so much of the history of the Credit Mobilier company as has any relation to myself. To render the discussion intelligible, I will first state briefly the offenses which that corporation committed, as found by the committees of the House.

The Credit Mobilier company is a corporation organized under the laws of the State of Pennsylvania, and authorized by its charter to purchase and sell various kinds of securities, and to make advances of money and credit to railroad, and other improvement companies. Its charter describes a class of business, which, if honestly conducted, any citizen may properly engage in.

On the 16th of August, 1867, Mr. Oakes Ames made a contract with the Union Pacific railroad company to build six hundred and sixty-seven miles of road, from the one hundredth meridian westward, at rates ranging from $42,000 to $96,000 per mile. For executing this contract he was to receive in the aggregate $47,925,000, in cash, or in the securities of the company.

On the 15th of October, 1867, a triple contract was made between Mr. Ames of the first part, seven persons as trustees of the second part, and the Credit Mobilier company of the third part, by the terms of which the Credit Mobilier company was to advance money to build the road, and to receive thereon seven per cent. interest, and two and one-half per cent. commission ; the seven trustees were to execute the Ames contract, and the profits thereon were to be divided among them, and such other stockholders of the Credit Mobilier company as should deliver to them an irrevocable proxy to vote the stock of the Union Pacific held by them. The principal stockholders of the Credit Mobilier company were also holders of a majority of the stock of the Union Pacific railroad.

On the face of this agreement, the part to be performed by the Credit Mobilier company as a corporation was simple and unobjectionable. It was to advance money to the contractors, and to receive therefore about ten per cent. as interest and commission. This explains how it was that, in a suit in the courts of Pennsylvania, in 1870, to collect the State tax on the profits of the company, its managers swore that the company had never declared dividends to an aggregate of more than twelve per cent. The company proper did not receive the profits of the Oakes Ames contract. The profits were paid only to the seven trustees, and to such stockholders of the Credit Mobilier as had delivered to them the proxies on their Pacific railroad stock. In other words, a ring inside the Credit Mobilier obtained the control, both of that corporation and of the profits of the Ames contract.

By a private agreement, made in writing, October 16, 1867, the day after the triple contract was signed, the seven trustees pledged themselves to each other so to vote all the Pacific railroad stock which they held in their own right, or by proxy, as to keep in power all the members of the then existing board of directors of the railroad company not appointed by the President of the United States, or such other persons as said board should nominate. By this agreement, the election of a majority of the directors was wholly within the power of the seven trustees. From all this it resulted that the Ames contract and the triple agreement, made in October, amounted, in fact, to a contract made by seven leading stock-holders of the Pacific railroad company with them-selves; so that the men who fixed the price at which the road was to be built were the same men who would receive the profits of the contract.

The wrong in this transaction consisted, first, in the fact that the stockholding directors of the Pacific railroad, being the guardians of a great public trust, contracted with themselves; and, second, that they paid themselves an exorbitant price for the work to be done; a price which virtually brought into their own possession, as private individuals, almost all the property of the railroad company. The six hundred and sixty-seven miles covered by the contract in-cluded one hundred and thirty-eight miles already completed, the profits on which inured to the benefit of the contractors.

The Credit Mobilier company had already been engaged in various enterprises before the connection with the Ames contract. George Francis Train had once been the principal owner of its franchises, and it had owned some western lands; (Wilson's Report, pp. 497-8;) but its enterprises had not been very remunerative, and its stock had not been worth par. The triple contract of October, 1867, gave it at once considerable additional value. It should be borne in mind, however, that the relations of the Credit Mobilier company to the seven trustees, to the Oakes Ames' contract, and to the Pacific railroad company, were known to but few persons until long afterward, and that it was for the interest of the parties to keep them secret. Indeed, nothing was known of it to the general public until the facts were ·brought out in the recent investigations.

In view of the facts above stated, it is evident that a purchaser of such shares of Credit Mobilier stock, as were brought under the operation of the triple contract, would be a sharer in the profits derived by that arrangement from the assets of the Pacific railroad, a large part of which consisted of bonds and lands granted to the road by the United States. The holding of such stock by a member of Congress would depend for its moral qualities wholly upon the fact whether he did or did not know of the arrangement, out of which the profits would come. If he knew of the fraudulent arrangement by which the bonds and lands of the United States, delivered to the Union Pacific railroad company for the purpose of constructing its road, were to be paid out at enormously extravagant rates, and the proceeds to be paid out as dividends to a ring of stockholders made by the Credit Mobilier company, he could not, with any propriety, hold such stock, or agree to hold it, or any of its pro-ceeds. And for a member of Congress, knowing the facts, to hold under advisement a proposition to buy this stock, would be morally as wrong as to hold it, and receive the profits upon it. If it was morally wrong to purchase it, it was morally wrong to hesitate whether to purchase it or not.

I put the case on the highest ethical ground, and ask that this rule be applied in all its severity in judging of my relation to this subject.

The committee found, as already stated, that none of the six members to whom Mr. Ames sold, or proposed to sell, the stock, knew of this arrangement. I shall, however, discuss the subject only in so far as relates to me, and shall undertake to establish three propositions:

First. That I never purchased, nor agreed to purchase, the stock, nor received any of its dividends.

Second. That though an offer was made, which I had some time under advisement, to sell me $1,000 worth of the stock, I did not then know, nor had I the means of knowing, the real conditions with which the stock was connected, or the method by which its profits were to be made.

Third. That my testimony before the committee is a statement of the facts as I have always understood them; and that neither before the committee, nor elsewhere, has there been, on my part, any prevarication or evasion on the subject.

My testimony was delivered before the investigating committee on the 14th of January. That portion which precedes the cross-examination, I had written out soon after the committee was appointed. I quote it, with the cross-examination, in full, as found recorded:

WASHINGTON, D. C., January 14, 1873.

J. A. Garfield, a member of the United States House of Representatives from the State of Ohio, having been duly sworn, made the following statement:

The first I ever heard of the Credit Mobilier was some time in 1866 or 1867—I cannot fix the date—when George Francis Train called on me and said he was organizing a company to be known as the Credit Mobilier of America, to be formed on the model of the Credit Mobilier of France; that the object of the company was to purchase lands and build houses along the line of the Pacific railroad at points where cities and villages were likely to spring up; that he had no doubt that money thus invested would double or treble itself each year; that subscriptions were limited to $1,000 each, and he wished me to subscribe. He showed me a long list of subscribers, among them Mr. Oakes Ames, to whom he referred me for further information concerning the enterprise. I answered that I had not the money to spare, and if I had, I would not subscribe, without knowing more about the proposed organization. Mr. Train left me, saying he would hold a place open for me, and hoped I would yet conclude to subscribe. The same day I asked Mr. Ames what he thought of the enterprise. He expressed the opinion that the investment would be safe and profitable.

I heard nothing further on the subject for a year or more, and it was almost forgotten, when some time, I should say during the long session of 1868, Mr. Ames spoke of it again; said the company had organized, was doing well, and he thought would soon pay large dividends. He said that some of the stock had been left, or was to be left, in his hands to sell, and I could take the amount which Mr. Train had offered me, by paying the $1,000 and the accrued interest. He said if I was not able to pay for it then, he would hold it for me till I could pay, or until some of the dividends were payable. I told him I would consider the matter ; but would not agree to take any stock until I knew, from an examination of the charter, and the conditions of the subscription, the extent to which I should become pecuniarily liable. He said he was not sure, but thought a stockholder would be liable only for the par value of his stock ; that he had not the stock and papers with him, but would have them after a while.

From the case, as presented, I should probably have taken the stock, if I had been satisfied in regard to the extent of pecuniary liability. Thus the matter rested for some time, I think until the following year. During that interval, I understood that there were dividends due, amounting to nearly three times the par value of the stock. But in the meantime, I had heard that the company was involved in some controversy with the Pacific railroad, and that Mr. Ames' right to sell the stock was denied. When I next saw Mr. Ames, I told him I had concluded not to take the stock. There the matter ended, so far as I was concerned, and I had no further knowledge of the company's operations until the subject began to be discussed in the newspapers last fall.

Nothing was ever said to me by Mr. Train or Mr. Ames to indicate or imply that the Credit Mobilier was, or could be, in any way connected with the legislation of Congress for the Pacific railroad, or for any other purpose. Mr. Ames never gave, nor offered to give, me any stock or other valuable thing as a gift. I once asked and obtained from him, and afterward repaid to him, a loan of $300; that amount is the only valuable thing I ever received from or delivered to him.

I never owned, received, or agreed to receive any stock of the Credit Mobilier, or of the Union Pacific railroad, or any dividends or profits arising from either of them.

(By the Chairman.)

Question. Had this loan you speak of any connection in any way with your conversation in regard to the Credit Mobilier stock?—*Answer.* No connection in any way except in regard to the time of payment. Mr. Ames stated to me that if I concluded to subscribe for the Credit Mobilier stock I could allow the loan to remain until the payment on that was adjusted. I never regarded it as connected in any other way with the stock enterprise.

Q. Do you remember the time of that transaction? —*A.* I do not remember it precisely. I should think it was in the session of 1868. I had been to Europe the fall before, and was in debt, and borrowed several sums of money at different times and from different persons. This loan from Mr. Ames was not at his instance. I made the request myself. I think I had asked one or two persons before him for the loan.

Q. Have you any knowledge in reference to any dealings of Mr. Ames with any gentlemen in Congress in reference to the stock of the Credit Mobilier? —*A.* No, sir; I have not. I had no knowledge that Mr. Ames had ever talked with anybody but myself. It was a subject I gave but little attention to; in fact, many of the details had almost passed out of my mind until they were called up in the late campaign.

(By Mr. Black.)

Q. Did you say you refused to take the stock simply because there was a lawsuit about it?—*A.* No ; not exactly that. I do not remember any other reason which I gave to Mr. Ames than that I did not wish to take stock in anything that would involve controversy. I think I gave him no other reason than that.

Q. When you ascertained the relation that this company had with the Union Pacific railroad company, and whence its profits were to be derived, would you have considered that a sufficient reason for declining it, irrespective of other considerations? —*A.* It would have been as the case was afterward stated.

Q. At the time you talked with Mr. Ames, before you rejected the proposition, you did not know whence the profits of the company were to be derived?—*A.* I did not. I do not know that Mr. Ames withheld, intentionally, from me any information. I had derived my original knowledge of the organization of the company from Mr. Train. He made quite an elaborate statement of it purposes, and I proceeded, in subsequent conversations, upon the supposition that the organization was unchanged. I ought to say for myself, as well as for Mr. Ames, that he never said any word to me that indicated the least desire to influence my legislative action in any way. If he had any such purpose, he certainly never said anything to me which would indicate it.

Q. You know now, and have known for a long time, that Mr. Ames was deeply interested in the legislation on this subject?—*A.* I supposed that he was largely interested in the Union Pacific railroad. I have heard various statements to that effect. I cannot say I had any such information of my own knowledge.

Q. You mean that he did not electioneer with you or solicit your vote? — *A.* Certainly not. None of the conversations I ever had with him had any reference to such legislation.

(By Mr. Merrick.)

Q. Have you any knowledge of any other member of Congress being concerned in the Credit Mobilier stock? — *A.* No, sir; I have not.

Q. Or any stock in the Union Pacific railroad? *A.* I have not. I can say to the committee that I never saw, I believe, in my life, a certificate of stock of the Union Pacific railroad company, and I never saw any certificate of stock of the Credit Mobilier, until Mr. Brooks exhibited one, a few days ago, in the House of Representatives.

Q. Were any dividends ever tendered to you on the stock of the Credit Mobilier, upon the supposition that you were to be a subscriber? — *A.* No, sir.

Q. This loan of $300 you have repaid, if I understand you correctly? — *A.* Yes, sir.

(By Mr. McCrary.)

Q. You never examined the charter of the Credit Mobilier to see what were its objects? — *A.* No, sir; I never saw it.

Q. If I understand you, you did not know that the Credit Mobilier had any connection with the Union Pacific railroad company? — *A.* I understood from the statement of Mr. Train that its objects were connected with the lands of the Union Pacific railroad company, and the development of settlements along that road; but that it had any relation to the Union Pacific railroad company, other than that, I did not know. I think I did hear, also, that the company was investing some of its earnings in the bonds of the road.

Q. He stated that it was for the purpose of purchasing land and building houses? — *A.* That was the statement of Mr. Train. I think he said, in that connection, that he had already been doing something of that kind at Omaha, or was going to do it.

Q. You did not know that the object was to build the Union Pacific railroad? — *A.* No, sir; I did not.

This is the case as I understand it, and as I have always understood it. In reviewing it, after all that has been said and written during the past winter, there are no substantial changes which I could now make, except to render a few points more definite. Few men can be certain that they give, with absolute correctness, the details of conversations and transactions, after a lapse of five years. Subject to this limitation, I have no doubt of the accuracy of my remembrance concerning this transaction.

From this testimony, it will be seen that, when Mr. Ames offered to sell me the stock in 1867–'68, my only knowledge of the character and objects of the Credit Mobilier company was obtained from Mr. Train, at least, as early as the winter of 1866–'67, long before the company had become a party to the construction contract. It has been said that I am mistaken in thinking it was the Credit Mobilier that Mr. Train offered me in 1866–'67. I think I am not. Mr. Durant, in explaining his connection with the Credit Mobilier, says:

I sent Mr. Train to Philadelphia. We wanted it (the Credit Mobilier) for a stock operation, but we could not agree what was to be done with it. Mr. Train proposed to go on an expanded scale, but I abandoned it. I think Mr. Train got some subscriptions; what they were I do not know.

It has been said that it is absurd to suppose that intelligent men, familiar with public affairs, did not understand all about the relation of the Credit Mobilier company to the Pacific railroad company. It is a sufficient answer to say that, until the present winter, few men, either in or out of Congress, ever understood it; and it was for the interest of those in the management of that arrangement to prevent these facts from being known. This will appear from the testimony of Hon. J. F. Wilson, who purchased ten shares of the stock in 1867. In the spring of 1869, he was called on professionally to give an opinion as to the right of holders of Pacific railroad stock to vote their own shares, notwithstanding the proxy they had given to the seven trustees. To enable him to understand the case, a copy of the triple contract was placed in his hands. He says:

Down to the time these papers were placed in my hands, I knew almost nothing of the organization and details of the Credit Mobilier, or the value of its stock, but then saw that here was abundant ground for future trouble and litigation; and, as one of the results, sold out my interest.

And again:

Q. Do you, or did you know, at the time you had this negotiation with Mr. Ames, the value of the Credit Mobilier stock? — A. I did not; and I wish to state here, in regard to that, that it was a very difficult thing to ascertain what was the value of the stock. Those who, as I say in my statement, possessed the secrets of the Credit Mobilier, kept them to themselves; and I never was able to get any definite information as to what the value of the stock was.

When, in the winter of 1867–'68, Mr. Ames proposed to sell me some of the stock, I regarded it as a mere repetition of the offer made by .Mr. Train, more than a year before. The company was the same, and the amount offered me was the same. Mr. Ames knew it had formerly been offered me, for I had then asked him his opinion of such an investment; and having understood the objects of the company, as stated by Mr. Train, I did not inquire further on that point.

There could not be the slightest impropriety in taking the stock, had the objects of the company been such as Mr. Train represented them to me. The only question on which I then hesitated, was the personal pecuniary liability attached to a subscription; and, to settle that question, I asked to see the charter, and the conditions on which the stock was based. I have no doubt Mr. Ames expected I would subscribe. But more than a year passed without further discussion of the subject. The papers were not brought, and the purchase was never made.

In the winter of 1869–'70, I received the first intimation I ever had of the real nature of the connection between the Credit Mobilier company and the Pacific railroad company, in a private conversation with the Hon. J. S. Black of Pennsylvania. Finding, in the course of that conversation, that he was familiar with the history of the enterprise, I told him all I knew about the matter, and informed him of the offer that had been made me. He expressed the opinion that the managers of the Credit Mobilier were attempting to defraud the Pacific railroad company, and informed me that Mr. Ames was pretending to have sold stock to members of Congress, for the purpose of influencing their action in any legistion that might arise on the subject.

Though I had neither done or said anything which placed me under any obligation to take the stock, I at once informed Mr. Ames, that if he was still holding the offer open to me, he need do so no longer, for I would not take the stock. This I did immediately after the conversation with Judge Black, which, according to his own recollection, as well as mine, was early in the winter of 1869–'70.

One circumstance has given rise to a painful conflict of testimony between Mr. Ames and myself. I refer to the loan of $300. Among the various criticisms that have been made on this subject, it is said to be a suspicious circumstance, that I should have borrowed so small a sum of money from Mr. Ames, about this time. As stated in my testimony, I had just returned from Europe, only a few days before the session began, and the expenses of the trip had brought me short of funds. I might have alluded in the same connection to the fact that, before going abroad, I had obtained money from a banker in New York, turning over to him advanced drafts for several months of my congressional salary, when it should be due; and, needing a small sum, early in the session, for current expenses, I asked it of Mr. Ames, for the reason that he had volunteered to put me in the way of making what he thought would be a profitable investment. He gave me the money, asking for no receipt, but saying, at the same time, that if I concluded to take the stock, we would settle both matters together. I am not able to fix the exact date of the loan, but it was probably in January, 1868.

Mr. Ames seems to have forgotten this circumstance, until I mentioned it to him, after the investigation began; for he said, in his first testimony, that he had forgotten that he had let me have any money. I neglected to pay him this money, until after the conversation with Judge Black, partly because of my pecuniary embarrassments, and partly because no conclusion had been reached in regard to the purchase of the stock. When I paid him, I took no receipt, as I had given none at the first.

Mr. Ames said once or twice, in the course of his testimony, that I did not repay it, although he says, in regard to it, that he does not know, and cannot remember.

On these differences of recollection between Mr. Ames and myself, it is not so important to show that my statement is the correct one, as to show that I have made it strictly in accordance with my understanding of the facts. And this I am able to show by proof entirely independent of my own testimony.

In the spring of 1868, Hon. J. P. Robison of Cleveland, Ohio, was my guest here in Washington, and spent nearly two weeks with me, during the trial of the impeachment of Andrew Johnson. There has existed between us an intimate acquaintance of long standing, and I have often consulted him on business affairs. On meeting him since the adjournment of Congress, he informed me that, while he was visiting me on the occasion referred to, I stated to him the offer of Mr. Ames, and asked him his opinion of it. The following letter, just received from him, states the conversation as he remembers it :

CLEVELAND, OHIO, May 1, 1873.

Dear General:—I send you the facts concerning a conversation I had with you (I think in the spring of 1868) when I was stopping in Washington for some days, as your guest, during the trial of the impeachment of President Johnson. While there, you told me that Mr. Ames had offered you a chance to invest a small amount in a company that was to operate in lands and buildings along the Pacific railroad, which he (Ames) said would be a good thing. You asked me what I thought of it as a business proposition, that you had not determined what you would do about it, and suggested to me to talk with Ames, and form my own judgment, and if I thought well enough of it to advance the money and buy the stock on joint account with you, and let you pay me interest on the one-half, I could do so. But I did not think well of the proposition as a business enterprise, and did not talk with Ames on the subject.

After this talk, having at first told you I would give the subject thought, and perhaps talk with Ames, I told you one evening that I did not think well of the proposition, and had not spoken to Ames on the subject.

Yours, truly,

J. P. ROBISON.

Hon. J. A. GARFIELD.

I subjoin two other letters, which were written about the time the report of the committee was made, and to which I refer in my remarks made on the 3d of March, in the House of Representatives. The first is from a citizen of the town where I reside; and the time of the conversation to which it alludes, was, as near as I can remember, in the fall of 1868, during the recess of Congress:

HIRAM, OHIO, February 18, 1873.

Dear Sir: — It may be relevant to the question at issue between yourself and Mr. Oakes Ames, in the Credit Mobilier investigation, for me to state that, three or four years ago, in a private conversation, you made a statement to me involving the substance of your testimony before the Poland committee, as published in the newspapers. The material points of your statement were these:

That you had been spoken to by George Francis Train, who offered you some shares of the Credit Mobilier stock; that you told him that you had no money to invest in stocks; that subsequently you had a conversation in relation to the matter with Mr. Ames; that Ames offered to carry the stock for you until you could pay for it, if you cared to buy it; and that you had told him in that case perhaps you would take it, but would not agree to do so until you had inquired more fully into the matter. Such an arrangement as this was made, Ames agreeing to carry the stock until you should decide. In this way, the matter stood, as I understood it, at the time of our conversation. My understanding was distinct that you had not accepted Mr. Ames' proposition, but that the shares were still held at your option.

You stated, further, that the company was to operate in real property along the line of the Pacific road. Perhaps, I should add that this conversation, which I have always remembered very distinctly, took place here, in Hiram. I have remembered the conversation the more distinctly from the circumstances that gave rise to it. Having been intimately acquainted with you for twelve or fifteen years, and having had a considerable knowledge of your pecuniary affairs, I asked you how you were getting on, and especially whether you were managing to reduce your debts. In reply, you gave me a detailed statement of your affairs, and concluded, by saying you had had some stock offered you, which, if you bought it, would probably make you some money. You then proceeded to state the case, as I have stated it above.

I cannot fix the time of the conversation more definitely than to say it was certainly three, and probably four, years ago.

Very truly, yours,

B. A. HINSDALE,
President of Hiram College.

Hon. J. A. GARFIELD, Washington, D. C.

The other letter was addressed to the Speaker of the House, and is as follows:

PHILADELPHIA, February 15, 1873.

My Dear Sir:—From the beginning of the investigation concerning Mr. Ames' use of the Credit Mobilier, I believe that General Garfield was free from all guilty connection with that business. This opinion was founded, not merely on my confidence in his integrity, but on some special knowledge of his case. I may have told you all about it in conversation, but I desire now to repeat it, by way of reminder.

I assert unhesitatingly that, whatever General Garfield may have done, or forborne to do, he acted in profound ignorance of the nature and character of the thing which Mr. Ames was proposing to sell. He had not the slightest suspicion that he was to be taken into a ring organized for the purpose of defrauding the public; nor did he know that the stock was in any manner connected with anything which came, or could come, within the legislative jurisdiction of Congress. The case against him lacks the *scienter* which alone constitutes guilt.

In the winter of 1869–'70, I told General Garfield of the fact that his name was on Ames' list; that Ames charged him with being one of his distributees; explained to him the character, origin and objects of the Credit Mobilier; pointed out the connection it had with congressional legislation, and showed him how impossible it was for a member of Congress to hold stock in it without bringing his private interests in conflict with his public duty. That all this was to him a perfectly new revelation, I am as sure as I can be of such a fact, or of any fact, which is capable of being proved only by moral circumstances. He told me, then, the whole story of Train's offer to him, and Ames' subsequent solicitation, and his own action in the premises, much as he details it to the committee. I do not undertake to reproduce the conversation; but the effect of it all was to convince me thoroughly that, when he listened to Ames, he was perfectly unconscious of anything evil. I watched carefully every word that fell from him on this point, and did not regard his narrative of the transaction, in other respects, with much interest, because, in my view, everything else was insignificant. I did not care whether he had made a bargain technically binding or not; his integrity depended upon the question, whether he acted with his eyes open. If he had known the true character of the proposition made to him, he would not have endured it, much less em-' braced it.

Now, couple this with Mr. Ames'. admission that he gave no explanation whatever of the matter to General Garfield; then, reflect that not a' particle of proof exists to show that he learned anything about it, previous to his conversation with me, and I think you will say that it is altogether unjust to put him on the list of those who, knowingly and willfully, joined the fraudulent association in question.

J. S. BLACK.

Hon. J. G. BLAINE,
  Speaker of House of Representatives.

To these may be added the facts, recently published by Colonel Donn Piatt of this city, that, in the winter of 1869–'70, he had occasion to look into the history of the Credit Mobilier company, and found the same state of facts concerning my connection with it, as are set forth in the letters quoted above.

Whether my understanding of the facts is correct or not, it is manifest, from the testimony given above, that, in the spring of 1868, and in the autumn of that year, and again in the winter of 1869, when I could have no motive to mis-represent the facts, I stated the

18

case to these gentlemen, substantially as it is stated in my testimony before the committee.

But it has been charged in the newspapers that, during the Presidential campaign, I denied any knowledge of the subject, or, at least, that I allowed the impression to be made upon the public mind that I knew nothing of it. To this answer, I wrote no letter on the subject, and made no statement in any public address, except to deny, in the broadest terms, the only charge then made,—that I had been bribed by Oakes Ames.

When the charges first appeared in the newspapers, I was in Montana Territory, and heard nothing of them until my return, on the 13th or 14th of September. On the following day, I met General Boynton, correspondent of the *Cincinnati Gazette*, and related to him, briefly, what I remembered about the offer to sell the stock. I told him I should write no letter on the subject, but if he thought best to publish the substance of what I had stated to him, he could do so. The same day he wrote and telegraphed from Washington, to the *Cincinnati Gazette*, under date of September 15, 1872, the following, which is a brief but correct report of my statement to him:

General Garfield, who has just arrived here from the Indian country, has to-day had the first opportunity of seeing the charges connecting his name with receiving shares of the Credit Mobilier from Oakes Ames. He authorizes the statement that he never subscribed for a single share of the stock, and that he never received, or saw a share of it. When the company was first formed, George Francis Train, then active in it, came to Washington, and exhibited a list of subscribers, of leading capitalists, and some members of Congress, to the stock of the company. The subscription was described as a popular one of $1,000 cash. Train urged General Garfield to subscribe, on two occasions, and each time, he declined. Subsequently, he was again informed that the list was nearly completed, but that a chance remained for him to subscribe, when he again declined; and to this day, he has not subscribed for, or received, any share of stock or bond of the company.

This dispatch was widely copied in the newspapers at the time, and was the only statement I made or authorized. One thing in connection with the case, I withheld from the public. When I saw the letters of Oakes Ames to Mr. McComb, I was convinced, from what Judge Black had told me, in 1869, that they were genuine, and that Ames had pretended to McComb that he had sold the Credit Mobilier stock for the purpose of securing the influence of members of Congress in any legislation that might arise touching his interests. I might have published the fact that I had heard this, and now believed Ames had so represented it; though, at the time Judge Black gave me the information, I thought quite likely he was mistaken. I did not know to what extent any other member of Congress had had negotiations with Mr. Ames; but knowing the members whose names were published in connection with the charges, and believing them to be men of the highest integrity, I did not think it just, either to them, or to the party with which we acted, to express my opinion of the genuineness of Ames' letters, at a time when a false construction would doubtless have been placed upon it.

Here, I might rest the case, but for some of the testimony given by Mr. Ames, in reference to myself. I shall consider it carefully, and shall make quotations of his language, or refer to it, as printed in the report, so that the correctness of my citations may, in every case, be verified.

To bring the discussion into as narrow a compass as possible, the points of agreement and difference between Mr. Ames and myself may thus be stated:

We agree that, soon after the beginning of the session of 1867–'8, Mr. Ames offered to sell me ten shares of the Credit Mobilier stock, at par and the accrued interest; that I never paid him any money on that offer; that I never received a certificate of stock; that after the month of June, 1868, I never received, demanded, or was offered any dividend, in any form, on that stock. We also agree that I once received from Mr. Ames a small sum of money. On the following points we disagree: He claims that I agreed to take the stock. I deny it. He claims that I received from him $329, and no more, as a balance of dividends on the stock. This I deny, and assert that I borrowed from him $300, and no more, and afterwards returned it; and that I have never received anything from him on account of the stock.

In discussing the testimony relating to myself, it

becomes necessary, for a full exhibition of the argument, to refer to that concerning others.

It has been said that in Mr. Ames' first testimony, he withheld, or concealed, the facts generally; and hence, that what he said at that time, concerning any one person, is of but little consequence. The weight and value of his first testimony, concerning any one person, can be ascertained only by comparing it with his testimony, given at the same examination, concerning others.

In that first examination, of December 17, Mr. Ames mentions, by name, sixteen members of Congress, who were said to have had dealings with him, in reference to Credit Mobilier stock. Eleven of these, he says, in that testimony, bought the stock; but he there sets me down among the five who did not buy it. He says: ' He [Garfield] did not pay for it or receive it.'

He was, at the same time, cross-examined, in regard to the dividends he paid to different persons; and he testified that he paid one or more dividends to eight different members of Congress, and that three others, being original subscribers, drew their dividends, not from him, but directly from the company. To several of the eight, he says, he paid all the dividends that accrued. But, in the same cross-examination, he testified that he did not remember to have paid me any dividends, nor that he had let me have any money. The following is the whole of his testimony concerning me, on cross-examination:

Q. In reference to Mr. Garfield, you say that you

agreed to get ten shares for him, and to hold them till he could pay for them, and that he never did pay for them, nor receive them?—*A.* Yes, sir.

Q. He never paid any money on that stock, nor received any money from it?—*A.* Not on account of it.

Q. He received no dividends?—*A.* No, sir; I think not. He says he did not. My own recollection is not very clear.

Q. So that, as you understand, Mr. Garfield never parted with any money, nor received any money on that transaction?—*A.* No, sir; he had some money from me once, some three or four hundred dollars, and called it a loan. He says that that is all he ever received from me, and that he considered it a loan. He never took his stock, and never paid for it.

Q. Did you understand it so?—*A.* Yes; I am willing to so understand it. I do not recollect paying him any dividend, and have forgotten that I paid him any money.

   *   *   *   *   *   *   *   *

Q. Who received the dividends?—*A.* Mr. Patterson, Mr. Bingham, James F. Wilson; and I think Mr. Colfax received a part of them. I do not know whether he received them all or not. I think Mr. Scofield received a part of them. Messrs. Kelley and Garfield never paid for their stock, and never received their dividends.

Certainly, it cannot be said that Mr. Ames has evinced any partiality for me; and if he was attempting to shield any of those concerned, it will not be claimed that I was one of his favorites.

In his first testimony, he claims to have spoken from memory, and without the aid of his documents. But he did, then, distinctly testify that he sold the stock to eleven members, and paid dividends to eight of them. He not only did not put me in either of those lists, but distinctly testified that I never took the stock, nor received the dividends arising from it.

His second testimony was given on the 22d of January, five weeks after his first. In assigning to this, and all his subsequent testimony, its just weight, it ought to be said, that before he gave it, an event occurred which made it strongly for his interest to prove a sale of the stock which he held as trustee. Besides the fact that McComb had already an equity suit pending in Philadelphia, to compel Mr. Ames to account to *him* for this same stock ; another suit was threatened, after he had given his first testimony, to make him account to the company for all the stock he had not sold as trustee. His first testimony was given on the 17th of December, and was made public on the 6th of January. On the 15th of January, T. C. Durant, one of the heaviest stockholders of the Credit Mobilier company, and, for a long time, its president, was examined as a witness, and said, ' The stock that stands in the name of Mr. Ames, as trustee, I claim belongs to the company yet ; and I have a summons in a suit, in my pocket, waiting to catch him in New York to serve the papers.' Of course, if, as a trustee, he had made sale of any portion of this stock, and afterward, as an individual, had bought it back, he could not be compelled to return it to the company.

Nowhere in Mr. Ames' subsequent testimony does he claim to *remember* the transaction between himself and me, any differently from what he first stated it to be. But from the memoranda found, or made, after his first examination, he *infers* and declares that there was a sale of the stock to me, and a payment to me of $329, on account of dividends.

Here, again, his testimony concerning me should be compared with his testimony given at the same time concerning others.

The memoranda, out of which all his additional testimony grew, consisted of certificates of stock, receipts, checks on the sergeant-at-arms, and entries in his diary. I will consider these in the order stated.

To two members of Congress, he delivered certificates of Credit Mobilier stock, which as trustee he had sold to them ; and in a third case, he delivered a certificate of stock to the person to whom a member had sold it. But Mr. Ames testifies that he never gave me a certificate of stock ; that I never demanded one ; and that no certificate was ever spoken of between us.

In the case of five members, he gave to them, or received from them, regular receipts of payment on account of stock and dividends. But nowhere is it claimed, or pretended, that any receipt was ever given by me, or to me, on account of any dividends arising from it.

Again, to five of the members, Mr. Ames gave checks on the sergeant-at-arms, payable to them by name ; and these checks were produced in evidence. In the case of three others, he produced checks bearing on their face the initials of the persons to whom he claimed they were paid. But he nowhere pretended to have, or ever to have had any check bearing either my name or my initials, or any mark or indorsement connecting it with me.

In regard to dividends claimed, in his subsequent testimony, to have been paid to different members, in two cases, he says he paid all the dividends that accrued on the stock from December, 1867, to May 6, 1871. In a third case, all the accretions of the stock were received by the person to whom he sold it, as the result of a re-sale. In a fourth case, he claims to have paid money on the 22d of September, 1868, on account of dividends, and in a fifth case, he claims to have paid a dividend in full, January 22, 1869. One purchaser sold his ten shares in the winter of 1868-'69, and received thereon a net profit of at least $3,000. Yet Mr. Ames repeatedly swears that he never paid me but $329; that after June, 1868, he never tendered to me, nor did I ever demand from him, any dividend; and that there was never any conversation between us relating to dividends.

After Mr. Ames had stated that he remembered no conversation between us in regard to the adjustment of these accounts, the committee asked:

Q. Was this the only dealing you had with him in reference to any stock?—*A.* I think so.

Q. Was it the only transaction of any kind?—*A.* The only transaction.

Q. Has that $329 ever been paid to you?—*A.* I have no recollection of it.

Q. Have you any belief that it ever has?—*A.* No, sir.

Q. Did you ever loan General Garfield $300?—*A.* Not to my knowledge; except that he calls this a loan.

Q. There were dividends of Union Pacific railroad stock on these ten shares?—*A.* Yes, sir.

Q. Did General Garfield ever receive these?—*A.* No, sir. He never has received but $329. * * *

Q. Has there been any conversation between you and him in reference to the Pacific stock he was entitled to?—*A.* No, sir.

Q. Has he ever called for it?—*A.* No, sir.

Q. Have you ever offered it to him?—*A.* No, sir.

Q. Has there been any conversation in relation to it?—*A.* No, sir.

The assertion that he withheld the payment of dividends, because of the McComb suit, brought in November, 1868, is wholly broken down by the fact that he did pay the dividends to several persons during a period of two years, after the suit was commenced.

The only other memoranda offered as evidence are the entries in Mr. Ames' diary for 1868. That book contains a separate statement of an account with eleven members of Congress, showing the number of shares of stock sold, or intended to be sold, to each, with the interest and dividends thereon. Across the face of nine of these accounts, long lines are drawn, crossing each other, showing, as Mr. Ames says, that in each such case the account was adjusted and closed. Three of these entries of accounts are thus crossed off, and the three members referred to therein testify that they never bought the stock. The account entered under my name is one of the three that are not crossed off. Here is the entry in full.

GARFIELD.

10 shares Credit M.	$1,000	00
7 mos. 10 days	43	36
	$1,043	36
80 per ct. bd. div., at 97	776	00
	$267	36
Int'st to June 20	3	64
	271	00

1,000 C. M.
1,000 U. P.

This entry is a mere undated memorandum, and indicates neither payment, settlement or sale. In reference to it, the following testimony was given by Mr. Ames, on cross-examination:

Q. This statement of Mr. Garfield's account is not crossed off, which indicates, does it, that the matter has never been settled or adjusted? —*A.* No, sir, it never has.

Q. Can you state whether you have any other entry in relation to Mr. Garfield? — *A.* No, sir.

Comparing Mr. Ames' testimony in reference to me, with that in reference to others, it appears that when he testified from his memory alone, he distinctly and affirmatively excepted me from the list of those who bought the stock, or received the dividends ; and that subsequently, in every case save my own, he produced some one or more of the following documents as evidence, viz., certificates of stock ;

receipts of money or dividends ; checks bearing either the full names or the initials of the persons to whom they purported to have been paid; or entries in his diary, of accounts marked ' adjusted and closed.' But no one of the classes of memoranda here described was produced in reference to me ; nor was it pretended that any one such, referring to me, ever existed.

In this review, I neither assert nor intimate that sales of stock are proved in the other cases referred to. In several cases such proof was not made. But I do assert that none of the evidences mentioned above exist in reference to me.

Having thus stated the difference between the testimony relating to other persons, and that relating to me, I now notice the testimony on which it is attempted to reach the conclusion that I did agree to take the stock, and did receive $329 on account of it.

On the 22d of January, Mr. Ames presented to the committee a statement of an alleged account with me, which I quote, —

	J. A. G.,	Dr.
1868.	To 10 shares stock Credit Mobilier ol A.	$1,000 00
	Interest	47 00
June 19.	To cash	329 00
		$1,376 00

		Cr.
1868.	By dividend bonds, Union Pacific railroad, $1,000, at 80 per cent. less 2 per cent.	$776 00
June 17.	By dividend collected for your account .	600 00
		$1,376 00

This account, and other similar ones presented at the same time, concerning other members, he claimed to have copied from his memorandum-book. But when the memorandum-book was subsequently presented, it was found that the account here quoted was not copied from it, but was made up partly from memory, and partly from such memoranda as Mr. Ames had discovered after his first examination.

By comparing this account with the entry made in his diary, and already quoted, it will be seen that they are not duplicates, either in substance or form; and that in this account a new element is added, namely, an alleged payment of $329 in cash, on June 19. This is the very element in dispute.

The pretended proof, that this sum was paid me, is found in the production of a check drawn by Mr. Ames on the sergeant-at-arms. The following is the language of the check:

June 22, 1868.

Pay O. A., or bearer, three hundred and twenty-nine dollars, and charge to my account.

Oakes Ames.

This check bears no indorsement or other mark, than the words and figures given above. It was drawn on the 22d day of June, and, as shown by the books of the sergeant-at-arms, was paid the same day by the paying teller. But if this check was paid to me on the account just quoted, it must have been delivered to me three days before it was drawn; for the account says I received the payment on the 19th of June.

There is nothing but the testimony of Mr. Ames that in any way connects this check with me ; and, as the committee find that the check was paid to me, I call special attention to all the testimony that bears upon the question

When Mr. Ames testified that he paid me $329 as a 'dividend on account of the stock, the following question was asked him :

Q. How was that paid? — *A.* Paid in money, I believe.

At a later period in the examination :

Q. You say that $329 was paid to him. How was that paid ? — *A.* I presume by a check on the sergeant-at-arms. I find there are checks filed, without indicating who they were for.

One week later, the check, referred to above, was produced, and the following examination was had :

Q. This check seems to have been paid to somebody, and taken up by the sergeant-at-arms. Those initials are your own ? — Yes, sir.

Q. Do you know who had the benefit of this check ? — *A.* I cannot tell you.

Q. Do you think you received the money on it yourself ? — *A.* I have no idea. I may have drawn the money and handed it to another person. It was paid in that transaction. It may have been paid to Mr. Garfield. There were several sums of that amount.

Q. Have you any memory in reference to this check ? — *A.* I have no memory as to that particular check.

Still later in the examination occurs the following :

Q. In regard to Mr. Garfield, do you know wheth-

er you gave him a check, or paid him the money?—
A. I think I did not pay him the money. He got it from the sergeant-at-arms.

Still later, in the same examination, occurs the following:

Q. You think the check, on which you wrote nothing to indicate the payee, must have been Mr. Garfield's?—*A.* Yes, sir. That is my judgment.

On the 11th of February, twelve days later still, the subject came up again, and Mr. Ames said:

A. I am not sure how I paid Mr. Garfield.

Still later, in a cross-examination in reference to Mr. Colfax, the following occurs:

Q. In testifying in Mr. Garfield's case, you say you may have drawn the money on the check, and paid him. Is not your answer equally applicable to the case of Mr. Colfax?—*A.* No, sir.

Q. Why not?—*A.* I put Mr. Colfax's initials on the check, while I put no initials on Mr. Garfield's; and I may have drawn the money myself.

Q. Did not Mr. Garfield's check belong to him? —*A.* Mr. Garfield had not paid for his stock. He was entitled to $329 balance. But Mr. Colfax paid for his, and I had no business with his $1,200.

Q. Is your recollection in regard to this payment to Mr. Colfax any more clear than your recollection as to the payment to Mr. Garfield?—*A.* Yes, sir; I think it is.

And, finally, in the examination of Mr. Dillon, cashier of the sergeant-at-arms, the following is recorded:

O. There is a check payable to Oakes Ames. or bearer. Have you any recollection of that?—*A.*

That was paid to himself.   I have no doubt, myself, that I paid that to Mr. Ames.

Reviewing the testimony on this point (and I have quoted it all), it will be seen that Mr. Ames, several. times, asserts that he does not know whether he paid me the check or not. · He states positively that he has no special recollection of the check.   His testimony is wholly inferential.   In one of the seven paragraphs quoted, he says he paid me the money ; in another, he says he may have paid me the money ; in three of them, he thinks, or presumes, that he paid me the check; and in the other two, he says he does not know.

The cashier of the sergeant-at-arms has no doubt that Mr. Ames himself drew the money on the check. And yet, upon this vague and wholly inconclusive testimony, and almost alone upon it, is based the assumption that I received from Mr. Ames $329, as a dividend on the stock.   I affirm, with perfect distinctness of recollection, that I received no check from Mr. Ames.   The only money I ever received from him was in currency.

The only other evidence, in support of the assumption that he paid me $329, as a balance on the stock, is found in the entries in his diary for 1868. The value of this class of memoranda depends altogether upon their character, and upon the business habits of the man who makes them.   On this latter point, the following testimony of Mr. Ames is important :

Q. Is it your habit, as a matter of business, in conducting various transactions with different persons, to do it without making any memoranda? — *A.* This was my habit. Until within a year or two, I have had no book-keeper, and I used to keep all my own matters in my own way, and very carelessly, I admit.

The memorandum-book, in which these entries were made, was not presented to the committee until the 11th of February, one week before they made their report. This book does not contain continuous entries of current transactions, with consecutive dates. It is in no sense a day-book; but contains a loose, irregular mass of memoranda, which may have been made at the time of the transactions, or long afterward. Mr. Ames says of it in his testimony:

Q. What was the character of the book in which the memoranda were made? — *A.* It was in a small pocket memorandum, and some of it on slips of paper.

It is not pretended that this book contains a complete record of payments and receipts. And yet, besides the check, already referred to, this book, so made up, contains the only evidence, or pretended evidence, on which it is claimed that I agreed to take the stock. It should be remembered that every portion of this evidence, both check and book, is of Mr. Ames' own making. I have already referred to the undated memorandum of an account in this book, under my name, and have shown that it neither proved a sale of stock, or any payment on account of it.

There are but two other entries in the book relating to me, and they are two lists of names, substantially duplicates of each other, with various amounts set opposite each. They are found on pages 450 and 453 of the testimony. The word 'paid' is marked before the first name on one of these lists, and ditto marks placed under the word 'paid,' and opposite the remaining names. But the value of this entry, as proof of payment, will be seen from the cross-examination of Mr. Ames, which immediately follows the list:

Q. This entry, 'Paid S. Colfax $1,200,' is the amount which you paid by this check on the sergeant-at-arms? — *A.* Yes, sir.

Q. Was this entry upon this page of these various names intended to show the amount you were to pay, or that you had paid; was that made at this date? — *A.* I do not know; it was made about that time. I would not have written it on Sunday; it is not very likely. It was made on a blank page. It is simply a list of names.

Q. Were these names put down after you had made the payments, or before, do you think? — *A.* Before, I think.

Q. You think you made this list before the parties referred to had actually received their checks, or received the money? — *A.* Yes. sir; that was to show whom I had to pay, and who were entitled to receive the 60 per cent. dividend. It shows whom I had to pay here in Washington.

Q. It says 'paid?' — *A.* Yes, sir; well, I did pay it.

Q. What I want to know is, whether the list was made out before, or after payment? — *A.* About the same time, I suppose; probably, before.

The other list, bearing the same names and amounts,

shows no other evidence that the several sums were paid, than a cross marked opposite each amount. But concerning this, Mr. Ames testifies that it was a list of what was to be paid, and that the cross was subsequently added to show that the amount had been paid.

Neither of these lists shows anything as to the time or mode of payment, and would nowhere be accepted as proof of payment. By Mr. Ames' own showing, they are lists of persons to whom he *expected* to pay the amounts set opposite their names. They may exhibit his expectations, but they do not prove the alleged payments. If the exact sum of $329 was received by me at the time, and under the circumstances alleged by Mr. Ames, it implies an agreement to take the stock. It implies, furthermore, that Mr. Ames had sold Pacific railroad bonds for me ; that he had received, also, a cash dividend for me, and had accounted to me as trustee for these receipts, and the balance of the proceeds.

Now, I affirm, with the firmest conviction of the correctness of my statement, that I never heard until this investigation began, that Mr. Ames ever sold any bonds, or performed any other stock transactions on my behalf, and no act of mine was ever based on such a supposition.

The only remaining testimony bearing upon me, is that in which Mr. Ames refers to conversations between himself and me, after the investigation began. The first of these was of his own seeking, and occurred before he or I had testified. Soon after the investigation began, Mr. Ames asked me what I remembered of our talk in 1867–'68, in reference to the Credit Mobilier company.   I told him I could best answer his question by reading to him the statement I had already prepared to lay before the committee, when I should be called.   Accordingly, on the following day, I took my written statement to the Capitol, and read it to him carefully, sentence by sentence, and asked him to point out anything which he might think incorrect.   He made but two criticisms; one, in regard to a date, and the other, that he thought it was the Credit Foncier and not the Credit Mobilier that Mr. Train asked me to subscribe to in 1866–'67. When I read the paragraph in which I stated that I had once borrowed $300 of him, he remarked, 'I believe I did let you have some money, but I had forgotten it.'   He said nothing to indicate that he regarded me as having purchased the stock; and from that conversation, I did not doubt that he regarded my statement substantially correct.   His first testimony, given a few days afterward, confirmed me in this opinion.

I had another interview with Mr. Ames, of my own seeking, to which he alludes elsewhere; and for a full understanding of it, a statement of some previous facts is necessary.   I gave my testimony before the committee, and in Mr. Ames' hearing, on the morning of January 14.   It consisted of the statement I had already read to Mr. Ames, and of the cross-examination which followed my reading of the statement, all of which has been quoted above.

During that afternoon, while I was in the management of an appropriation bill in the House, word was brought to me that Mr. Ames, on coming out of the committee-room, had declared, in the hearing of several reporters, that 'Garfield was in league with Judge Black to break him down ; that it was $400, not $300, that he had let Garfield have, who had not only never repaid it, but had refused to repay it.' Though this report of Mr. Ames' alleged declaration was subsequently found to be false, and was doubtless fabricated for the purpose of creating difficulty, yet there were circumstances which, at the time, led me to suppose that the report was correct. One was, that Judge Black (who was McComb's counsel in the suit against Ames) was present at my examination, and had drawn out on cross-examination my opinion of the nature of Mr. Ames' relation to the Credit Mobilier company and the Union Pacific company ; and the other was, that in Mr. Ames' testimony of December 17, he had said, 'He (Mr. Garfield) had some money from me once, some three or four hundred dollars, and called it a loan.' The sum of four hundred dollars had thus been mentioned in his testimony, and it gave plausibility to the story that he was now claiming that, as the amount he had loaned me.

Supposing that Mr. Ames had said what was reported, I was deeply indignant ; and, with a view of drawing from him a denial or retraction of the statement, or, if he persisted in it, to pay him twice over, so that he could no longer say or pretend that there existed between us any unsettled transaction, I drew some money from the office of the sergeant-at-arms, and, going to my committee-room, addressed him the following note :

HOUSE OF REPRESENTATIVES,
January 14, 1873.

Sir :—I have just been informed, to my utter amazement, that, after coming out of the committee-room this morning, you said in the presence of several reporters that you had loaned me four, instead of three, hundred dollars, and that I had not only refused to pay you, but was aiding your accusers to injure you in the investigation.   I shall call the attention of the committee to it, unless I find I am misinformed.   To bring the loan question to an immediate issue between us, I inclose herewith $400.   If you wish to do justice to the truth and to me, you will return it, and correct the alleged statement, if you made it.   If not, you will keep the money, and thus be paid twice and more. Silence on your part will be a confession that you have deeply wronged me.

J. A. GARFIELD.

Hon. OAKES AMES.

After the House had adjourned for the day, I found, on returning to my committee-room, that I had omitted to inclose the note with the money, which had been sent to the House post-office.   I immediately sought Mr. Ames to deliver the note, but failed to find him at his hotel, or elsewhere, that evening. Early the next morning, January 15, I found him, and delivered the note.   He denied having said, or claimed, any of the things therein set forth, and wrote on the back of my letter the following :

WASHINGTON, January 15, 1873.

Dear Sir :—I return you your letter with inclosures, and I utterly deny ever having said that you refused to pay me, or that it was four, instead of three hundred dollars, or that you was aiding my accusers. I also wish to say that there has never been any but the most friendly feelings between us, and no transaction, in the least degree, that can be censured by any fair-minded person. I herewith return you the four hundred dollars as not belonging to me.

Yours, truly,

OAKES AMES.

Hon. J. A. GARFIELD.

From inquiry of the reporters, to whom the remarks were alleged to have been made, I had become satisfied that the story was wholly false; and when Mr. Ames added his denial, I expressed to him my regret that I had written this note in anger and upon false information. I furthermore said to Mr. Ames that, if he had any doubt in reference to the repayment of the loan, I wished him to keep the money. He refused to keep any part of it, and his conversation indicated that he regarded all transactions between us settled.

Before I left his room, however, he said he had some memoranda which seemed to indicate that the money I had of him was on account of stock; and asked me, if he did not, some time in 1868, deliver to me a statement to that effect. I told him if he had any account of that sort, I was neither aware of it, nor responsible for it; and thereupon I made substantially the following statement :

Mr. Ames, the only memoranda you ever showed me was in 1867–'68, when speaking to me of this proposed sale of stock, you figured out, on a little piece of paper, what you supposed would be realized from an investment of $1,000; and, as I remember, you wrote down these figures:

$$\begin{array}{r} 1,000 \\ 1,000 \\ 400 \\ \hline 2,400 \end{array}$$

as to the amounts, you expected to realize.

While saying this to Mr. Ames, I wrote the figures, as above, on a piece of paper lying on his table, to show him what the only statement was, he had ever made to me.   It is totally false that these figures had any other meaning than that I have here given; nor did I say anything, out of which could be fabricated such a statement.

In his testimony of January 29, Mr. Ames gives a most remarkable account of this interview.   Remembering the fact, by him undisputed, that there had been no communication between us on this subject, for more than four years before this investigation began, notice the following:

Q. Did you have any conversation, in reference to the influence this transaction would have on the election last fall? — *A.* Yes, he said it would be very injurious to him.

Q. What else, in reference to that? — *A.* I am a very bad man to repeat conversation; I cannot remember.

That is, he makes me, on the 15th of January, 1873,

express the fear that this transaction will injure me in the election of October, 1872.

Again:

Q. You may state whether, in conversation with you, Mr. Garfield claims, as he claims before us, that the only transaction between you was borrowing $300. — *A.* No, sir; he did not claim that with me.

Q. State how he did claim it with you; what was said? — *A.* I cannot remember half of it. * * He [Garfield] stated, that when he came back from Europe, being in want of funds, he called on me, to loan him a sum of money. He thought he had repaid it. I do not know; I do not remember. * *

Q. How long after that transaction [the offer to sell Credit Mobilier stock] did he go to Europe? — *A.* I believe it was a year or two. * *

Q. Do you not know that he did not go to Europe for nearly two years afterward? — *A.* No, I do not. It is my impression, it was two years afterward, but I cannot remember dates.

I should think not, if this testimony is an example of his memory!

It is known to thousands of people, that I went to Europe in the summer of 1867, and at no other time. I sailed from New York on the 13th of July, 1867, spent several days of August, in Scotland, with Speaker Blaine and Senator Morrill of Vermont, and returned to New York on the 9th of the following November — three weeks before the beginning of the session of Congress.

The books of the sergeant-at-arms of the House show that, before going, I had assigned several months' pay, in advance, to a banker, who had advanced me money, for the expenses of the trip. To break the weight of this fact, which showed why I came to need a small loan, Mr. Ames says I did not go to Europe till nearly two years afterward.

If a reason be sought why he gave such testimony, it may perhaps be found on the same page from which the last quotation is made:

Q. How did you happen to retain that little stray memorandum? — *A.* I do not know. I found it in my table two or three days afterward. I did not pay any attention to it at the time, until I found there was to be a conflict of testimony, and I thought that might be something worth preserving.

How did he find out, after that time, that 'there was to be a conflict of testimony?' The figures were made on that piece of paper, January 15, the day after I had given my testimony, and four weeks after he had given his first testimony. There was no conflict, except what he himself made; and that conflict was as marked between his first statement and his subsequent ones, as between the latter and mine.

There runs through all his testimony, now under consideration, an intimation that I was in a state of alarm, was beseeching Mr. Ames to 'let me off easy,' 'to say as little about it as possible,' 'to let it go as a loan,' 'to save my reputation,' that I 'felt very bad,' was 'in great distress,' 'hardly knew what I said,' and other such expressions.

I should have been wholly devoid of sensibility, if I had not felt keenly the suspicions, the false accusations, the reckless calumnies with which the public mind was filled, while the investigation was in progress. But there is not the smallest fragment of truth in the statement, or rather the insinuation, that I ever asked, or wanted, anything from Mr. Ames, on this subject, but simple justice and the truth.

The spirit in which a portion of the public treated the men whose conduct was being investigated, may be understood from the following questions, put to Mr. Ames, in the midst of an examination, not at all relating to me:

Q. In that conversation, with Mr. Garfield, was anything said, by him, about your being an old man, near the end of your career, and his being comparatively a young man? — *A.* No, sir; nothing of that sort.

It is manifest that this question was suggested by some of the inventive bystanders, in hopes of making an item for a new sensation.

The most absurd and exaggerated statements were constantly finding their way into the public press, in reference to every subject and person connected with the investigation, and this question is an illustration.

In no communication with Mr. Ames, did I ever say anything inconsistent with my testimony before the committee.

Conscious that I had done no wrong, from the beginning to the end of this affair, I had nothing to conceal, and no favors to ask, except that the whole truth should be known. I was in the committee-room but once, during the investigation, and I went then, only when summoned to give my testimony.

From a review of the whole subject, the following conclusions are fairly and clearly established:

I. That the Credit Mobilier company was a State corporation, regularly organized; and that neither its charter, nor the terms of its contract, of October 15, 1867, disclosed anything which indicated that the company was engaged in any fraudulent or improper enterprise.

II. That a ring of seven persons, inside the Credit Mobilier company, calling themselves trustees, obtained the control of the franchises, and of a majority of the stock, of both the Credit Mobilier and of the Union Pacific railroad company; and, while holding such double control, they made a contract with themselves, by which they received, for building the road, an extravagant sum, greatly beyond the real cost of construction; and, in adjusting the payments, they received stock and bonds of the railroad company, at a heavy discount.

*   *   *   *   *   *

That these exorbitant profits were distributed, not to the stockholders of the Credit Mobilier proper, but to the ring of seven trustees, and their proxies — the holders of this ring stock — and that this arrangement was kept a close secret by its managers.

III. That, in 1867–'8, Mr. Ames offered to sell small amounts of this stock to several leading members of Congress, representing it as an ordinary investment, promising fair profits; but, in every such offer, he concealed from such members the real nature of the arrangement, by which the profits were to be made, as well as the amount of dividends likely to be realized. While thus offering this stock, he was writing to one of his ring associates, that he was disposing of the stock 'where it would do most good,' intimating by that, he was thereby gaining influence in Congress, to prevent investigation into the affairs of the road. His letters, and the list of names, which he gave to McComb, represent many persons as having bought the stock, who never did buy or agree to buy it, and also represent a much larger amount sold than he did actually sell. Mr. Ames' letters and testimony abound in contradictions, not only of his own statements, but also of the statements of most of the other witnesses; and it is fair, in judging of its credibility, to take into account his interests involved in the controversy.

IV. That in reference to myself, the following points are clearly established by the evidence:

1. That I neither purchased, nor agreed to purchase, the Credit Mobilier stock, which Mr. Ames offered to sell me; nor did I receive any dividend arising from it. This appears from my own testimony; and, from the first testimony given by Mr. Ames, which is not overthrown by his subsequent statements; and is strongly confirmed by the fact that, in the case of each of those who did purchase the stock, there was produced, as evidence of the sale, either a certificate of stock, receipt of payment, a check drawn in the name of the payee, or entries in Mr. Ames' diary, of a stock account marked, adjusted,

and closed; but, that no one of these evidences exists, in reference to me. This position is further confirmed by the subsequent testimony of Mr. Ames, who, though he claims that I did receive $329 from him on account of the stock, yet he repeatedly testifies that, beyond that amount, I never received or demanded any dividend, that he did not offer me any, nor was the subject alluded to, in conversation between us.

Mr. Ames admits, that after December, 1867, the various stock and bond dividends, on the stock he had sold, amounted to an aggregate of more than 800 per cent.; and, that between January, 1868, and May, 1871, all these dividends were paid to several of those who purchased the stock. My conduct was wholly inconsistent with the supposition of such ownership; for, during the year 1869, I was borrowing money, to build a house here, in Washington, and was securing my creditors by giving mortgages on my property; and, all this time, it is admitted that I received no dividends, and claimed none.

The attempt to prove a sale of the stock to me, is wholly inconclusive; for it rests, first, on a check payable to Mr. Ames himself, concerning which, he several times says he does not know to whom it was paid; and second, upon loose, undated entries in his diary, which neither prove a sale of the stock nor any payment on account of it.

The only fact from which it is possible for Mr. Ames to have inferred an agreement to buy the stock, was the loan to me, of $300. But that loan was made months before the check of June 22, 1868, and was repaid in the winter of 1869; and, after that date, there were no transactions of any sort between us.

And finally, before the investigation was ended, Mr. Ames admitted that, on the chief point of difference between us, he might be mistaken.

He said he 'considered me the purchaser of the stock, unless it was borrowed money I had of him;' and, at the conclusion of his last testimony, he said:

Mr. Garfield understands this matter as a loan; he says I did not explain it to him.

Q. You need not say what Mr. Garfield says. Tell us what you think.

A. Mr. Garfield might have misunderstood me. *

* I supposed it was like all the rest, but when Mr. Garfield says he mistook it for a loan; that he always understood it to be a loan; that I did not make any explanation to him, and did not make any statement to him; I may be mistaken. I am a man of few words, and I may not have made myself understood to him.

2. That the offer which Mr. Ames made to me, as I understood it, was one which involved no wrong or impropriety. I had no reason for supposing that behind this offer to sell me a small amount of stock lay hidden any scheme to defraud the Pacific railroad, or imperil the interests of the United States. I was not invited to become a party to any scheme of spoliation, much less was I aware of any attempt to influence my legislative action, or any subject connected there-

with. And, on the first intimation of such a nature of the case, I declined any further consideration of the subject.

3. That whatever may have been the facts in the case, I stated them in my testimony, as I have always understood them; and there has been no contradiction, prevarication, or evasion, on my part.

This is demonstrated by the fact that I stated the case to Mr. Robison, in the spring of 1868, and to Mr. Hinsdale, in the autumn of that year, and to Judge Black, in the winter of 1899-'70, substantially as it is stated in my testimony before the committee.

I have shown that, during the presidential campaign, I did not deny having known anything about the Credit Mobilier company; that the statement published in the *Cincinnati Gazette*, September 15, is substantially in accord with my testimony before the committee; and finally, that during the progress of the investigation, there was nothing in my conversation, or correspondence with Mr. Ames, in any way, inconsistent with the facts as given in my testimony. To sum it up, in a word: out of an unimportant business transaction, the loan of a trifling sum of money, as a matter of personal accommodation, and out of an offer, never accepted, has arisen this famous fabric of accusation and suspicion.

If there be a citizen of the United States, who is willing to believe that, for $329, I have bartered away my good name, and to falsehood, have added perjury, these pages are not addressed to him. If there be one who thinks that any part of my public life has been gauged on so low a level as these charges would place it, I do not address him — I address those who are willing to believe that it is possible for a man to serve the public without personal dishonor. I have endeavored, in this review, to point out the means by which the managers of a corporation, wearing the garb of honorable industry, have robbed and defrauded a great national enterprise, and attempted, by cunning and deception, for selfish ends, to enlist in its interest those who would have been the first to crush the attempt, had their objects been known.

If any of the scheming corporations, or corrupt rings, that have done so much to disgrace the country, by their attempts to control its legislation have ever found in me a conscious supporter, or ally, in any dishonorable scheme, they are at full liberty to disclose it.   In the discussion of the many grave and difficult questions of public policy, which have occupied the thoughts of the nation, during the last twelve years, I have borne some part; and I confidently appeal to the public records for a vindication of my conduct."

There was another political disturbance, in connection with the vote of Congress, in 1872, to increase the salary of its members, and for which General Garfield voted under protest, as the measure was combined with others he wished very much to see passed.   General Garfield sent to his constituents an explanation of the matter, when he saw how sadly they had misconstrued his motives and his action. It is a complete history of the affair in itself, and is given in full :

HIRAM, OHIO, April 21, 1873.

ON the 3d day of March, the day that completed the tenth year of my service as your Representative in Congress, I cast a vote, in company with one hundred and one other Representatives, on account of which it appears that the following resolution has lately been adopted by a convention of delegates at Warren, called to nominate a member of the State Constitutional Convention :

Resolved, That James A. Garfield, in voting for the retroactive salary bill, has forfeited the confidence of his constituents, and, therefore, we, the representatives of the Republican party of Trumbull County, in convention assembled, ask him to resign forthwith his office as our Representative in Congress.

The officers of that convention have not favored me with a copy of the resolution, and I have learned of its terms only through the press and private communications. Presuming that the above is the correct text of the resolution, and waiving all question of the jurisdiction and authority of that convention to sit in judgment on the subject, I respond to the resolution itself. In doing so I assume that those who framed it were animated only by a sense of public duty. I will assume also that they were willing and even anxious to do me justice, and to state fairly and truthfully my alleged offense. This, however, they have not done.

The language of the resolution implies that I voted to give additional back pay to members of Congress. It assumes that the retroactive pay was the chief provision of the bill for which I did vote. Now, just such a bill as that language describes was brought into the House, for the purpose of fastening it as an amendment to one of the leading appropriation bills. That effort I resisted at every stage. The bill for which I did vote now fills twenty-seven pages of the national statute-book. The offensive retroactive clause is contained in three lines of the statute.

Whether I ought or ought not to have voted for the appropriation bill, with the retroactive salary clause incorporated in it, depends upon the merits and demerits of the bill as a whole. Whether I am in any way responsible for its offensive provisions depends upon what efforts I made, or failed to make, to prevent their adoption.

That it may be clearly understood what I did on this subject, I will briefly state the facts.

As Chairman of the Committee on Appropriations it was my duty to see that the annual appropriation bills were acted upon in the House before the Forty-Second Congress expired. To do this it was necessary to press them constantly, and to the exclusion of a great mass of other business. For this purpose chiefly the House was in session from ten to fifteen hours in each twenty-four during the last week of the term.

I had special charge of the legislative appropriation bill, upon the preparation of which my committee had spent nearly two weeks of labor before the meeting of Congress. It was the most important of the twelve annual bills. Its provisions reached every part of the machinery of the Government in all the States and Territories of the Union. The amount appropriated by it was one-seventh of the total annual expenditures of the Government, exclusive of the interest on the public debt. It contained all the appropriations required by law for the legislative

department of the Government; for the public printing and binding; for the President and the officers
and employes at the Executive Mansion; for the
seven executive departments at Washington, and all
their bureaus and sub-divisions; for the sub-treasu-
ries and public depositaries in fourteen cities of the
Union; for all the officers and agents employed in
the assessment and collection of the internal revenue;
for the governments of the nine Territories and of
the District of Columbia; for the mints and the
assay offices; for the land offices and the surveys of
public lands; and for all the courts, judges, district
attorneys, and marshals of the United States. Besides this, during its progress through the two
Houses, many provisions had been added to the bill
which were considered of vital importance to the
public interests. A section had been added in the
Senate to force the Pacific railroad companies to pay
the arrears of interest on the bonds loaned to them
by the United States, and to commence refunding
the principal.

An investigating committee of the House had
unearthed enormous frauds committed by and against
these companies, and as the result of two months'
labor had framed a bill of several sections to provide
for bringing suits in the courts to recover the vast
sums of which the road and Government had been
plundered, and to prevent further spoliation. That
bill had also been made a part of the appropriation
bill.

While the bill was first passing through the
House, repeated efforts were made to increase the
salaries of different officers of the Government; in
every instance I resisted these efforts, and but little
increase was made until forty-eight hours before the
Congress expired, when the House loaded upon this
bill an amendment increasing the salaries of the

President, Vice-President, judges of the Supreme Court, and members of Congress, including those of the Forty-Second Congress.

An unsuccessful effort had been made three weeks before to fasten that amendment upon another appropriation bill of which I had charge. In the struggle to fasten it upon this bill there was a lengthy debate, in which its merits and demerits were fully discussed. In that debate I bore my full share in opposing the amendment. Before it was finally adopted there were eighteen different votes taken in the House and the Committee of the Whole on its merits and its management. On each and all of these I voted adversely to the amendment. Six years ago, when the salaries of Congressmen were raised and the pay was made to date back sixteen months, I had voted against the increase; and now, bearing more responsibility for the appropriations than ever before, I pursued the same course. No act of mine during this struggle can be tortured into a willingness to allow this amendment to be fastened to the bill. But all opposition was overborne by majorities ranging from three to fifty-three, and the bill with this amendment added was sent to the Senate Saturday evening, the 1st of March. If the Senate had struck out the amendment, they could have compelled the House to abandon it or take the responsibility of losing the bill. But the Senate refused, by a vote of nearly two to one, to strike out the salary clause or any part of it; and many Senators insisted that with the abolition of mileage and other allowances $6,500 was no real increase, and that the rate should be greater. The bill then went to a conference committee with sixty-five unadjusted amendments pending between the two Houses.

The battle against the salary clause was fought and lost before the appropriation bill went to the conference committee. The Speaker of the House and the President of the Senate both recognized the fact in appointing their respective committees of conference. In announcing the committee of conference on the part of the House, the Speaker said :

"There are several points of difference between the two Houses of exceeding importance. It is the duty of the Chair to adjust the conference so as to represent those points upon which the House most earnestly insists. The three points of difference especially involved are the subject of salaries of members and other officers, what is styled the Morrill amendment, and the provision in regard to the Pacific railroad. The Chair thinks that so far as he can analyze the votes of the House on these propositions, that the following conferees will fairly represent the views of the House on the various questions : Mr. GARFIELD of Ohio, Mr. BUTLER of Massachusetts, and Mr. RANDALL of Pennsylvania."

I was appointed chairman because I had charge of the bill. Messrs. Butler and Randall were appointed because they represented the declared will of the House on the salary question. They were not members of the Committee on Appropriations, and were not familiar with the other provisions of the bill. The salary clause was the first of the sixty-five amendments referred to the committee, and six full hours were spent in considering it. Notwithstanding the fact that the battle against the salary clause was already lost, I made the best effort I could to retrieve it in the conference committee. I faithfully presented the considerations urged against it by the minority in the House, and moved to strike out the clause relating to congressional salaries. The Senate conferees were unanimous against the motion, and my two associates agreed with them. I moved to strike out the retroactive feature, and the vote stood as before. By the same majority the amount was fixed at $7,500. There was no longer any doubt that the salary clause must stand or fall with the bill.   It was clear that a majority of the committee represented the judgment of the two Houses.

In this situation there were but two courses before me: one was to refuse to act with the conference committee, abandon the bill to Mr. Butler, the next on the conference, and go into the House and oppose its final passage; the other was to stand by the bill, make it as perfect as possible, limit and reduce the amount of the appropriation as much as could be done, and report it to the House for passage.

In a word, I was called upon to decide this question: Is the salary amendment so impolitic, so unwise, so intolerable, that in order to prevent its becoming a law the whole bill ought to be defeated? If so, it was the duty of both the Senate and the House to defeat it; and if they passed it, it was the duty of the President to veto it.   Upon the decision I then made, and the reasons for and against it, I invoke the judgment of my constituents; for there, if anywhere in the course of this legislation, I forfeited my claim to their confidence.

If the enactment of this amendment into a law was itself a crime, then any bill, however important it might be, to which it was attached, ought to be defeated.   No public emergency can justify theft or robbery.   But bad as this amendment was in some of its provisions, it is an abuse of language and of truth to call it either theft or robbery.   On the contrary, many of the items of increase were acknowledged to be just, even by those who opposed the amendment most earnestly.   It was clearly within the constitutional power of Congress to pass that clause.   The Constitution makes it their duty to fix the salary of all officers of the Government, including their own.

The retroactive pay provided for in this amendment, unwise, indelicate, and indefensible as I believe it to have been, was in accordance with all the precedents, for every increase of pay of members of Congress since the adoption of the Constitution has applied to the whole term of the Congress that authorized it. It was not a crime, and we have no right to say that those who advocated it were thieves and robbers. I opposed the whole scheme of increase of salaries chiefly on two grounds:

First. That officers at the national Capital were already receiving higher rates of pay than many of those serving at a distance; and that if we began to increase salaries at the Capital, and particularly our own, it would be indecent and unjust not to go through the whole list and make the increase general. To do this would greatly increase the expenditures already overgrown by the results of the war; and,

Second. I opposed it because I thought it peculiarly impolitic for the Forty-Second Congress to give any new cause for bringing itself into public odium. Much had already occurred to throw discredit upon it, and this would add a new shade to the colors in which it was being painted.

On the other hand, there were grave objections to the defeat of the appropriation bill. Everybody knew that its failure would render an extra session of the new Congress inevitable. It is easy to say now that this would have been better than to allow the passage of the salary clause. Present evils always seem greater than those that never come. The opinion was almost universal that an extra session would be a serious evil in many ways, and especially to the Treasury. Its cost, directly and indirectly, would far exceed the amount appropriated for retroactive salaries. An unusual amount of dangerous legislation was pressing upon Congress for action. A measure to refund the cotton tax, which would take seventy millions from the Treasury, was pressed by a powerful organization in and out of Congress, and its consideration had only been prevented by interposing the appropriation bills. A vast number of doubtful claims growing out of the war were ready to follow in the wake of the cotton tax. To organize a new Congress, which would require the appointment and organization of new committees, and to begin this bill anew, perfect its details, and pass it, would require many weeks. In the meantime the field would be clear for pushing all schemes against the Treasury.

But more than this, the defeat of the bill would carry with it the defeat of the only legislation by which Congress has attempted for many years to check the career of those greedy corporations whose powers have become so dangerous to the public welfare. For the first time Congress was thoroughly aroused to the danger; and the sections concerning the Pacific railroad, which had been added to this bill, empowered and directed the executive, through the courts, to strike an effective blow against those who had already robbed the Pacific railroad at the expense of the National Treasury. If these sections failed, it was by no means certain that the new Congress would pass them; and if it did, the interests of the Government would greatly suffer by the delay.

Only a single day and night remained before the final adjournment, and three other great appropriation bills were still unfinished.

These considerations were inseparably connected with the defeat of this appropriation bill. I knew that if it failed from any act of mine, the responsibility for its failure would rest more heavily on me than upon any other member. I had been made responsible for its management, but was in no way responsible for the adoption of the salary amendment.

After weighing the case as well as I could, I concluded it was my duty to stand by the bill; and I did so.

I remained in the conference, and did what I could to perfect the bill and reduce the amount appropriated by it. On my motion the following proviso was made a part of the bill: "*Provided*, That in settling the pay and allowances of members of the Forty-Second Congress, all mileage shall be deducted, and no allowances shall be made for expenses of travel." The sum deducted from the additional back pay, under this proviso, amounted in the aggregate to nearly $400,000; and the pay to the members of the late Congress is made less than those of the next Congress by the total amount of actual traveling expenses.

The other sixty-four amendments to the bill were satisfactorily adjusted, after many hours of deliberation. Having done what I could to perfect the bill, I signed the conference report and presented it to the House; but in doing so I stated that I alone had opposed the salary clause in the conference committee, and had done what I could to strike it out, and that I had signed the report rather than run the risk of losing the bill. I then voted for the bill, not for the increase of salaries nor for the retroactive clause, for I was opposed to both, but for the bill as a whole.

It is clear that it would have passed if I had voted against it. But believing that it was better to pass the bill, even with the salary amendment included, than risk the consequences of its failure, I voted for it. It would have been an inconsistent and cowardly act on my part to vote against it merely to escape criticism.

If the bill, as reported from the conference committee, ought to have been defeated, there was one well-known and very easy way to do it. One-fifth of the members present, by dilatory and filibustering motions and calling the ayes and noes, could have prevented a vote on the report till the end of the session. Should the ninety-six members who voted against the conference report be censured for not preventing its adoption? Less than half of their number could easily have done so. But no one of . them, so far as I know, thought it his duty to defeat the bill. Certainly I did not think it the duty of the chairman of the Committee on Appropriations to lead such a movement.

It has been said that the conference report might have been recommitted for a further attempt to strike off the salary clause. The answer to this is, that the House, on an aye and no vote, by nineteen majority, ordered the question to be put on the adoption of the report.

The plain fact is, that the final vote on the bill was not a test of the sentiments of members of the House on the salary question. The responsibility for the increase of salaries rests upon those who forced the amendment upon the bill.

There is one feature of the case to which I refer with great reluctance, and with a deep sense of the injustice that is done me. It is charged that I voted for the bill for the purpose of putting $5,000 of back pay into my own pocket. I fearlessly appeal to friends and enemies alike to say whether any act of my public life has warranted them in imputing to me unworthy and mercenary motives. The point here raised is one to which I did not intend to refer in this letter. I preferred to leave my personal motives to the future for vindication. But already, without my knowledge or procurement, a paragraph has found its way to the press which makes it proper for me to say what I did not wish paraded in public, that I not only did not receive the back pay nor any part of it, but I ordered it so covered into the general Treasury as to be placed beyond the reach of myself or my heirs.

I have thus stated the facts in the case, that you may know precisely what I did, and the reasons for it. I desire that this and every other act of my public life shall be fully known to you. Ten years ago you called me from another field of duty and honor to represent you in the national Legislature. Since then you have expressed your confidence and esteem in many ways, and in none more strikingly than in the five re-elections with which you have honored me.

I have not been insensible to these evidences of your approval. I have conscientiously sought to serve you and the country with the best of my ability. I have spared neither time nor labor faithfully to discharge the duties of the place assigned me.

Doubtless I have made my full share of mistakes and blunders, and my vote on this bill may have added another to the list. I respect no man the less for thinking so, but in this as in all my official conduct I acted for what I regarded the public good. Whether wise or unwise, defensible or indefensible, that vote had the approval of my judgment, and I do not shrink from any responsibility growing out of it.

But I do not affect to conceal my surprise and disappointment at the construction which has been given to that vote. Probably no man who, conscious of his own integrity, has served a constituency as long as I have served you could see the basest of motives attributed to him and listen to a public demand for his instant resignation with indifference.

Certainly I cannot.   Were I to follow my own inclinations merely, I would at once abandon a position so difficult to fill acceptably, and which the assaults of calumny have rendered on so many accounts undesirable.   But the charge on which the demand of the Warren convention is based is an injustice to which I cannot consent.   The principle on which it is made rises above any merely personal consideration.   If I ought to resign for casting this vote, every elective officer should resign whenever any of his official acts, done in good faith, are strongly disapproved by those who elected him.   If the delegates believe that the retroactive clause is so infamous that I ought to resign for voting for the appropriation bill to which it was attached, will they follow out their logic and insist that the President ought to resign for signing it? My vote did not make it a law.   His signature did.   I do not consent to the logic that leads to such a conclusion.

The facts are before you.   I am ready anywhere and at any time to make good the statements herein set forth, and upon the facts I appeal from the action of the convention to your more deliberate judgment.

Very respectfully,
JAMES A. GARFIELD.

Immediately upon receiving the check for the increase of his salary, General Garfield sent it to the United States treasurer, and it was covered into the treasury.

CHAPTER XVIII.

LABORS IN CONGRESS.

APPOINTMENT ON COMMITTEES. — VARIETY OF WORK. — HIS LEADER-
SHIP. — LIST OF SPEECHES. — THE ELECTORAL COMMISSION. — A
SPEECH IN WALL STREET. — VIEWS ON FINANCES. — RESUMPTION
OF SPECIE PAYMENTS.

GENERAL GARFIELD'S labors in Congress were of
the most varied and arduous character. It seems
incredible that one man could make so many speeches, write out so many bills, attend so many committee hearings, and appear so punctually in his seat as
he has done. He carried the affairs of the Military
committee as its practical head, until the chairman-
ship of the Ways and Means committee, which was
given him, took him into a wider field. For many
years he was the leader of the House in matters re-
quiring hard work ; and after the election of Mr.
Blaine to the Senate, he was regarded by the Republican party as their leader and oracle, in all their
debates and controversies with the other party. He
studied, wrote and spoke about a vast variety of topics,
concerning widely different themes, and, as all admit,
with ability and good judgment. He delivered addresses in the House, which have often been quoted
with respect by eminent scholars, upon public lands,

river navigation, contagious diseases, revenue, currency, duties, specie payments, Arctic explorations, science, schools, manufactories, commerce, agriculture, appropriations, law trials, Chinese immigration, diplomatic affairs, war claims, fisheries, polygamy, pensions, constitutional amendments, banks, slavery, treaties with foreign nations, trade with Canada, electoral count, reconstruction, State rights, and hundreds more ; and, all the while, was assiduously at work as a member of the most important committees. His eminent legal knowledge pointed him out at once as the proper statesman for the examination of the Louisiana trouble, for drafting constitutional amendments and impeachment reports, and for a place on that most august of all our national tribunals, the electoral commission, for adjusting the contested election case between R. B. Hayes and Samuel J. Tilden, the claimants for the presidential chair.

His study, at odd moments, of questions of science and education, made him a prominent member of the Board of regents of the Smithsonian Institute, and his love of literature secured the honorary membership in many of the leading literary societies in this country, and of the " Cobden Club," in London, on motion of John Bright.

During those years of restless activity, he wrote articles for magazines, and the many addresses which he delivered, at schools, colleges, celebrations, anniversaries and political meetings. Among his speeches, none seems to have given him greater celebrity, than the short exclamation which he made to the crowd in Wall street, on the evening after the assassination of President Lincoln. The accounts in the public press gave it as follows :

An enormous crowd had gathered at the Wall street Exchange. The wrath of the workingmen was simply uncontrollable, and revolvers and knives were in the hands of thousands of Lincoln's friends, ready to avenge the death of the martyred president, without being careful to consider who deserved penalty. Speeches from Butler and Dickinson had done nothing to appease the gathering wrath of the mob. Two men had been beaten — one lay dead, the other dangerously wounded — for declaring that Lincoln ought to have been hung long ago. Some had made a rude gallows out of scantling, with a looped halter hanging from it. Suddenly some one raised a shout, "The World! the World! the office of the World!". It was the signal for a surging movement which a moment later would have been a terrible march. Just then a man stepped forward, with a small flag in his hand, and beckoned to the crowd. Another telegram from Washington! And then, in the awful stillness of the crisis, taking advantage of the hesitation of the crowd, a right arm was lifted skyward, and a voice clear and steady, loud and distinct, spoke out: "Fellow citizens! Clouds and darkness are round about Him! His pavilion is dark waters and thick clouds of the skies! Justice and judgment are the establishment of his throne! Mercy and truth shall go before his face! Fellow citizens! God reigns, and the government at Washington still lives!" The effect was tremendous. The crowd stood riveted to the ground in awe, gazing at the motionless orator, and thinking of God and the security of the government in that hour. As the boiling wave subsides and settles to the sea, when

some strong wind beats it down, so the tumult of
the people sank and became still.   All took it as a
divine omen.   It was a triumph of eloquence, inspired by the moment, such as falls to but one man's
lot, and that but once in a century.

His political speeches were made the texts of his
party, and his services were eagerly sought for in
every doubtful State.   His published speeches are
well worth preserving, and of being read again and
again.   Some of his addresses, including as large a
variety as possible, in order to show the versatility
of his talents, are included in this volume.

During his first session he declared his views upon
the finances of the nation ; and, as the consistency
of his career on matters of finance may be of interest to all who study his life, extracts from two of his
speeches are given here together.   The first is a brief
statement of his views in 1866; the second is a more
elaborate discussion, made in Chicago in 1879.   The
remarks in Congress in 1866, were as follows :

Mr. Speaker, there is no leading financier, no
leading statesman now living, or one who has lived
within the last half century, in whose opinion the
gentleman can find any support.   They all declare,
as the Secretary of the treasury declares, that the
only honest basis of value is a currency, redeemable
in specie, at the will of the holder.   I am an advocate
of paper money, but that paper money must represent what it professes on its face.   I do not wish to
hold in my hands the printed lies of the government
I want its promises to pay, signed by the high officers of the government, sacredly kept in the exact
meaning of the words of the promise.

21

Let us not continue this conjurer's art, by which sixty cents shall discharge a debt of one hundred cents. I do not want industry, everywhere, to be thus crippled and wounded, and its wounds plastered over with legally authorized lies.

An Extract from General Garfield's speech upon the suspension and resumption of Specie Payments, before the Honest Money League of Chicago, January 2, 1879, was printed as follows :

Successful Resumption will greatly aid in bringing into the murky sky of our politics, what the signal service people call " clearing weather." It puts an end to a score of controversies which have long vexed the public mind, and wrought mischief to business. It ends the angry contention over the difference between the money of the bond-holder and the money of the plow-holder. It relieves enterprising Congress-men of the necessity of introducing twenty-five or thirty bills a session to furnish the people with cheap money, to prevent gold-gambling, and to make cus-tom duties payable in greenbacks. It will dismiss to the limbo of things forgotten, such Utopian schemes as a currency based upon the magic circle of intercon-vertibility of two different forms of irredeemable paper, and the schemes of a currency, " based on the public faith," and secured by " all the resources of the na-tion," in general, but upon no particular part of them. We shall still hear echoes of the old conflict, such as " the barbarism and cowardice of gold and silver," and the virtues of " fiat money;" but the theories which gave them birth will linger among us like belated ghosts, and soon find rest in the political grave of dead issues. All these will take their places in history alongside of the resolution of Varsittart, in 1811, that " British paper had not fallen, but gold had risen in value, and the declaration of Castlereagh, in the House of Commons, that "the money standard is a sense of value in reference to currency as compared with commodities," and the opinion of another member, who declared that the standard is neither gold nor silver, but something set up in the imagination to be regulated by public opinion."

When we have fully awakened from these vague dreams, public opinion will resume its old channels, and the wisdom and experience of the fathers of our constitution will again be acknowledged and followed.

We shall agree, as our fathers did, that the yardstick shall have length, the pound must have weight and the dollar must have value in itself, and that neither length, nor weight, nor value can be created by the fiat of law. Congress, relieved of the arduous task of regulating and managing all the business of our people, will address itself to the humbler but more important work of preserving the public peace, and managing wisely the revenues and expenditures of the government. Industry will no longer wait for the legislature to discover easy roads to sudden wealth, but will begin again to rely upon labor and frugality, as the only certain road to riches. Prosperity, which has long been waiting, is now ready to come. If we do not rudely repulse her, she will soon revisit our people, and will stay until another periodical craze shall drive her away.

CHAPTER XIX.

HIS PRESENT POSITION.

ELECTION AS SENATOR. — A SCHOLAR. — AN ORATOR. — A POOR MAN. —
WINS THE RESPECT OF THE DEMOCRATIC PARTY. — SPEECH BEFORE
THE OHIO LEGISLATURE. — THE CHICAGO CONVENTION. — GENERAL
GARFIELD'S SPEECH. — HIS NOMINATION. — HIS LETTER OF ACCEPT-
ANCE. — CONCLUSION.

THIS volume appears at a time when the subject
of this biography is most prominently before the
American people, as a candidate for the office of
President of the nation. It is but a few months
since he was elected to the United States Senate by
the unanimous vote of his party in the Ohio legislature. Thus, while he has not seen active service in
the Senate, he has been promoted in the political
ranks, step by step, until now the highest office is
also offered.

Coming thus to the close of this book, it is fitting
that a view should here be taken of his present social
and political position. As a scholar, he holds a high
rank in our nation, and his talents as a thinker,
writer and orator, have long been recognized by our
greatest philosophers, teachers, and essayists.

He is a poor man, and never was in affluent cir-

Private Residence of Gen. James A. Garfield, Mentor, Ohio.

cumstances. He has a modest house at Washington, and a comfortable little farm and dwelling at Mentor, Ohio. ·But these represent more than his actual financial worth, inasmuch as he is not out of debt. He can not have cheated the people, nor can he have swindled the government, as has been so often charged against candidates for office; for he possesses very little property, and lives in a very frugal style. His house, his carriage, and his clothing, are plain and cheap, having nothing about them suggestive of opulence or display.

He is a genial, sociable companion, and a kind neighbor. His neighbors love and honor him most. The citizens of his Congressional district seem to idolize him beyond reason. He is more than popular. He is loved.

He holds the respect of his political opponents, and with all his hard blows, they never accuse him of insincerity, or of dishonorable intention. They say that he treats them fairly; and often quote his speech before the Ohio legislature, January 14, 1880, the day after his election as U. S. Senator, as a characteristic act. In that he said:

I recognize the importance of the place to which you have elected me; and I should be base, if I did not also recognize the great man whom you have elected me to succeed. I say for him, Ohio has had few larger-minded, broader-minded men in the records of our history, than that of Allen G. Thurman. Differing widely from him as I have done in politics, and do, I recognize him as a man high in character and great in intellect; and I take this occasion to refer to what I have never before referred to in public, that many years ago, in the storm of party fighting, when the air was filled with all sorts of missiles aimed at the character and reputation of public men, when it was even for his party interest to join the general clamor against me and my associates, Senator Thurman said in public, in the campaign, on the stump — when men are as likely to say unkind things as at any place in the world — a most generous and earnest word of defense and kindness for me, which I shall never forget as long as I live. I say, moreover, that the flowers that bloom over the garden wall of party politics are the sweetest and most fragrant that bloom in the gardens of this world; and where we can early pluck them and enjoy their fragrance, it is manly and delightful to do so.

The nomination for the presidency came to him, as all his promotions have come, unasked and unsought by him. The Republican convention of 1880 was held in session seven days, at Chicago, completing its nomination on June 9. To that convention General Garfield was a delegate. He had no expectation of the nomination. But the two wings of that party were so antagonistic over the strenuous endeavors of one to nominate General U. S. Grant, and of the other to nominate James G. Blaine, that there was no hope of success for either. Under these circumstances the delegates, after several days of discussion and balloting, turned to look for another name as potent as those before the convention, and to whom none could be opposed. In that situation the name of General Garfield attracted immediate attention.

General Garfield had labored and hoped for the nomination of the Hon. John Sherman of Ohio, and had nominated him in a model speech, a part of which is here inserted :

Mr. President:—I have witnessed the extraordinary scenes of this convention with deep solicitude. No emotion touches my heart more quickly than sentiment in honor of a great and noble character ; but as I sat on these seats and witnessed these demonstrations, it seemed to me that you were a human ocean in a tempest. I have seen the sea lashed into fury and tossed into spray, and its grandeur moves the soul of the dullest man. But I remember that it is not the billows, but the calm level of the sea, from which all hights and depths are measured ; when the storm has passed, and the hour of calm settles on the ocean, when the sunlight bathes its smooth surface, then the astronomer and surveyor take the level from which they measure all terrestrial hights and depths.

Gentlemen of the convention, your present temper may not mark the healthful pulse of our people. When our enthusiasm has passed, when the emotions of this hour have subsided, we shall feel that calm level of public opinion below the storm from which the thoughts of a mighty people must be measured, and by which their final action will be determined.

Not here in this brilliant circle, where 15,000 men and women are assembled, is the destiny of the Republican party to be decreed. Not here, where I see the enthusiastic faces of 756 delegates, waiting to cast their votes into the urn, and determine the choice of the republic, but by 4,000,000 Republican firesides where the thoughtful voters, with wives and children about them, with the calm thoughts inspired by love of home and love of country, with the history of the past, the hopes of the future, and the knowledge of the great men who have adorned and blessed our nation in days gone by. There, God prepares the verdict that shall determine the wisdom of our work to-night. Not in Chicago, in the heats of June, but in the sober quiet that comes to them between now and November, in the silence of deliberate judgment, will this great question be settled.

But no sooner had the possibility of General Garfield's nomination entered the minds of the delegates, than the current of opinion turned so rapidly towards

THE WHITE HOUSE.

him, as to cause men to say, who had no knowledge of the coming votes, " I feel that Garfield will certainly be nominated." With the sudden impulse of great and excitable bodies, and amid enthusiasm, bustle and wild excitement, his name was given to the country as the choice of a great party. It was another providential approval of a great statesman and an honest man.

The letter which he wrote, accepting the nomination, was an important document to himself, to his party and to the country, and was printed as follows:

MENTOR, O., July 12, 1880.

Dear Sir: — On the evening of the 8th of June last, I had the honor to receive from you, in the presence of the committee of which you were the chairman, the official announcement that the Republican national convention of· Chicago had that day nominated me for their candidate for President of the United States. I accept the nomination with gratitude for the confidence it implies, and with a deep sense of the responsibilities it imposes. I cordially indorse the principles set forth in the platform adopted by the convention. On nearly all the subjects of which it treats, my opinions are on record among the published proceedings of Congress. I venture, however, to make special mention of some of the principal topics which are likely to become the subject of discussion, without reviewing the controversies which have been settled during the last twenty years, and with no purpose or wish to revive the passions of the late war.

It should be said that, while the Republicans fully recognize, and will strenuously defend, all the rights retained by the people, and all the rights reserved by the States, they reject the pernicious doctrine of State supremacy, which so long crippled the functions of the national government and at the time brought the union very near to destruction. They insist that the United States is a nation, with ample power of self-preservation; that its constitutions and laws, made in pursuance thereof, are the supreme law of the land; that the right of the nation to determine the method by which its own legislature shall be created, cannot be surrendered without abdicating one of the fundamental powers of government; that the national laws relating to the election of representatives in Con. gress shall neither be violated nor evaded; that every elector shall be permitted freely, and without intimidation, to cast his lawful ballot at each election, and have it honestly counted, and that the potency of his vote shall not be destroyed by the fraudulent vote of any other person. The best thoughts and energies of our people should be directed to those great questions of national well-being in which all have a common interest. Such efforts will soonest restore perfect peace to those who were lately in arms against each other, for justice and good-will will outlast passion. But it is certain that the wounds of the war cannot be completely healed, and the spirit of brotherhood cannot fully pervade the whole country, until every citizen, rich or poor, white or black, is secure in the free and equal enjoyment of every civil and equal right guaranteed by the constitution and the laws. Wherever the enjoyment of these rights is not assured, discontent will prevail, immigration will cease, and the social and industrial forces will continue to be disturbed by the migration of laborers and the consequent diminution of prosperity. The national government should exercise all its constitutional authority to put an end to these evils, for all the people and all the States are members of one body, and no member can suffer without injury to all. The most serious evils which now afflict the South arise from the fact that there is not such freedom and toleration of political opinion and action that the minority party can exercise an effective and wholesome restraint upon the party in power. Without such restraint, party rule becomes tyrannical and corrupt. The prosperity which is made possible in the South, by its great advantages of soil and climate, will never be realized until every voter can freely and safely support any party he pleases.

Next in importance to freedom and justice is popular education, without which neither justice nor freedom can be permanently maintained. Its interests are intrusted to the States and to the voluntary action of the people. Whatever help the nation can justly afford should be generously given to aid the States in supporting common schools ; but it would be unjust to our people and dangerous to our institutions to apply any portion of the revenues of the nation, or of the States, to the support of sectarian schools. The separation of the Church and the State in everything relating to taxation should be absolute.

On the subject of national finances, my views have been so frequently and fully expressed, that little is needed in the way of an additional statement. The public debt is now so well secured, and the rate of annual interest has been so reduced by refunding, that right economy in expenditures, and the faithful application of our surplus revenues to the payment of the principal of the debt will gradually, but certainly, free the people from its burdens, and close with honor the financial chapter of the war. At the same time, the government can provide for all its ordinary expenditures, and discharge its sacred obligations to the soldiers of the union and to the widows and orphans of those who fell in its defense. The resumption of specie payments, which the Republican party so courageously and successfully accomplished, has removed from the field of controversy many questions that long and seriously disturbed the credit of the government and the business of the country. Our paper currency is now as national as the flag, and resumption has not only made it everywhere equal to coin, but has brought into use our share of gold and silver. The circulating medium is more abundant than ever before, and we need only maintain the equality of all our dollars to insure to labor and capital a measure of value, from the use of which no one can suffer loss. The great prosperity which the country is now enjoying should not be endangered by any violent changes or doubtful financial experiments.

In reference to our custom laws, a policy should be pursued which will bring revenues to the treasury, and enable labor and capital, employed in our great industries, to compete fairly in our own markets with the labor and capital of foreign producers. We legislate for the people of the United States, not for the whole world; and it is our glory that the American laborer is more intelligent and better paid than his foreign competitors. Our country cannot be independent unless its people, with their abundant natural resources, possess the requisite skill at any time to clothe, arm and equip themselves for war, and in time of peace produce all the necessary implements of labor. It was the manifest intention of the founders of the government to provide for the common defense, not by standing armies alone, but by raising a greater army of artisans, whose intelligence and skill should powerfully contribute to the safety and glory of the nation.

Fortunately for the interests of commerce, there is no longer any formidable opposition to appropriation for the improvements of our harbors and great navigable rivers, provided that the expenditures for that purpose are strictly limited to works of national importance. The Mississippi river, with its great tributaries is of such vital importance to so many millions of people, that the safety of its navigation requires exceptional consideration. In order to secure to the nation the control of all its waters, President Jefferson negotiated the purchase of a vast territory extending from the Gulf of Mexico to the Pacific Ocean. The wisdom of Congress should be invoked to devise some plan by which that great river shall cease to be a terror to those who dwell upon its banks, and by which its shipping may safely carry the industrial products of 25,000,000 of people. The interests of agriculture, which is the basis of all our material prosperity, and in which seven-twelfths of the population are arrayed, as well as the interest of manufactures and commerce, demand that the facilities for cheap transportation shall be increased by the use of all our great water courses.

The material interests of this country, the traditions of its settlement and the sentiment of our people, have led the government to offer the widest hospitality to emigrants who seek our shores for new and happier homes, willing to share the burdens as well as the benefits of our society, and intending that their posterity shall become an undistinguishable part of our population. The recent movement of the Chinese to our Pacific coast partakes but little of the qualities of such an emigration, either in its purposes or its result. It is too much like an importation to be welcomed without restriction ; too much like an invasion to be looked upon without solicitude. We cannot consent to allow any form of servile labor to be introduced among us, under the guise of immigration. Recognizing the gravity of this subject, the present administration, supported by Congress, has sent to China a commission of distinguished citizens, for the purpose of securing such a modification of the existing treaty as will prevent the evils likely to arise from the present situation. It is confidently believed that these diplomatic negotiations will be successful, without the loss of commercial intercourse between the two powers, which promises great increase of reciprocal trade and the enlargement of our markets. Should these efforts fail, it will be the duty of Congress to investigate the evils already felt, and prevent their increase by such restrictions as, without violence or injustice, will place upon a sure foundation the peace of our communities, and the freedom and dignity of labor.

The appointment of citizens to the various executive and judicial offices of the government is, perhaps, the most difficult of all duties which the constitution has imposed upon the Executive. The convention wisely demands that Congress shall co-operate with the executive departments in placing the civil service on a better basis. Experience has proved that, with our frequent changes of administration, no system of reform can be made effective and permanent without the aid of legislation. Appointments to the military and naval service are so regulated by law and custom, as to leave but little ground for complaint. It may not be wise to make similar regulations by law for the civil service ; but, without invading the authority or necessary discretion of the Executive, Congress should devise a method that will determine the tenure of office, and greatly reduce the uncertainty which makes that service so uncertain and unsatisfactory. Without depriving any officer of his rights as a citizen, the government should require him to discharge all his official duties with intelligence, efficiency and faithfulness. To select wisely, from our vast population, those who are best fitted for the many offices to be filled, requires an acquaintance far beyond the range of any one man. The Executive should, therefore, seek and receive the information and assistance of those whose knowledge of the communities, in which the duties are to be performed, best qualifies them to aid in making the wisest choice.

The doctrines announced in the Chicago convention, are not the temporary devices of a party to attract votes and carry an election ; they are deliberate convictions, resulting from a careful study of the spirit of our institutions, the events of our history and the best impulses of our people. In my judgment, these principles should control the legislation and administration of the government. In any event, they will guide my conduct until experience points out a better way. If elected, it will be my purpose to enforce strict obedience to the constitution and the laws, and to promote, as best I may, the interest and honor of the whole country, relying for support upon the wisdom of Congress, the intelligence and patriotism of the people and the favor of God.

With great respect, I am

Very truly yours,

J. A. GARFIELD.

To Hon. George F. Hoar,
Chairman of the Committee.

Awaiting the future events in this great mans career with intense interest, and feeling that whatever may be his experience or success hereafter, " the past at least is secure ; " and that his example as a boy, scholar, teacher, general and statesman, which is now so fortunately brought to the attention of the people, is a valuable heritage to bequeath to the youth of our land, we lay down this pen, and turn to other tasks.

" Lives of great men all remind us
We can make ourlives sublime."

SKETCH OF THE LIFE

GEN. CHESTER A. ARTHUR

OF NEW YORK.

CHESTER A. ARTHUR was born, October 5, 1830 in a small town in Franklin County, Vermont. His father, Rev. William Arthur, D.D., was a somewhat noted Baptist clergyman, and was a very learned man. It is said, by those who remember him, that he possessed an unusual knowledge of general literature, and was a ready and entertaining writer, on matters of public interest. As a theologian, he was an unshaken believer in his creed, and was one of its stoutest and most persistent champions. His success and chief merit, as a preacher, lay in his wonderful memory, and his talent as a writer, rather than in his oratorical powers. He was a cautious thorough student, and was frequently made the umpire in theological disputes among his brethren in the ministry.

He was pastor of the Baptist churches at Bennington, Hinesburg, Fairfield and Williston, in the State of Vermont, and in. Greenwich, Perry, York, Schenectady, Lansingburg, Hoosic, New York City, West Troy and Newtonville, in the State of New York.

Fearless in his expression of theological opinions, uncompromising in regard to those customs and sports of the time which he considered sinful, he often made enemies among fashionable people, and sometimes was at variance with the ministers of other denominations. This was by no means his universal experience, but was one of the necessary results of unmoved fidelity to his religious faith.

He is said to be a man who cared but little for appearances, and was too much devoted to his books to take much care of his dress, or to pay much attention to the rules of fashionable society. A noble, brave, devoted, sincere preacher of the gospel, as he understood it, and wholly given to his ministerial work.

His study of English literature, was carried on by him to fit himself better for his sacred work.

He published several small volumes and pamphlets, mostly upon theological matters ; the most of them, however, were printed at the request, and at the expense, of his parishioners, or the town authorities. His noted book upon "Family Names," shows a marvelous amount of research and skill, and has given him a place among the most erudite of scholars.

Like a great number of his profession in his time, he was a poor man during the larger part of his life, and was never wealthy. He had two sons and five daughters, and he labored very hard and lived most economically, that he might be able to give them an education. He was a self-made man, coming to this country, from Antrim, Ireland, when he was eighteen years old, and the prejudice against his nationality, with his reduced circumstances, made his early life a laborious and trying one.

He died at Newtonville, New York, October 27, 1875, honored, respected, and sincerely mourned, by thousands of Christian men and women.

Chester was the oldest child in the family of seven, and, in his early days, had but few luxuries or toys, with which to make life attractive. The very worst, and the most disagreeable, situation in which a child can be placed, is to be the son of a preacher of the gospel. In the atmosphere of a rigid adherence to the set rules of morality, with a consciousness of a constant watchfulness on the part of his parents, lest he should do something improper, hampers and irritates him into uneasiness, and usually into chronic rebellion. He is flattered and petted by the parishioners, who hope thus to please their dear pastor ; and finding that the opinion, which other people tell him they have of his goodness and smartness, does not agree with the estimation in which he is held by his father and mother, he naturally adopts the most agreeable conclusion, and believes the inconsiderate flatterers, and loses respect for the advice or commands of his parents. Then, being the center of attention on the part of so many people, over whom the preacher is desirous to exert a good influence no less by example than precept, the preacher goes to the other extreme, and tries to make staid and sensible old people of his children, while they are yet in early childhood. This frets and sours them, until they hate the name of a church, and disrespect all things connected with it. It is a bondage, from which the children persistently attempt to escape, and too often they succeed in shaking off all restraint, and end their lives in debauchery or crime.

Such is the record of many ministers' sons; and when one has the natural character, and chooses the path to greatness, in spite of all these hinderances, he is worthy of a double honor.

The difficulties and temptations which usually beset a preacher's son, were not strangers to Chester, and it is said that he sometimes exhibited that independence of restraint, and dislike of parental control, which is so universal with such boys. He is said, by the old neighbors, to have been a boy who was full of life and roguishness, having a far greater interest in his sports than in his books. Yet his affection for his parents was very strong, and he could not bear to grieve them. That was his anchor as a boy. To please them, he would study or work, or do disagreeable tasks, which no amount of driving would compel him to do. He was sharp and quick in his studies, and found much time for play, while other boys were pursuing their lessons.

He had many advantages over other boys, in the help which his father readily gave him, and in the guides and hints concerning his lessons, which his father's library supplied.. His father's circumstances were such that the eldest son was compelled to labor frequently, and was a most vigorous workman in such farm work, or shop jobs, as he could get.

The greater portion of his time, however, was given to study with his father, or at school. At the early age of fourteen, he was prepared to enter Union College.

At that time, he is represented as a rather slender boy, eager in play, and always the leader among his school-mates in all their sports. Especially was this the case when anything that appeared dangerous or venturesome was undertaken by them. He always took an active interest in parades and political processions, and was always on hand with his torch, whenever a party jubilee was held. He was not distinguished, in his college life, beyond the general record of his class, and must have found it difficult work to keep pace with a class of young men so much older than he. He is said to have been a great lover of athletic sports, and was a favorite with his class.

When he left Union College, he had no capital

but his education, with which to begin life, and his father was neither disposed, nor able, to give him further assistance. He then succeeded in finding a country school in Vermont, to which he was recommended by some of his father's acquaintances, and where he taught, through the winter months, for two years. Having determined to pursue the study of the law, he began to procure such books as were preparatory to it, and worked with great diligence, and saved his money with great care, in order to secure the necessary education to admit him to the bar. In 1850 he had saved nearly five hundred dollars, and he determined to go to New York, and study law in an office. In that city, he secured a place in the office of the Hon. E. D. Culver, and, living as cheaply as possible, he applied himself wholly to his books. His legal abilities were remarkable, and his progress very rapid ; so that he at once attracted the attention and commendation of distinguished lawyers, with whom he became acquainted. His room-mate, Henry D. Gardiner, was also an active and brilliant young man, and Chester became quite intimate with him. This social friendship at last ripened into a determination to form a partnership, which was accomplished as soon as they were admitted to the bar. But they did not then propose to remain in the great city of New York, where it seemed so difficult for young men to get a foothold, in the practice of the law. They dreamed of wider fields, and larger fees, in the great new West.

With the hope of finding some place to locate, the

young men started for the Western States, and wandered about for some time, finding no satisfactory opening. Reluctantly, they turned homeward, and, soon after, opened an office in New York. To the surprise of themselves and many older lawyers, they secured a profitable practice at once, and within three years were known to the whole city as lawyers of standing and ability. Two or three important cases connected with matters of public interest contributed much towards their success.

One of these cases was the celebrated Lemmon slave case, which attracted the angry attention of the whole nation.

Jonathan Lemmon of Virginia, brought a suit to recover possession of eight slaves that had been declared free by Judge Paine of the superior court of New York. Lemmon had been incautiously passing through New York with his slaves, intending to ship them to Texas, when they were discovered and freed by order of Judge Paine. The judge was of the opinion that the fugitive slave law did not hold these slaves when once they were brought within the territory of New York. The state of Virginia directed its attorney-general to appeal from Judge Paine's decision. The legislature of this State responded to the challenge, by requesting the governor to employ counsel to defend the case. The Hon. E. D. Culver and Joseph Blunt, Esq., were appointed. Afterward they withdrew, and young Arthur, who had been a student in Mr. Culver's office, was appointed. He associated with himself William M. Evarts, Esq., as counsel, and argued the case before the Supreme Court, Charles O'Connor, being one of the counsel for the slave-holder. That court sustained Judge Paine's decision. The case was then appealed to the court of appeals. There also the judgment of Judge Paine was affirmed — and henceforth, no slave-holder dared venture into New York State with his slaves.

In 1856, colored people were not permitted to ride on the Fourth avenue horse cars in New York. Lizzie Jennings, a colored woman of excellent character, superintendent of a Sunday-school, was roughly expelled from a Fourth avenue car because she was black. Arthur brought a suit against the railroad company in her behalf. He argued the case before Judge Rockwell in a Brooklyn court. The jury gave a verdict of five hundred dollars' damages in favor of the colored woman. The damages were paid by the railroad company, and henceforth, colored people rode without question on the cars of all the street lines in New York.

He became known as the champion of the colored people, and his docket was filled with cases at each session of the court. He became naturally interested in the negro race, and a determined opponent of slavery. He was one of the original advocates of the formation of the Republican party, and attended its first meeting at Saratoga.

He seems never to have sought political promotion; but being a genial, good-natured man, naturally enjoying good fellowship and lively company, he took pleasure in the companionship which military associations gave, and contracted, through them, a love for military manœuvres and parades.

His interest in military matters, and his known abilities as a lawyer, secured for him the appointment, in 1858, of judge-advocate of the 2d brigade of the New York militia. This was soon followed by a promotion to be chief engineer on the staff of Governor Morgan of New York, and, two years later, by the promotion to the office of inspector-general of that State.

At the opening of the war, when the difficulties of supplying the New York troops with clothing and provisions, seemed almost insurmountable, General Arthur accepted the important trust of quartermaster-general which he held until the expiration of Morgan's term of office. No higher encomium can be passed upon him than the mention of the fact that the war account of the State of New York was at least ten times larger than that of any other State, yet it was the first audited and allowed in Washington, and without the deduction of a dollar, while the quartermaster's accounts from other States were reduced from $1,000,000 to $10,000,000. During the term of office, every present sent to him was immediately returned. Among others, a prominent clothing house offered him a magnificent uniform, and a printing house sent him a costly saddle and trappings. Both gifts were indignantly rejected. When General Arthur became quartermaster-general, he was poor. When his term expired he was poorer still. He had opportunities to make millions unquestioned. He had to provide for the clothing, arming and transportation of hundreds of thousands of men. But with a rigid simplicity in his own life and the enforcement of economy upon subordinates, he, by example and command, saved to the State great sums of money. He took great pains to carry on all his public business so openly, justly and carefully as to avoid the possibility of loss or suspicion of fraud. One of his favorite sayings at this time, when his friends felt that he was too precise in his drafts and accounts of army contracts, was a quotation from Plutarch's life of Cæsar,—"Cæsar's wife must be above suspicion."

In conversation with an acquaintance in 1862, he said, "If I had misappropriated five cents, and on walking down town saw two men talking on the corner together, I would imagine they were talking of my dishonesty, and the very thought would drive me mad."

At the expiration of Governor Morgan's term, General Arthur returned to his law practice. Business of the most lucrative character poured in upon him, and the firm of Arthur & Gardiner prospered exceedingly. Much of their work consisted in the collection of war claims, and the drafting of important bills for speedy legislation, and a great deal of General Arthur's time was spent in Albany and Washington, where his uniform success won for him a national reputation. For a short time, he held the position of counsel to the board of tax commissioners of New York, at $10,000 per annum.

He secured the nomination and the election of the

Hon. Thomas Murphy as State senator. He also took an active and friendly. interest in securing the appointment of Mr. Murphy as collector of the port of New York, and when Mr. Murphy resigned on November 20, 1871, President Grant nominated General Arthur to the vacant position. And four years later, when his term expired, re-nominated him, an honor that had never been shown to any previous collector in the history of the port.

In 1878, a difference arose between General Arthur and President Hayes with reference to the interpretation of the civil service rules adopted by the government. Collector Arthur believed that the same efficiency and honesty might be secured by less troublesome machinery than that which Mr. Hayes insisted upon his using, and the difference of opinion was made by both a matter of conscience in view of their duty to the nation. President Hayes removed him from the office during a vacation of Congress, notwithstanding the fact that two special Congressional committees made searching investigation into his administration, and both reported themselves unable to find anything upon which to base a charge against him. In announcing the change, both President Hayes and Secretary Sherman bore official witness to the purity of his acts while in office.

He has been an active and liberal man in political matters, and holds the position of Chairman of the New York State Republican Central committee.

General Arthur is considered by artists to be a very handsome person, having an intelligent, pleasant countenance, broad shoulders, strong, full muscles, and being over six feet tall. .

He was married in 1852 to Miss Herndon, daughter of Lieutenant Herndon of the United States navy, whose widow received a gold medal from Congress in recognition of his bravery. General Arthur's wife died in 1879.

General Arthur furnishes another example of the general rule, that the greatest men are self-made men.

On the 18th of July, 1880, General Chester A. Arthur accepted the Republican nomination for Vice-president, in the following letter:

New York, July 15, 1880.

Dear Sir: — I accept the position assigned me by the great party whose action you announce. The acceptance implies approval of the principles declared by the convention, but recent usage permits me to assume expression of my views, thoughts and duty. To secure honesty and order, in popular elections, is a matter so vital that it must stand in front. The authority of the national government to preserve from fraud and force, elections at which its own officers are chosen, is a chief point on which the two parties are plainly and intensely opposed. Acts of Congress for ten years, in New York and elsewhere, have done much to curb the violence and wrong to which the ballot and the count have been again and again subjected, sometimes despoiling great cities, sometimes stifling the voice of a whole State, often seating, not only in Congress, but on the bench and in the legislature, numbers of men never chosen by the people. The Democratic party, since gaining possession of the two Houses of Congress, has made these just laws the object of bitter, ceaseless assault, and, despite all resistance, has hedged them with restrictions, cunningly contrived, to baffle and paralyze them. This aggressive majority boldly attempted to extort from the Executive his approval of various enactments, destructive of the election laws, by the revolutionary threat that the constitutional exercise of the veto power would be punished by withholding the appropriations necessary to carry on the government; and these threats were actually carried out, by refusing the needed appropriations, and by forcing an extra session of Congress, lasting for months, and resulting in concessions to this usurping demand, which are likely, in many States, to subject the majority to the lawless will of a minority. Ominous signs of public disapproval alone subdued this arrogant power into a sullen surrender, for the time being, of a part of its demands. The Republican party has strongly approved the stern refusal of its representatives to suffer the overthrow of statutes, believed to be salutary and just. It has always insisted, and now insists, that the government of the United States of America is empowered, and in duty bound, to effectually protect the elections denoted by the constitution as national. More than this, the Republican party holds, as a cardinal point in its creed, that the government should, by every means known to the constitution, protect all American citizens, everywhere, in the full enjoyment of their civil and political rights. As a great part of the work of reconstruction, the Republican party gave the ballot to the emancipated slave, as his right and defense. A large increase in the number of members of Congress, and of the electoral college, from the former slave-holding States, was the immediate result. The history of recent years abounds in evidence that in many ways and in many places, especially where their number has been great enough to endanger Democratic control, the very men by whose elevation to citizenship this increase of representation was effected, have been debarred and robbed of their voice and their vote. It is true that no State statute or constitution, in so many words, denies or abridges the exercise of their political rights, but the modes employed to bar their way are no less effectual. It is a suggestive and startling thought, that the increased power, derived from the enfranchisement of a race, now denied its share in governing the country, wielded by those who lately sought the overthrow of the government, is now the sole reliance to defeat the party which represents the sovereignty and nationality of the American people, in the greatest crisis of our history. Republicans cherish none of the resentments which may have animated them during the actual conflict of arms. They long for a full and real reconciliation between the sections which were needlessly and lamentably at strife; they sincerely offer the hand of good will, but they ask, in return, the hand of good faith. They deeply feel that the party, whose career is so illustriously great in patriotic achievements, will not fulfill its destiny until peace and prosperity are established in all the land, nor until liberty of thought, conscience, and action, and equality of opportunity, shall not be merely cold formalities of statutes, but living birthrights, which the humble may confidently claim, and the powerful dare not deny.

The resolution referring to the public service seems to be deserving of approval. Surely no man should be the incumbent of an office, the duties of which he is, for any cause, unfit to perform, who is lacking in the ability, in the fidelity or integrity which a proper administration of such office demands. This sentiment would doubtless meet with general acquiescence, but opinion has been widely divided upon the wisdom and practicability of the various reformatory schemes which have been suggested, and of certain proposed regulations governing appointments to public office. The efficiency of such regulations has been distrusted, mainly because they have seemed to exalt mere educational and abstract tests above general business capacity, and even special fitness for the particular work in hand. It seems to me that the rules which should be applied to the management of the public service may properly conform, in the main, to such as regulate the conduct of successful private business. Original appointments should be based on ascertained fitness. The tenure of office should be stable. Positions of responsibility should, so far as practicable, be filled by the promotion of worthy and efficient officers. The investigation of all complaints, and the punishment of all official misconduct, should be prompt and thorough. These views, which I have long held, repeatedly declared, and uniformly applied, when called upon to act, I find embodied in the resolution, which, of course, I approve. I will add that, by the acceptance of public office, whether high or low, one does not, in my judgment, escape any of his responsibilities as a citizen, nor lose or impair any of a citizen's rights; that he should enjoy absolute liberty to think and speak and act in political matters, according to his own will and conscience, provided, only, ·that he honorably, faithfully and fully discharges all his official duties.

The resumption of specie payment, one of the fruits of the Republican party, has brought the return of abundant prosperity and the settlement of many distracting questions. The restoration of sound money, the large reduction of the public debt and of the burden of interest, the high advancement of the public credit, — all attest the ability and courage of the Republican party to deal with such financial problems as may hereafter demand solution. Our paper currency is now as good as gold, and silver is performing its legitimate functions for the purposes of change. The principles which should govern the relations of these elements of the currency are simple and clear. There must be no deteriorated coin, no depreciated paper, and every dollar, whether of metal or paper, should stand the test of the world's fixed standard.

The value of popular education can hardly be over-stated, although its interests of necessity must be chiefly confided to voluntary effort and the individual action of the several States. They should be encouraged, so far as the constitution permits, by the generous co-operation of the national government. The interests of the whole country demand that the advantage of our American school system should be brought within the reach of every citizen, and that no revenue of the realm or of the State should be devoted to the support of sectarian schools. Such changes should be made in the present tariff and system of taxation as will relieve any overburdened industry or class, and enable our manufacturers and artisans to compete successfully with those of other lands. The government should aid works of internal improvement national in their character, and should promote the development of our watercourses and harbors, wherever the general interests of commerce require it. Four years ago, as now, the nation stood at the threshold of a presidential election, and the Republican party founded its hope of success, not upon its promises, but upon its history. Its subsequent course has been such as to strengthen the claims which it then made to the confidence and support of the country. On the other hand, considerations more urgent than have ever before existed forbid the elevation of their opponents to power. Their success, if success attends them, must chiefly come from the united support of that section which sought the forcible disruption of the union, and which, according to all the teachings of our past history, will demand ascendancy in the councils of the party, to whose triumph it will have made by far the largest contribution.   There is the gravest reason for apprehension that exorbitant claims on the public treasury, by no means limited to the hundreds of millions already covered by bills introduced in Congress, within the past four years, would be successfully urged if the Democratic party should succeed in supplementing its present control of the national legislature, by electing the Executive also.   There is danger in intrusting the control of the whole law-making power of the government to a party which has, in almost every Southern State, repudiated obligations quite as sacred as those to which the faith of the nation now stands pledged.   I do not doubt that success awaits the Republican party, and that its triumph will assure a just, economical and patriotic administration.   I am respectfully, your obedient servant,

C. A. ARTHUR.

To Hon. GEORGE F. HOAR, President of the Republican National Convention.